I0554301

BUTTERCREAM BETRAYAL

Cupcake Catering Mystery Series Book 5

KIM DAVIS

Cinnamon & Sugar Press

Buttercream Betrayal

Kim Davis

Chapter 1

"Piper, Missy, stop! Stay, come, stop, sit!" My voice cracked as I yelled to get my dogs' attention. My mouth continued to spew every command I'd recently learned, and then some, in the dog training course we'd just finished. I watched with mounting horror as the two dogs careened toward Eloise Parker. Of course, the two dogs didn't listen to me. They never did unless Eloise's son, Shawn, who also happened to be the dog trainer, was around.

Piper finally noticed the woman and tried to make a course correction. But with her growing momentum, along with Missy hot on her tail, the two dogs couldn't help but sideswipe Eloise. The ceramic pie dish, cradled in her hands, crashed to the floor.

She raised a bony, ring-laden hand and pointed at me. "You and your dogs have been nothing but trouble from the very start. Get them out of here."

I guess I didn't move fast enough to suit her.

"I didn't mean tomorrow, Emory. Get those dogs out now!"

I tore my gaze from her glare and watched my two dogs

run out the wide-open glass double doors. Several other dogs followed, barking. Torn between collecting the leashes and slinking away from the clubhouse and abandoning their graduation certificate or grabbing paper towels to clean up Eloise's award-winning apple pie, I stood frozen in place. The need to slink away was strong, but concern over the dogs injuring themselves on the shattered pie plate won out.

Before I could take a step toward the kitchen to find paper towels, a loud whistle pierced the air.

"Sit!" The dog trainer's voice was loud and commanding. I felt the urge to sit right where I was. The dogs ceased to bark, and from my vantage point, I saw most of them sit, their tongues lolling from the sides of their mouths. Naturally, Missy and Piper were having too much fun to listen, and they both jumped into the community pool. I probably never should have introduced them to swimming with my nieces over the summer.

Eloise noticed as well. She threw a murderous glower my way. "I'll be sending you the bill for cleaning and disinfecting the pool."

She fluffed her ash-blonde, shoulder-length hair, straightened her heavily starched button-down shirt, brushed a speck of pie crust from her black slacks, and stomped toward her son on four-inch stilettos. The shattered pie sat, untended to, in the middle of the floor. Several of the other dog owners got up from their tables, abandoning their glasses of wine, and slunk off to collect their wayward pets. They all avoided my gaze.

"I have a feeling we're going to flunk dog training," Vannie, my half sister, muttered beneath her breath as she sidled up to me. She swiped a strand of frizzy red hair from her freckled face, which resembled my own, then began tearing sheets of paper towel from the roll she held. "Shawn's going to be livid his mother's pie was destroyed. They've both been bragging about it ever since Cheryl decided to organize this doggie graduation party."

Vannie had moved from Spain at the end of June. She'd planned on staying with Tillie, her grandmother, who'd become not only my employer but my best friend, for only a few weeks until she could find an apartment. But three months later, she hadn't moved and, instead, appeared to be settling in. Tillie was in no hurry for her only granddaughter to move out and had proved quite persuasive in getting Vannie to stay put. One evening, over a pitcher of gimlets, we decided it would be fun to participate in six sessions of doggie obedience training held on Saturdays, since Piper and Missy seemed to egg on each other's mischievousness. The dogs' misbehavior only seemed to ramp up as the sessions progressed.

"We can at least say we lasted the entire six weeks and gave it a good try." I sighed as I took the roll of paper towels from Vannie and knelt beside her to help clean up the broken shards of the plate and the splattered apple pie. "I can't believe Eloise left this mess knowing dogs are running around. What if one of the dogs had snatched up a piece of the pie and eaten a shard of glass along with it?"

"I have a feeling Eloise never has to clean up her own messes and expects everyone else to jump in and fix things." Vannie stood and gathered the soiled paper towels. "I'll toss these and bring back some wet ones. I want to make sure there aren't any tiny shards we missed and that there isn't any pie left to attract any doggie licks."

She quickly returned, and we finished cleaning up the floor. It became obvious that the rest of the floor in the condo association's clubhouse needed a thorough cleaning after we compared it to the large patch we'd scrubbed. I wondered if Eloise, as president of the homeowners' association, would facilitate that or if she'd turn a blind eye.

I looked out the door to make sure Piper and Missy were

entertaining themselves in the pool. They were. I wasn't worried about their safety since they were both strong swimmers and we'd worked on teaching them how to get out of the pool on their own. Plus, I felt mostly confident that Shawn and Eloise would keep a close eye on them to make sure they didn't get into any more mischief.

"Let me find some paper plates to leave the golden appletini cupcakes on, and then we can grab the girls and get out of here. I'm pretty sure I have a couple clean towels left in my SUV from the last time we took them to the beach." I began opening cupboards in the spacious kitchen. The condo association hadn't stinted when they'd built the clubhouse.

"I'll bring the towels from the car; otherwise we'll be soaked when we pull them from the pool." Vannie swiped a cupcake from my decorative platter and took a bite. She hummed. "You're going to make more of these for the family dinner tomorrow night, aren't you? I love the bite from the Goldschläger."

"They're already made." I swiped a fingerful of frosting from her cupcake and stuck it in my mouth. "I'm planning on making a batch of kid-friendly apple pie–filled cupcakes that I've been experimenting with for Brian to serve at Oceana. You can all give me your input."

My boyfriend, Brian, owned Oceana, a highly sought-after restaurant in Laguna Beach. Brian also happened to be Vannie's half brother… well, it was quite confusing to explain the twists and turns of our parentage, but rest assured, Brian and I were not, in any way, related.

Instead, my mother, Addie, and Brian's father, David, had had a college romance, and the unexpected baby, Vannie, had been given up for adoption. The couple parted ways, and it was only the previous year that we'd been able to track Vannie down and connect with her. Oh, and to make it even more confusing when people first met us, I have a twin sister, Carrie.

The three of us are close to identical and all have red hair, although Carrie somehow was graced with a lack of freckles and frizz.

I started transferring the cupcakes to disposable plates so I could slink out with my good platters and not worry about having to return to pick them up later. I needed them for another party I was catering the following day.

Vannie plucked my SUV keys from my pocket and left to retrieve the towels.

"What are you doing?" Cheryl, vice president of the homeowners' association, stood in the doorway with her hands on her plump hips. Her face was red, and she was out of breath.

"I'm leaving the cupcakes here, and then Vannie and I will take our dogs home." I handed Cheryl a cupcake when she came to stand next to me. "Shawn is going to flunk us, so we thought we'd better disappear instead of making a scene."

"You're not leaving. Piper and Missy completed the course and deserve a certificate." Cheryl bit into the cupcake. Her eyes widened. "Wow, there's a hit of something in this. It's insanely delish."

"It's Goldschläger and Sour Apple Pucker Schnapps." I went back to transferring the cupcakes. Cheryl had determined that the potluck get-together should have an apple theme. "What did you bring?"

"The apple cider maple meatballs."

"Are those the ones in the slow cooker?"

"Yep. It's super easy." She leaned in toward me conspiratorially and lowered her voice. "I cheated and used premade frozen meatballs."

I couldn't help but laugh. "They smell divine, but I won't tell if you don't want me to."

She shrugged. "Guess it doesn't much matter, but Eloise is kind of a snob about taking shortcuts. Not that she does any cooking herself. I heard she has a private chef come in when she doesn't want to go out to dinner."

"Speaking of Eloise, she's going to kill us for ruining her *award-winning* apple pie."

Cheryl sniggered as I mimicked Eloise's intonation of "award-winning." "Be that as it may, I want you to stay. You and Vannie are the only reason Precious and I survived these last six weeks. It's been…"

Precious was Cheryl's six-month-old pug. Cheryl confided that she'd purchased the pup from Shawn after Eloise had pressured her into it, and then the mother and son had pressured her again to sign up for the training sessions.

"A little like being in military boot camp?" I eyed a cupcake then decided I'd better skip the unneeded calories.

"Yeah. It wasn't what I expected."

"Me either, but Shawn's got some great reviews and seems to come highly recommended. But still, it was way too intense for what my dogs and I could handle."

Tillie had found Shawn's training sessions for us. I suspected she'd picked his services because of the photos plastered all over his website. Tall and muscular, the blond, blue-eyed man exuded alpha-male appeal as he posed with his German Shepard, Spike, in locations around Southern California, often with his shirt off to show his rippling six-pack abs. There were multiple shots of the pair at the beach, mountains, and desert, and in each pose, they both appeared intimidating.

When we'd arrived at the training facility, which was a basic warehouse in an industrial park in Irvine, I'd been disconcerted to learn that Spike would be in the training sessions. My unease only blossomed as Shawn had allowed his dog to bully the much smaller dogs. When I expressed my concern, he told me that dogs learn much faster when a true alpha dog corrects their behavior. At least the German

Shepard wasn't at the clubhouse today; otherwise, I had a feeling my two dogs would've been Spike's lunch.

Cheryl washed her hands then smoothed back her graying bob. A frown deepened the furrows in her forehead. She apparently didn't follow the typical regimen of regular Botox injections as so many women did in our coastal area. "Precious hasn't seemed herself since the training started. She's become nervous and, well, not to provide TMI, she's had tummy troubles that aren't going away. Plus, she gets short of breath for no reason at all. The vet wants to do a lot more tests to find out what's wrong. I spent more than I should've by going through Shawn to get her, and I've already spent more than I can really afford on vet bills. But we do what we have to for our fur babies, don't we?"

"Poor Precious. She's seemed okay when she's romping around with Piper and Missy."

"She loves your dogs, and they're gentle with her." She looked over her shoulder to make sure no one was within earshot then turned back to me and lowered her voice. "I overheard someone gossiping how earlier this year, Spike attacked one of the participating dogs during a session. Shawn somehow managed to not have to pay the vet bills, and he didn't even refund the training fees when the owner dropped out. I would've dropped out when I heard about it, but well, you know Eloise. She'd make my life unbearable, and we have to work together."

"OMG, that's awful! You'd think Shawn would stop using Spike during the sessions if that happened."

"You'd think." Cheryl's tone was wry.

"Emory, I have the towels." Vannie hustled into the kitchen. "Are you ready to grab the girls and get out of here? They're sun-napping right now, so it might be a good time to corral them before they get into any more trouble."

"I've decided you're not leaving." Cheryl flashed a smile at Vannie. "Precious and I need your company."

"Um, about that." Vannie's cheeks reddened. "Shawn and Eloise really laid into me and told me, in no uncertain terms, that we have to leave."

"This is a non-training social event held at a private facility not associated with Shawn's Dog Training Solutions. You're staying, and I'll deal with the Parkers." Cheryl's face turned puce as she stomped off to confront the trainer.

Chapter 2

"I feel uncomfortable causing another scene with Shawn and Eloise." Vannie picked up my empty platter and washed it. "It might be better to leave like they asked."

I was torn. While I didn't much like confrontation, given the way the humans and dogs alike had been bullied over the last six weeks, I wanted to stand up to Shawn and his mother for once. Especially if Cheryl was going to stand up for us. "If Cheryl is already pleading our case, then I think we owe it to her to hang around."

"You're right."

We both paused as the sound of women noisily arguing got louder as they headed our way.

"You have no right to kick them out, Eloise," Cheryl said.

"If I wanted your opinion, I would have asked for it." Eloise's tone was harsh. "I suggest you go take care of your dog and leave this to me."

"But this is a private event, and I personally booked the clubhouse. You can't force them to leave since they're my guests." Cheryl's voice went an octave higher.

They rounded the corner and entered the kitchen.

Cheryl's face and chest had turned an alarming shade of red, and Eloise had a pinched look on her face.

"Ms. Martinez and Ms. Crawford." Eloise's tone was sharp, and she'd reverted to calling us by our last names instead of our first. "As president of the association, I have every authority to remove troublemakers, no matter what the vice president might suggest. Therefore, this is your warning that you have five minutes to vacate the premises, along with your dogs. Otherwise, I'll be forced to contact the police."

"Whoa! There's no need to threaten us, Eloise." Vannie stood straight and pulled her shoulders back. "We'll be out of here in two minutes. And you can count on us leaving a one-star review for Shawn's Dog Training Solutions. This is the sorriest program I've ever encountered."

Eloise sputtered. "This has nothing to do with my son and everything to do with your inability to control your dogs."

"It has everything to do with your son since he guaranteed we could train our dogs when we handed over the exorbitant fee to join his program." Vannie took a step toward Eloise, who backed up.

"Now, now, let's not be hasty. Perhaps this has all been a misunderstanding, and you can keep your dogs on a leash while you stay." Eloise held her hands up, palms facing the ceiling.

"Don't be ridiculous, Eloise. Piper and Missy were overly excited, and they've worn themselves out now. Let Emory and Vannie stay for lunch without worrying about their dogs." Cheryl walked over to stand next to us in a show of solidarity. "I don't know why you're here since you don't even have a dog." Cheryl whispered, but it was loud enough for Eloise to hear. "She has a cat. She doesn't like dogs even though Shawn's company pays all her bills."

"You don't need to be spreading rumors, Cheryl," Eloise sputtered. "Fine, you two can stay and enjoy the luncheon even if it's only potluck."

She said "potluck" as if it was a dirty word. When Cheryl had made the suggestion, all twelve people participating in the training program had readily agreed that a potluck made the most sense. Henri, who had a schnauzer-mix dog named Blossom, had offered to make homemade apple dog treats for the canine participants. I had every intention of getting the recipe from him should Piper and Missy like the treats. Who was I kidding? Those two dogs had yet to find any food they didn't love.

"You still haven't explained why you're here, Eloise." Cheryl crossed her arms.

"I'm here to support and help promote my son's business. Something you wouldn't know about." Eloise spun around on her heels, the red soles flashing, and left the kitchen.

Cheryl's face had drained of color, and her fists were clenched. I touched her shoulder. "Are you okay?"

She seemed to shake herself, muttered "Fine," then followed Eloise out of the kitchen.

"What was that all about?" Vannie asked.

"I have no idea. Whatever it is, I think Eloise knew exactly how to hurt Cheryl the most." I picked up two disposable plates holding the cupcakes, not bothering to retransfer them to my decorative platter. "Can you grab that third plate of cupcakes and help me get them onto the dessert table? It's probably time for lunch."

The main room of the clubhouse was bright and airy. Large windows lined the east and west sides of the room, and they'd been opened to let in the cool ocean breeze. The north side held the large double glass doors that led onto the patio and the Olympic-sized pool. Cheryl had covered five banquet tables with dog paw–printed tablecloths. In the center of each table, sunflowers sat in mason jars with raffia twine bow accents. Bowls, platters, and a few slow cookers filled with food sat upon an additional banquet table that had been covered with a disposable paper tablecloth, and another table held an assortment of desserts.

A line had formed for the food, and a few dogs nudged their owners' legs, begging for morsels. Other dogs, Missy and Piper included, sprawled on the cool terra cotta tile flooring, deep in slumber. I hoped the pair continued napping so we could enjoy our lunch without further shenanigans. Vannie and I quickly rearranged a few of the desserts and placed the cupcakes on the table. Joining the end of the food line, I scanned the room for Cheryl, but I didn't see her.

However, it was hard not to notice Shawn and Eloise huddled in the corner. Their discussion appeared to be quite tense given the frowns that creased both their faces and the way Shawn held his arms tightly crossed over his rock-hard chest. They appeared to be arguing, although quietly enough that I couldn't hear what they were saying. Eloise poked her son in the chest. It must've been hard enough to hurt, because he rubbed the area, and his face flamed red. She tried poking him again, but he shoved her hand away before she connected.

Vannie nudged me as the line moved forward. "Take some of the apple-and-sausage tortellini dish I made and let me know what you think. The recipe called for spicy Italian sausage, but I thought chicken-apple sausage went with the theme better."

"You and your tender palate." I giggled. "This is California. We like things spicy."

"I know. It's just hard to get used to." While Vannie wasn't terribly forthcoming about her childhood, I had found out she hadn't been exposed to eating jalapeños and other spicy foods.

"We'll make a Californian out of you yet." I peeked at the table Eloise and Shawn had been sitting at and found it empty. Neither of the Parkers were anywhere in sight.

Vannie giggled and began loading her disposable plate, starting with a slice of chunky applesauce-smothered pork tenderloin. I scooped up a spoonful of pumpkin-apple-three-cheese mac and cheese, according to the note the cook had included next to the slow cooker. At the end of the table, I plucked two dog bone–shaped dog treats from a Tupperware container and put them onto a small plate for the dogs. Once our plates were full—with more than we needed to eat—we found a spot to sit. Not one of the other participants opted to sit with us, and I presumed it was so they wouldn't be associated with the troublemakers.

Cheryl finally came back in, shuffling her feet. Her face was blotchy and her hair mussed. She still looked distraught.

"I'll be right back. Cheryl looks like she could use some assistance." I stood and made my way to her side.

She startled when I placed my hand on her shoulder. "Oh! I suppose I should be watching where I walk." Cheryl skittered away from my touch.

"It's all right. I wanted to help you get a plate of food, and then you can sit with me and Vannie." I gestured in the direction of our table. "We're feeling like we're back in junior high, where no one wants to sit at the geek table."

Cheryl mustered a wan smile. "I was one of those geeks, so I get it. I'll be over in a minute."

I returned to the table, where I found Piper curled up at Vannie's feet, probably hoping a tidbit of food would be dropped for her to snatch up. Missy still snoozed in the patch of sunlight that filtered through a window.

"Cheryl's going to join us." I tugged at a piece of flaky pastry that pinwheeled around apples, sausage, and cheese.

"She looks like she could use a friend." Vannie popped a cocktail-sized apple cider–sauced meatball into her mouth and chewed. Once she swallowed, she speared a plain-looking meatball from my plate and ate that too.

"Hey, that was mine." I mimicked a whiney tone. I couldn't keep up the pretense for long and chuckled. "How was it?"

"Okay, but not as good as the ones Cheryl brought. It tasted like sausage with some apple mixed with baking mix." Vannie's eyes grew misty. "My mom used to make something similar for her bridge group when I was a kid."

I reached over and clasped her hand. Vannie's parents had been killed in a hit-and-run accident, and she had been instrumental in bringing the person responsible to justice.

"Am I interrupting anything?" Cheryl stood two feet away from the table.

I pulled my hand back from Vannie's and pointed at the chair beside me. "Please, have a seat. We were reminiscing about food that reminds us of lost family members."

Cheryl's face clouded over for a moment, but then she placed her sparsely loaded plate on the table.

"Your meatballs are delicious. I'd love to get the recipe from you if you don't mind sharing." Vannie speared another meatball—this time from her own plate—and popped it into her mouth.

"Like I said before, they're easy-peasy when you start with premade meatballs. I'll email the sauce recipe to you." Cheryl shuffled the food around on her plate but didn't take a bite.

I scanned the room but still didn't see Eloise or Shawn anywhere. The other participants were engrossed in conversations. I leaned my head toward Cheryl and lowered my voice. "Eloise's comment seemed to distress you, and you still seem upset. Is there anything we can do to help?"

She shook her head.

Vannie leaned over the table toward Cheryl. "Sometimes, just talking about it with someone who's not involved helps."

Cheryl worried her lower lip, and her eyes grew teary. "My son's been in prison, and it's all Shawn's fault. He's the one who should have served the time."

Vannie and I exchanged a glance. Neither of us expected this. "How devastating for you and your family. When will he be released?"

A tear leaked down her cheek. "Kai got out last month but won't come home after being in for five years."

"Was he close enough for you to at least visit on occasion?" Vannie handed the distraught woman a tissue.

"He was up the coast, in San Luis Obispo." Cheryl wiped her eyes. "It was a long trek, and I couldn't afford to take much time off of work or spend money on a motel room. I only saw him a handful of times, and now, I might not ever see him again."

My curiosity was getting the better of me, and even though I knew I shouldn't try to pry the details from her, I wanted—no, needed—to know how Shawn was responsible. "Do you mind if I ask how Shawn caused this and why he wasn't in prison too?"

"My kid isn't a saint and has always looked for an easy way to make cash." She picked up her fork and toyed with the scoop of Waldorf salad sitting on her plate. I admired the creator's use of both red and green apples along with red and green grapes. "About seven years ago, Shawn convinced him to help start training pit bulls for dogfighting. Once the dogs were trained, Kai took over the gambling aspect of their partnership—he's always been good with numbers. After a year, Shawn added drug deals to the gambling, along with breeding dogs for clients. They were both making more money than they knew what to do with."

Cheryl's mouth quivered, and tears threatened to spill over. "Someone turned in their operation to the police, and Kai was left holding the bag. The building that housed the pit bulls was in Kai's name, and clients who'd been picked up for questioning all implicated Kai. Not one of them mentioned Shawn, including Kai."

"Why is that?" I was horrified that dogfighting had been going on in our area. It also explained Shawn's approach to dog training.

"Kai wouldn't tell me." She swiped at the tear that had

trickled down her cheek. "All he'd say was that if I wanted him to survive his incarceration, I needed to keep my mouth shut."

Vannie gasped, and my mouth fell open. I reached over and grasped Cheryl's cold hand. "Why are you telling us then? You can count on us to keep this confidential, but you shouldn't be discussing it with anyone aside of law enforcement."

"I can't go to the police." She lowered her voice to barely above a whisper. "Some of their clients were officers. If they found out, it could mean big trouble for Kai even though he doesn't live around here now."

"Again, why tell us?" I pulled my hand back and pushed my plate away. My appetite had vanished.

"I've heard you've solved some murders and thought you could maybe find a way to implicate Shawn. I don't believe for a minute that he's not doing anything illegal." She scanned the room then continued. "I think his dog training business is a front for something. Rebecca told me she bought a purebred poodle puppy from Shawn last year for a ridiculous amount. She'd planned on competing and then eventually breeding the dog but then found out Shawn had lied to her. The dog wasn't purebred, and he wouldn't refund her money. The contract she'd signed, without reading all the fine print, had plenty of loopholes and clauses that absolved him of any wrongdoing. Then the poor thing has had all sorts of health issues. The vet said it had most likely come from a puppy mill."

I shuddered. Puppy mills and dogfighting rings were ghastly, and anyone who operated or profited from one needed to be arrested. "Who is Rebecca? I don't recall that name from our training group."

"Oh. Sorry. I forget you're not associated with the condos here." She gestured at the other participants. "The majority of people here live at the condos. Eloise has pressured a lot of us to adopt puppies and then use Shawn to train our fur babies."

"And Rebecca?" Vannie reminded Cheryl.

"Oh. Right. Rebecca Brighton. She's the homeowners' association treasurer."

"Did Rebecca confront Eloise about her dog?" I studied Cheryl's face as she worried her lower lip. "Maybe she could intervene with her son?"

She finally shrugged. "I know she'd planned on talking to her, but when I asked her about it, she told me to drop it. It wouldn't surprise me if Shawn threatened her or something. He's quite intimidating."

Chapter 3

"Cheryl!" Eloise stood in the doorway, her hands fisted on her hips. "I need to talk to you right now."

The fork Cheryl had been holding clattered to the plate. "But I'm eating. Can't it wait?"

I couldn't help but notice the tremor in Cheryl's voice.

"This will only take a moment." Eloise glowered at us. "Now."

Cheryl pushed her chair away from the table and slowly stood. The rest of the room had fallen silent, but everyone studiously examined the food on their plates as Cheryl slowly walked toward the imposing woman. As soon as she reached the doorway, Eloise grabbed her arm and pulled her onto the patio and away from the entrance. Probably so no one would eavesdrop on their conversation. Within a minute or two, Cheryl returned. Her face was beet red, and she wouldn't meet my gaze.

"Is everything all right?" I asked.

"Fine. It was just about something Eloise needs me to take care of first thing Monday morning."

Vannie and I exchanged a look that said we didn't believe her.

"Is she upset at you for some reason?" Vannie asked.

Cheryl shook her head. "Everything's fine. Really."

Eloise returned to the room and clapped her hands. She waited until the chatter quieted before she spoke. "I'm sorry that Shawn had other business to attend to and couldn't be here to pass out graduation certificates to those who qualify." She glared at me before continuing. "He'll email the certificates to you next week."

Without another word, she spun on her heels and left. Several attendees muttered amongst themselves, but I caught the gist. They thought Shawn was a cheapskate and had probably never intended to pass out printed certificates with their dogs' names imprinted on them.

Vannie and I ate the rest of our meal in relative silence. Cheryl didn't respond to our attempts at chitchat, even about the silly antics of our dogs, nor did she eat more than a bite or two of the food on her plate.

When people started hitting the dessert table, I stood and collected our plates. "I'll throw these away and bring back an assortment of desserts for us to share. Is there anything in particular you'd like?"

Cheryl pushed her plate toward me. "Thanks. I'd like one of your cupcakes if you don't mind."

"Of course. Vannie, did you see something you'd like to try?"

"Just bring back one of everything, and we'll be good." Her cheeks rounded with the huge smile she gave me.

"That's a great plan." I picked up Cheryl's plate and added it to the ones I already held.

After disposing of the plates, I joined the short line for the delectable goodies. A stocky woman, perhaps in her early forties, stood in front of me. I searched my memory for her name but came up blank. I blamed my shortcoming on Shawn discouraging any social interaction within the group—humans and dogs alike—during the training.

She turned to face me and brushed magenta bangs out of her eyes. "You're Emory, right? I have a hard time telling you and your sister apart."

"Yes, and you're Anna...?"

"Actually, it's Arabelle, but I go by Belle." She snorted and tugged on her snug black T-shirt. "Not that Lord Trainer would stoop to call me by my nickname."

Heat flooded my face, but I got the sense that she was another unhappy client of Shawn and his heavy-handed ways. "Sorry about that. He did make it difficult to get to know each other."

She snorted again. "How'd you get roped into this?"

"My sister's grandmother surprised us with the course."

Belle raised her eyebrows. "Not your grandmother?"

I shook my head. "Long story, but no. Tillie's an honorary grandmother to me."

Belle inched closer to the dessert table as the line moved. I followed.

"How about you? How did you find this trainer?"

"Probably the same way most of us ended up here: coerced into buying a dog from Shawn and then coerced into purchasing the training session." She leaned toward me and lowered her voice. "Don't ever move into these condos. It's a racket."

I drew my eyebrows together. "Can't the homeowners join together and do something about it?"

She shook her head. "The last time a few tried, they ended up with legal bills out the wazoo and then had a heck of a time trying to sell to get out of here. Like I said, it's a racket, and it's best to just keep your head down and go along with it."

We finally reached the dessert table, and my mouth watered over the yummy treats. I placed a couple of each on my plate. When Belle pointedly looked at my hoard, my face heated again. "I'm sharing with my table."

She peered over at Cheryl and Vannie. "Be careful what you say in front of Cheryl. She's in Eloise's back pocket."

"From my perspective, it looks like Eloise and Shawn are coercing her just as much as everyone else."

"Maybe. I'd still be careful."

Since we were the only two remaining at the dessert table, I settled my plate onto the surface. "Do you mind if I ask about the dog you purchased from Shawn? What breed did you get, and do you feel like your pet is healthy?"

"Brutus is a Chihuahua. And I know for a fact I paid too much for a dog that has joint issues." Her mouth turned downward. "I'm sure that Shawn is involved in a puppy mill, given what my vet said about Brutus. But what am I going to do? I have no way to prove it."

"I'm so sorry about Brutus."

"Me too, but at least he has a loving home now." Belle stiffened and turned to leave. "I need to get back to my table."

Without another word, she scurried over to the table she shared with five other attendees. I looked around to see what had spooked her. It was Eloise. She stood in the doorway and surveyed the room. Her gaze landed on me, and her mouth moved into a grim line. I tried to ignore her as I picked up my filled plate, along with three empty paper plates, and returned to Vannie and Cheryl.

"Sorry for taking so long." I placed the plate in the middle of the table and handed each of my tablemates an empty plate. Mindful of Belle's warning, I decided to tell a white lie. "That woman asked for my cupcake recipe."

"That takes a lot of nerve." Cheryl's voice rose. "Doesn't she know you're a cupcake caterer?"

"No. Why would she?" I picked up an oatmeal, apple, and white chocolate chip cookie from the plate. "We never had the opportunity to socialize during the training sessions. I didn't even know her name until now."

"Hmph." Cheryl took the cupcake from the plate and

peeled back the red-and-black dog bone–printed paper wrapper. She took a bite and fell quiet as she chewed. Her eyes even closed for a brief moment before she swallowed. "I hope you told her to order some if she wanted them."

I broke the cookie in half and handed a piece to Vannie before taking a bite. The cinnamon-y apple flavor flooded my mouth, and the white chocolate chips added a pleasing sweetness.

Once Vannie had taken a bite, her eyes widened. "That is good, but how did they get so much apple flavor in it? It seems more intense than if only fresh apples were used."

Cheryl wiped her mouth with a paper napkin. "Simone gave me the recipe. She uses apple crisps and frozen concentrated apple juice in the dough instead of fresh apples. It really makes the apple flavor pop."

"Apple crisps? What's that?" Vannie picked up another cookie, split it in two, and handed me a piece.

"It's some kind of dried apples that are like potato chips, just made from apples. Her son loves them, even when they're not in cookies." Cheryl took another bite of cupcake and might have uttered a soft moan.

"Is Simone the woman with the eight-year-old boy?" I jutted my chin toward the table farthest from us, where a thin, petite woman, probably in her early thirties, sat. Her coffee-brown hair was cut short and spiked on the top. A row of earrings glittered along her ears. Her son wasn't with her.

"Yep. His name is Carter. Cute kid but too much energy." Cheryl licked the frosting from her fingers then wiped her hands on the napkin. "I think his dad picked him up right before lunch."

"Which dog belongs to them?" I gazed around the room.

"It's the black miniature poodle." Cheryl chuckled. "Carter named him Thor. He's into mythology and stuff. Carter is, not Thor."

I was happy to see Cheryl acting more like herself instead

of seeming so withdrawn. Maybe the combination of sugar and booze from the cupcake had helped revive her mood. "Did they get Thor from Shawn?"

A shadow passed over Cheryl's face. "Thankfully, no. I believe it was a puppy from his grandparents' dog. As far as I know, Thor is in good health."

I divided the remaining desserts between our plates. Someone had gone all out with an apple crumb cake, while another person had baked an apple Bundt cake drizzled with glaze. We sampled maple-glazed apple blondies, apple fritter bread, and caramel-apple-pie bars. They were all amazing, and I ate every last crumb despite being stuffed.

Vannie popped the last bite of apple fritter bread into her mouth. "There wasn't one thing here today that I didn't like."

I agreed then checked to make sure Eloise was nowhere in sight. "Do you think it would be worthwhile for me to talk to everyone who purchased a dog from Shawn? They might have some information that you don't."

Cheryl twisted her mouth then sighed. "About that. It's best we just drop the whole thing. I can't risk my son's safety."

Vannie gawped. "Were you threatened? Did Eloise say something when she called you outside earlier?"

Her face blanched. "No. Not at all. I've just had time to think about it, and there's no sense in stirring anything up."

"I promise if we talk to anyone, it'll be low-key. Eloise and Shawn won't find out."

Cheryl fixed her watery-gray eyes on us. "Eloise and Shawn *always* find out."

Chapter 4

O nce the desserts had been consumed, the party quickly ended. Participants gathered their dogs along with their dishes and belongings and straggled out into the bright sunshine.

Cheryl began clearing our table.

"What can we do to help clean up?" Vannie began folding the tablecloth as soon as Cheryl had cleared the last plate.

"If you could gather the cloth tablecloths, that would be great. I bought them myself, and I'd like to keep them." She tossed the soiled plates and napkins into a large trash bin. "The cleaning crew is scheduled to come in late tonight, and they can take care of the rest."

"What about the leftover desserts?" I perused the table that still held four of my cupcakes along with an assortment of cookies and bars that had been transferred to disposable plates.

"If you don't want any, then the cleaning crew will eat them or take them back to their office."

"We don't need any of it," Vannie said as she plucked another cookie from the table.

My sister was right, of course. I had cupcakes waiting for

us at home, and Vannie typically kept a container filled with homemade cookies in Tillie's pantry.

Between the three of us, the tables were quickly stripped of the linens, and we headed home. Piper and Missy had clearly worn themselves out and gently snored from the back seat of my cherry-red SUV once I'd given them the home-made dog treats. As I'd suspected, they'd gobbled the dog bone-shaped treats up then begged for more.

"Any plans for the rest of the day?" Vannie asked.

"I need to bake one hundred birthday cupcakes for a little girl's party. I have to deliver them by ten tomorrow morning on Lido Isle, and all I've accomplished is getting the mermaid tails done." I turned my blinker on to merge onto the Pacific Coast Highway, known as PCH by locals. "She wants me to replicate mermaid-themed cupcakes she found on Pinterest, and all I can say is they're the most labor-intensive things I've come across."

"I'll bet they're adorable once you get them done." Vannie yawned. "Maybe you should make a few extras for Sophie, Kaylee, and Tommy for dinner tomorrow night."

"I planned on doing that. I'm so glad we already cele-brated our nieces' birthday. I'm not sure I ever want to dupli-cate this design for so many people again, but at least I'm being well compensated for it."

My twin, Carrie, had birthed twin girls, who had just turned six the previous month. Fortunately for me, they'd wanted a cookie-decorating party so they and their friends could decorate their treats themselves instead of having me produce an elaborate, time-consuming design. My sister, a professional caterer, had made an ice cream cake to consume poolside at my home. In addition to her two daughters, Carrie had a son, Tommy, who was now a sturdy eighteen-month-old despite having been premature.

"How about you? Any plans this evening?" I slowed the

vehicle and came to a stop as the stoplight turned red. I turned and smiled at my sister.

"Teresa asked if I'd like to join her at a jazz supper club tonight." Vannie's cheeks turned pink. She'd recently started working at a local high school as an English teacher. Teresa was the Spanish teacher and had also spent a few years in Spain in her early twenties. They had a lot in common and had developed a close friendship in the short month since they'd met. I wondered if Vannie's blush indicated there was a romance developing between the pair, not that I felt free to ask. Yet. My half sister was reticent about anything to do with her current or even former private life. We were still in the stage of trying to define our relationship, no matter how well we got along. Tillie might know, but I didn't feel comfortable going behind Vannie's back to satisfy my curiosity.

"That sounds like fun. Is it the one up in Seal Beach?" I pressed on the accelerator when the light turned green, more than thankful that the summer hordes of tourists had left. During peak summer season, it wasn't uncommon to sit through two or even three red-light cycles before getting to cross the intersection.

"That's the one. Have you been there?"

"No. My ex wasn't a jazz fan, and when I dated Randall, he could barely sit still long enough to eat a burger much less sit through a music session."

"Brian enjoys jazz. I'm surprised he hasn't taken you." Vannie examined her phone screen. "It's not that far a drive from Newport Beach."

"The restaurant has consumed him, and it's only recently that he's started taking Sunday and Monday evenings off on a consistent basis." What little time we had together, we hadn't wanted to spend with anyone other than our close family and friends.

"Assuming I'm going to love the club as much as I think, I'll put a bug in his ear to take you." Vannie nudged my arm, which rested on the center console. "You both have kind of become homebodies."

"Yeah, about that. If I stay home, I have less chance of finding a dead body." I'd stumbled across and been involved in too many murders over the last couple of years.

"You're living in denial. I know you've found victims at your pool house."

I groaned. "You really don't need to remind me."

"That's what sisters are for. To keep you honest with yourself."

I would have flashed her a pointed look had I not been driving. Instead, I changed the subject. "What do you think we should do about the information Cheryl shared about Eloise and Shawn? If it's true, I'm super creeped out."

"I know. Don't you think it's weird that she changed her mind about us getting involved right after Eloise pulled her from the clubhouse?"

"It's certainly suspicious." I used my garage door remote to open the door and parked. "I think we should find a way to contact each participant and see if anyone else bought a puppy from Shawn that's now experiencing issues, without getting Cheryl involved."

"That's a good plan."

I opened the vehicle's door then stopped. "I forgot to tell you. I talked to Belle—the one with the magenta hair—while at the dessert table. She said she'd had the same experience as Cheryl in that she was coerced into buying a dog from Shawn and then signing up for the training sessions. Plus, her vet suspects her little Chihuahua is from a puppy mill since it has some health issues."

"I watched a documentary on puppy mills, and it was utterly heartbreaking. If Shawn's running one, we need to do something to shut it down and bring him to justice." Vannie opened her door and stepped out. "I didn't see or hear anything out of the ordinary at his training facility."

Shawn's Dog Training Solutions was located in a large warehouse in an industrial park close to the Santa Ana airport. It wasn't unusual to feel as if the planes were flying right over us as they took off. The first few times I'd experienced it had been startling, and the dogs had been quite upset as well.

"I think if he'd installed the puppy mill there, we would have heard a lot of barking. Right?"

"You're right. He must have it somewhere else. Maybe out in the desert where no one would complain about the noise?" Vannie popped the trunk of the SUV and extracted her covered casserole dish. "Where are your platters?"

"Ugh. I left them at the clubhouse in the kitchen." My stomach dropped. "I bought them specifically for tomorrow's birthday party."

"Use something else." Vannie slung her purse over her shoulder.

"The platters will complement the mermaid cupcakes perfectly, and for the price I've charged, I feel like I have to go back and pick them up." I eyed Vannie hopefully.

"Sorry, no can do. Teresa is picking me up in thirty minutes, and I desperately need a shower and makeup fix." She slung her free arm around me and bussed my cheek. "Text Cheryl and see if she can meet you there."

"I should have gotten her phone number. I'll send her an email, and hopefully she'll see it right away." I opened the back door of the SUV and lifted Piper and Missy down one at a time. "Can you put them in my backyard before you head to the shower? I need to pick up those platters and get back here and start baking."

She saluted me. "I'm on it. And don't worry. If you're still up baking and decorating when I get home, I'll come help out."

"You're the best. Thank you!" I waited until Vannie had corralled the two dogs and gotten them safely into my backyard then sent Cheryl a quick email before pulling out of the garage.

Traffic was even lighter than it had been on our drive home, and I hit green lights most of the way. It took a mere twenty minutes to arrive back at the clubhouse in Huntington Beach. Cheryl still hadn't answered my email, but I decided to try the glass doors to the clubhouse anyway. They were unlocked and opened when I tugged on the handle. The overhead chandelier lights were on, and the main room appeared empty aside from the tables and chairs. The dessert table had been cleared of plates and the goodies. Only a few crumbs had been left behind. I wondered if the cleaning crew had arrived earlier than what Cheryl had said. If so, I desperately hoped they'd left my platters behind.

"Hello?" I raised my voice. No one answered. "I'm here to pick up some platters from the event this afternoon."

Not a peep. I made my way toward the kitchen area and wondered why the cleaning crew would have taken the desserts but hadn't cleaned up the crumbs left on all the tables and floors.

The smell of natural gas along with burnt coffee assaulted my nose as I rounded the corner and walked into the kitchen. Had someone left a burner on and the flame had gone out? I pulled my T-shirt up to cover my nose.

That was when I saw the stilettos. The red soles faced the doorway I'd just walked through. The stiletto-clad feet were attached to black pants-covered legs and stuck out from behind the stainless-steel island. Even without seeing the person, I was fairly certain it was Eloise. Not one other attendee today had been wearing stilettos or black slacks.

The hiss of gas coming from the professional eight-burner stovetop caught my attention and made me stop in my tracks. My gaze swept the rest of the kitchen to ascertain if I was alone. No one else was here aside from the body. My attention returned to the coffee maker that had been left on, right next to the stovetop. The dregs were beginning to scorch in the glass carafe. If the glass shattered, would it cause an explosion with all the gas filling the air? I wasn't sure, but I didn't want to take any unnecessary chances. I rushed to the stovetop, my T-shirt pressed firmly over my mouth and nose.

As I attempted to hold my breath, I couldn't help but gasp when the full form of Eloise came into view. She was lying, face up, on the floor. Buttercream had been smeared over her face, and a cupcake had been crammed into her mouth. Her arctic-blue eyes stared, unblinking.

Chapter 5

I tore my gaze away from Eloise and stepped around her to reach the source of the gas. With shaking hands, I fumbled with the stovetop's knobs, switching them all to the off position. Trying not to breathe in the deadly fumes, I darted to the windows and cautiously opened each one, not sure what might cause the gas to ignite before it dissipated. At each window—there were four of them—I pressed my face against the screen and gulped in fresh air.

As soon as the windows were open and I'd filled my lungs with fresh air, I grabbed the coffee carafe and walked through the main dining area and out onto the patio. After placing the carafe on a table, I fumbled with my phone and called 911.

"What's your emergency?" The dispatcher sounded congested.

"I found a body, and someone left all the gas burners on." My voice quaked, and I was certain my words were barely discernable.

"Ma'am, do you need medical attention?"

"I'm all right, but you need to send the police, fire, and ambulance. Someone tried to blow up the clubhouse to cover up the murder."

"What's your location, ma'am?" Despite my frantic demands, the dispatcher's voice remained calm and soothing.

"I'm at the clubhouse at the Oceanview condos. It's at Sandy Beach and Sandpiper Way."

"Have you vacated the building, and are you safe?"

"Yes. I'm on the patio, but I'll make my way to the parking area to wait for the police."

"They've been dispatched and should reach you in a few minutes." Clicking keys filled my ear. "Could you provide your name?"

"Emory Martinez." I still hadn't done anything about changing my last name after my divorce. I'd thought I would revert to my maiden name, but when I found out my dad wasn't really my dad, I felt adrift and didn't know what last name I should claim. My stepdad, Lars Whitendale, would have been delighted for me to take his name, but since I was inching closer to thirty, it didn't seem as important as when I was a kid and he'd given us a home. Back then, I'd been a bratty preteen and balked at his offer to officially adopt Carrie and me. I had been certain my own father would come back to claim us. He never did.

"And is this your personal cell phone number that you're calling from?"

"Yes."

"Would you like for me to stay on the line with you while you wait for emergency personnel?"

"There's no need. I think I can hear the sirens already."

"All right. Be safe." He disconnected the call before I could respond.

I trotted to my SUV and climbed inside. With the doors securely locked, I nervously waited for the emergency personnel while I pondered who might have wanted to kill Eloise. One thing was certain: I'd be a suspect, and I hoped the investigating detective would have a fair and open mind. It was unfortunate that Newport Beach detectives wouldn't be assigned the case, which had happened in Huntington Beach. I had two detective friends on the Newport Beach force, and I trusted them to not arrest me, although they sometimes might want to because of my meddling.

It didn't take long for a police car, closely followed by a fire truck and a paramedic truck, to pull into the parking lot, lights flashing and sirens blaring. I climbed from the SUV and stood while they parked. The police officer was the first to jump from his vehicle, and I strode to meet him by the walkway that led to the glass-doored clubhouse entrance. The firemen and paramedics weren't far behind.

"You called about a body and a gas leak?" Officer Reed, according to the name tag pinned to his uniform, looked at least ten years younger than me. He was fresh-faced, and a permanent dimple accented his rosy apple cheeks. His wheat-blond hair was cut military short, which emphasized his light-blue eyes.

Clasping my shaking hands, I nodded. "It's Eloise Parker. She's the homeowners' association president. I found her in the kitchen just lying on the floor. She's clearly deceased."

A fireman interrupted me. "And the gas leak? Is it in the kitchen?"

"It's not a leak. Someone turned on all eight burners on the stovetop but without the flames. I turned the burners off and opened all the windows." I turned my attention to the police officer. "Someone left a carafe of coffee dregs on the coffeepot burner and set it right next to the stovetop. I got the impression someone was trying to cause an explosion and make it look like an accident."

"The investigating detective will make that determination." The young officer's youthful voice softened his statement, so I didn't feel like I was getting a lecture. "Can you show us the kitchen?"

"Hold up. We need to make sure the area is safe before anyone enters the building." The fireman held up his hand in the stop position. He was tall, with well-proportioned muscles. His wavy black hair, coffee-brown eyes, and chiseled jaw made him a firemen's calendar-worthy model. If he hadn't reminded me so much of my ex-husband, I might have swooned a bit. "How long have the windows been open?"

"Maybe ten minutes? I didn't pay attention to the time. My only thought was to turn off the burners and get out of there." I pointed to the gate that led to the pool. "I brought the coffee carafe outside but didn't turn off the coffee machine. I wasn't sure if the switch would spark and ignite the gas."

"You did the right thing." The fireman motioned for another man, dressed in the same yellow fireman gear, to follow him.

The three paramedics clustered around their vehicle, medical bags in hand. I presumed they'd wait until the building was declared safe.

"Ma'am?" The young police officer tapped on an iPad. He shuffled his feet and appeared a little nervous. "A detective will be here soon. He'd like me to get your contact information and a brief statement while we wait."

I provided my name and address, grateful he didn't seem to associate me with my ex-husband, Officer Philip Martinez, who worked in the same department.

"And what were you doing here at this time of day?"

"I was here for a luncheon with about twenty-five other people." A few of the attendees had brought their spouses and children. "We'd just finished the last session of dog training and wanted to celebrate. I'd forgotten a couple of my platters, and I need them for tomorrow morning, so I came back. I'm a cupcake caterer, and I have a delivery to make first thing tomorrow morning."

The motion of the paramedics entering the clubhouse caught my eye. The gas must've dissipated. I unrealistically hoped they could revive Eloise, but deep down, I knew it was too late.

Officer Reed looked up from his iPad. His eyebrows shot toward his hairline, and his eyes widened. "You're *that* Emory? Philip's ex-wife?"

Why, oh why, did I have to mention the cupcakes? "Uh, yes. That's me."

He took a step backward. "Okay. I think I have all the information I need. The detective will be here soon."

I couldn't help but frown. What had Philip been saying about me to his fellow officers? I had thought we'd sorted out our issues and had parted amicably, despite him being a lying, cheating snake who'd left me deeply in debt.

Before the officer could trip over his own two feet in his haste to get away, I held up my hand. "Wait. What has Philip been saying about me?"

His cheeks reddened. "Uh. Nothing?"

"Oh, c'mon, you know I don't believe you. I promise I won't tell him where I heard it." My ex could be a bit vindictive.

Officer Reed's gaze darted around. "Uh, it's really nothing to worry about."

I lifted an eyebrow and tapped my foot.

He caved. "Um, um, he said you were a murder magnet."

I barked out a laugh. It wasn't funny except that this wasn't the first time I'd been called a murder magnet.

"And he said anyone in their right mind would steer clear of you." He kept his head lowered. "Sorry."

"It's not your fault. Besides, Philip's said much worse to me and about me." I held up my empty ring finger. "It's one of the many, many reasons he's my ex."

He nodded then heaved a sigh of relief when an unmarked black sedan pulled into the parking lot. I turned and watched as the vehicle came to a stop, and once the engine had turned off, a large man unfolded from the seat and stood. He was tall, at least a foot taller than my five-two frame, and his bulky build looked like pure muscle without an ounce of pudginess, the exact opposite of my build. As the detective —it couldn't be anyone else—ambled toward me, Officer Reed stepped even farther back.

Chapter 6

The detective stopped three feet from me then tapped on his iPad, tapped a few more times, and scrolled. He finally lifted his gaze to meet mine. His hazel eyes were flecked with gold, which complemented his caramel skin tone. Gray sprinkled his short black hair, and I guessed he was in his late forties. Dressed in a crisp white button-down shirt, which had no wrinkles despite the lateness of the day, and pressed black slacks, he exuded a no-nonsense air.

"Ms. Martinez, I'm Detective Hawkins." Instead of shaking my hand, he extended a business card. "I understand you found a body and believe someone intentionally tried to blow up the building?"

I took the card and tucked it into my pocket. "Yes."

Before I could elaborate, the fireman strode up to us and extended his hand to the detective. "Nathan. Nice to see you despite the circumstances."

"It's great to see you too, Larry." The detective shook the offered hand. "How's the wife and new little one?"

"They're doing fine. Sarah's turning one next week. Can you believe it?"

Detective Hawkins whistled. "The adage is true. Time flies."

"You're right about that." The fireman jerked his thumb over his shoulder. "It's safe to enter the building and examine your victim. It's a doozy."

The two men turned their attention to me, and Larry pointed in my direction. "This young woman probably saved the day with her quick thinking by turning off the burners and opening the windows. I took a look at the burnt coffeepot, and it was probably only a matter of thirty minutes or so before it would have caught fire. Someone put an accelerant in the pot. My guess is kerosene or maybe paint thinner, but the lab will be able to tell for sure."

My face heated, especially when it seemed that Detective Hawkins let his attention linger on me much too long. "I didn't do this."

"Ms. Martinez, why don't you wait in your car while I take a look. I have a lot of questions I need answers to." Detective Hawkins didn't wait for a reply. "Larry, you can walk through the crime scene with me."

The two men walked toward the clubhouse and entered. I headed to my SUV to wait for what would surely be a long, drawn-out interview. I mentally kicked myself for procrastinating on making the cupcakes that had to be delivered the following morning. It was going to be a long, long night with zero sleep.

With nothing to keep myself occupied while I waited, I opened the notes app on my phone and started a list of suspects—er, attendees—from the potluck. This wasn't the first body I'd found nor was it the first time I'd been accused of murder. So far, Detective Hawkins hadn't come right out and said he thought I was guilty nor had he hinted as such either.

Still, it didn't hurt to write down everything I recalled from the events of the day. I also needed to get all the email addresses—and phone numbers if available—of the training participants. I hoped Cheryl would be willing to divulge the information. Assuming I ever made it home this evening, I'd make her a batch of apple pie–filled cupcakes to sweeten my request.

Shawn was at the top of my list. While I wouldn't have called it an argument, he'd obviously been upset with his mother before he bailed out on our, well, the attendees' graduation celebration. Cheryl appeared to have plenty of motives for killing Shawn, but I just didn't see her murdering Eloise and, most especially, staging the clubhouse to blow up.

Then there were people who had purchased dogs from Shawn only to find that they'd had health issues due to Shawn's supposed puppy mill conditions. If Shawn had been the victim, they'd all have solid reasons for killing him, but it didn't make any sense to target Eloise. I racked my brain to remember the names and came up with Belle, Cheryl, and the condo association treasurer. I'd have to ask Cheryl for the woman's name again. I wrote down the names with question marks as a header.

A rap on my window made me jump, and I fumbled with my phone. Detective Hawkins motioned for me to roll down my window. I complied.

"Ms. Martinez, I assume the cupcakes that are part of the crime scene are yours?"

"Yes. But how did you know?" My hands began to tremble, so I tucked them beneath my legs.

"I know exactly who you are and what trouble you've gotten into before this." His lips mashed together to form a grim line.

"I promise you, I had nothing to do with her death or with trying to blow up the clubhouse." The tremble in my voice was impossible to control.

He gave a slight nod. "I have your contact information from Officer Reed. Head home, and I'll be in contact with you tomorrow to get your full statement. For some reason, the lad neglected to get all the details."

I couldn't help but smile wryly. "Ah, yes. It seems my ex has embellished my, uh, reputation. I think Officer Reed is just a bit frightened of me."

"I'll have a chat with Officer Martinez and put an end to his rumor and innuendo mongering." Detective Hawkins turned to head back to the clubhouse.

"Wait."

He turned back toward me.

"You'd really tell Philip to stop spreading rumors about me?"

"For whatever reason the universe has, you've been involved in several murders in the last couple of years. Not only have you survived the attempts on your life, but you've found out crucial details that solved the cases." Detective Hawkins placed his large hand on his narrow hip. "I'd like to tell you to leave the investigating to the experts, such as myself, but I fully recognize that most people aren't open or chatty when talking to the police. On the other hand, if they feel like they're merely gossiping or chatting while indulging in your cupcakes, they're more apt to share information we wouldn't otherwise get. I can't have an officer spreading detrimental rumors that might hinder you obtaining that information."

"Thank you. I appreciate your confidence." I could scarcely believe what he was saying. Instead of arresting me, he was encouraging me to bake cupcakes and gossip? "Does that mean I'm not a suspect?"

"Let's just say I'm inclined to believe your innocence and will keep your name at the bottom of my suspect list for now." He tapped the SUV's window frame. "Head on home. I understand you're delivering mermaid cupcakes for Amanda's birthday party tomorrow morning, and I'm sure you have a lot to do before then."

My mouth fell open. "How do you know that?"

He grinned. "She's my goddaughter and has been talking about them nonstop for the last month."

Before I could snap my mouth closed or respond, Detective Hawkins turned and jogged back to the clubhouse. I sat, stunned, for half a minute then started the engine. Before I pulled out of the parking lot, I called Brian on the SUV's Bluetooth connection.

"Hey, what's up?" The sounds of banging pans, chattering prep chefs, and knives thudding into wooden chopping boards practically drowned out his voice.

"I know you're super busy right now, but I wanted to let you know I'm safe. I found another body this afternoon."

"Hang on." The noise of the kitchen receded, and I surmised Brian was walking toward his office. A door closed, and it was quiet. "Did you just say you found another body?"

I nodded then remembered he couldn't see me. "Yes. I came back to the condo clubhouse to get the platters I'd forgotten to take home after our lunch. That was when I found the homeowners' association president."

"Are you okay? Was she murdered?" Brian's voice held concern and not irritation that I'd found another victim.

"I'm fine, but unfortunately, yes, it was a murder. But the good news is the detective says I'm not really a suspect, or at least I'm not at the top of his list."

"Em, what aren't you telling me?" Brian could always tell when I was glossing over something.

"Welllll…" I gulped. "The killer left on all eight stovetop burners in the kitchen—that's where I found her—and a coffeepot left on that had burned down and had started to smoke."

"You got out of there the second you saw that, right?" Brian's voice held agitation now.

"I turned the burners off, opened all the windows, and took the coffeepot outside. I couldn't risk leaving it like that. What if it blew up when the firefighters got there?"

"You're right. You did the brave thing, but oh my god, what if it'd blown up while you were there? I don't know what I'd do if something happened to you." His voice trembled. "I'm taking off, and I'll be at your house in about an hour."

"Brian, really, there's no need." I rushed to reassure him when I heard his sharp inhalation of breath. "Of course, I'd love to see you, but I still have to bake cupcakes for the mermaid party tomorrow, and it's going to take me all night to get it done. Besides, Saturdays are your busiest night of the week, and you can't disappoint your foodie fans by leaving."

He blew out a long breath. "I know you're right, but I still feel like I should be there to show my support in person."

"I'm safe, and the cupcakes will keep me preoccupied tonight." I smiled. "How about you come show me your support around noon tomorrow? I should be home from delivering the cupcakes and have all my chores completed by then."

"It's a date. I'll bring something for lunch." A knock sounded on Brian's office door, followed by a murmur of voices. "Sorry about that. I really have to get back to the kitchen."

"No problem. I'll see you tomorrow." After our declarations of love for each other, I disconnected the call.

Piper and Missy weren't in the yard nor were they in the house. Worried just a tad, I sent Tillie a quick text asking if she'd picked them up.

She responded immediately but called instead of sending her usual text. She jumped in without any preamble. "I'm sorry. I meant to send you a text to let you know I brought them over to my place. John ended up flying back to London today instead of next week as planned, so I'm home."

John was Tillie's beau, at least when he visited Southern California several times a year. A real-live English baron, he divided his time between London, Newport Beach, and his villa in Italy. He'd hinted that he would love nothing more than for Tillie to join him on his travels, but as of yet, she'd declined.

"Oh? Is everything all right?"

"As far as I know. He didn't mention why his plans changed." Tillie rustled a bag, and the two dogs whined.

"Are you feeding them more treats?" I pulled butter from the refrigerator and began chopping it into small cubes to help soften it more quickly.

"Well…" Tillie chuckled. "Busted."

I glanced at the clock built into the double ovens. It was five already. "I have mermaid cupcakes to bake and decorate for delivery tomorrow, so I'd planned on reheating tortilla soup leftover from a couple days ago. Would you like to join me, or do you have other plans?"

"That sounds perfect. John took me out for a huge lunch before he left for the airport, so I'm not terribly hungry." Tillie rustled the treat bag again.

"You're spoiling them too much, and they're not going to want to eat their dinner either."

"Fine. Have it your way." Tillie covered the phone with her hand and proceeded to tell the dogs what a mean lady I was.

"Tillie, what time would you like to come over?"

"The girls and I will be there in about fifteen minutes. Does that work for you?"

"Perfect. I'll have the soup ready along with a margarita, or would you rather have a gimlet?"

"Water is fine. John and I had a few too many mimosas with lunch, and I want to keep a clear head over dinner to discuss your new investigation."

"Wait. What? How did you hear about that already?"

"Your sister told me the briefest of details before she left on her date."

Was Tillie giving me a clue that romance was brewing

between Vannie and Teresa? "But how did she know? I didn't call her."

"Teresa's cousin was one of the paramedics who responded to the scene. He's met Vannie several times and, at first, thought it was her, so he called Teresa, who called your sister."

"Bad news still travels fast, I see." I was a bit hurt that Vannie hadn't bothered to check to make sure I was all right. And why had Teresa introduced Vannie to her family on multiple occasions when we knew next to nothing about her?

Tillie must've heard something in the tone of my voice. "Don't go and start feeling sorry for yourself. Vannie was set on canceling her date and heading back to the site to be with you. I put my foot down and insisted she go out. It's important to me that she put roots down here, and there's no better way than by making close friends and finding love."

Well, that answered my question about her relationship with Teresa. But she could have at least called me, and I said as much.

"She started to call you, and then I reminded her that you'd be talking to the police and wouldn't be able to answer the phone anyway. I also promised her that you'd send her a text letting her know you're back home and safe."

"You make a good point." I still felt out of sorts, but it was most likely from the horror of finding Eloise and almost getting blown up. I knew I shouldn't take it out on my sister or Tillie.

"Good. Text her as soon as we hang up."

"I will, and I'll see you soon. And Tillie? No more treats for the dogs today."

She blew a raspberry. "Whatever."

I chuckled as we disconnected the call. Though she was in her eighties, Tillie's elegant appearance belied her exuberant sprightliness, much to her son's consternation. I'd been hired by David to prepare meals for Tillie and keep a watchful eye on her when she'd broken her arm by tumbling down the stairs. David was concerned that she was unsteady on her feet and had been exhibiting some signs of dementia. However, no one knew the real story of why she'd fallen aside from myself, Tillie, and the man she'd been sexting while traversing the staircase.

I texted Vannie, who responded with a kiss emoji, then poured the leftover soup into a saucepan and set it over medium-low heat while I made guacamole to go with tortilla chips. There's nothing easier or better than fresh, homemade guacamole. All it takes is mashing ripe avocados with a squeeze or two of fresh lime juice, salt, and pepper. Of course, adding some minced garlic and/or *pico de gallo* makes it even more delicious. I even liked chopped cilantro in my guac, but Tillie is part of the population who says it tastes like soap. When Brian teased her about it, she pulled up a proven scientific article on her phone that explained the genetic reason her taste buds reacted negatively to cilantro.

According to the article, Tillie had a variation in a group of olfactory-receptor genes that picks up the aldehydes in cilantro genes. So now we served cilantro on the side instead of mixing it into the dishes we were preparing. I frequently got a chuckle when Tillie brought up her olfactory-receptor gene whenever Brian or I served her something she didn't care for. We both try hard to make sure she eats plenty of fresh veggies and fruit even when she'd rather indulge in rich pastries for breakfast or cocktail appetizers before dinner—cheese, crackers, and salami-type meats—to go with her gimlets.

Chapter 7

T illie sashayed into the pool house, carrying a bottle of chardonnay—a very expensive bottle from her extensive wine cellar. She set it on the counter and kissed my cheek. "I changed my mind about drinking and thought we could both use a glass or two of wine with dinner."

Piper and Missy scurried into the kitchen and came to a sliding halt in front of their food and water bowls. They sat on their haunches and eagerly watched our every move. I ignored them and turned toward Tillie. "Oh?"

She opened the cupboard to the right of the kitchen sink and grabbed two wineglasses. "You sounded down, and with the day you've had, you deserve to be spoiled a bit."

"Thank you. I won't say no to a small glass, but that's it." I gestured to the cupcake ingredients lining my counter. "I have too much work to do tonight to overindulge."

"A little birdie told me you'll have a couple extra sets of hands to help out a bit later." Tillie filled a glass, practically to the brim, and handed it to me. "Here's your one glass of wine."

I took a sip. It was exquisite, as were all the wines I'd

indulged in from Tillie's wine cellar. "Vannie's bringing Teresa here to help me?"

"That's the plan. Unless you'd rather they not come over?" Tillie filled her glass to the halfway level then clinked it to mine.

"I'm happy to have their help, and even more importantly, I can't wait to meet Teresa."

"She's a darling girl, well, young woman." Tillie put a scoop of kibble into each of the dog bowls then stepped back as Piper and Missy rushed to eat. Apparently, the swimming and all the mischief they'd gotten into earlier had made them extra hungry, or else Tillie hadn't fed them as many treats as I'd assumed.

"You've met her already?" I poured the heated soup into bowls and placed them on the table.

"When she picked Vannie up late this afternoon." Tillie sat down and spread the napkin over her lap.

I retrieved the guacamole from the refrigerator and placed it beside the bowlful of tortilla chips on the table. "So, are they dating or just good friends?"

A twinkle lit up Tillie's eyes. "Vannie hasn't said, but they exchanged quite a few goo-goo-eyed looks when Teresa showed up, which makes me think there's more to it than just friendship. Your sister is a very private person, so I don't pry as much as I'd like."

I couldn't help but laugh. "It must be killing you to show such remarkable restraint."

"You don't know the half of it." She toasted me with her wineglass. "Now, dear, tell me all about the murder."

As we ate our soup and munched on chips and guac, I shared every detail I could recall. Tillie was a good sounding board and had proved to be a valuable asset in solving the other murders I'd had the misfortune of being involved in. She clenched her teeth, and her eyes hardened when I told her I suspected Shawn ran a puppy mill and had trained dogs for the fight ring.

"There's got to be a way to close him down for good and make him pay for abusing those poor animals." Tillie bent down and stroked Missy's ears. "You be sure to tell that detective what you heard."

"You can count on it. I'm just as appalled as you are."

Piper, not wanting to be left out of the attention, placed her head on my leg, so I obliged and stroked her ears.

Once the dogs were satiated with the attention, they flopped onto the floor and closed their eyes. I stood and began clearing away the empty bowls and plates from the table as I continued telling her about going back to retrieve my platters… which I still didn't have for tomorrow's party.

"The door to the clubhouse was unlocked, but no one was around. All the desserts left for the cleaners had been taken, so I assumed they'd arrived early. When no one answered, I walked back to the kitchen." I closed my eyes for a moment, realizing once again how close to death I'd been today. "When I walked in, I could smell gas. It was impossible to breathe. But even worse was the pot of coffee dregs that had been left on and was almost completely burned down. Someone had intentionally placed it next to the stovetop."

Tillie brought her palm to her mouth and held it there. Her eyes widened. She placed her free hand on top of mine and squeezed tight before releasing it.

"I covered my nose and mouth with my T-shirt and turned the cooktop burners off then opened the windows."

"Is that when you found the body?"

"She was lying right there between the island and the cooktop. I couldn't avoid seeing her." I shuddered then took a gulp of wine. "Someone smeared my cupcake buttercream all over her face and crammed a cupcake into her mouth."

"Oh, my dear." Tillie's hand found mine again and held tight. "I hope you didn't linger to examine the scene."

"Not at all. I grabbed the coffeepot but didn't turn off the machine since I wasn't sure it wouldn't spark and blow the place up. Then I ran outside and called 911."

Tillie released my hand and splashed more wine into both our glasses. "Do you think her death has something to do with the puppy mill business, or could it be something else?"

"I've been mulling over that question all afternoon. If Shawn were the victim, then I'd definitely say it was because of his abuse of animals, but I'm not sure about Eloise. I don't know how involved she was in Shawn's business aside from coercing condo residents to buy puppies from him and spend a boatload of money on his training sessions."

"I'm sorry I got you mixed up in this." Tillie shook her head. "It's all my fault. I shouldn't have gotten sucked in by his handsome face and his impressive six-pack abs. Whoever designed his website knew what they were doing."

"Don't blame yourself. All the reviews were stellar, but it makes me wonder if he or Eloise coerced those too." I stood and began measuring ingredients for the cupcakes. It was one of the things I loved about my charming pool house. The living space was wide open to the kitchen, so I could work and still chat with any of my visitors. "But back to your question. It's possible Eloise elicited rage in one of the condo residents. Even Cheryl—she's the association vice president and today's potluck organizer—had issues with Eloise and Shawn. And then her son was arrested and sentenced to five years in prison because of his association with Shawn, while Shawn got off scot-free."

"You didn't mention this before. What happened with Cheryl's son?"

I slapped my just-washed hand onto my forehead. "I completely forgot about the tiff Cheryl and Eloise got into. It's good I'm talking to you now so I'll have my facts lined up when I speak with the detective tomorrow. Eloise basically taunted Cheryl over her son's incarceration without actually saying it. Poor Cheryl was devastated. I can't believe she actually has to, er, had to deal with Eloise on a daily basis."

I quickly explained what Cheryl had told us about her son's involvement with Shawn's business and subsequent conviction.

"There you go. You have your number-one suspect right there." Tillie stood and opened my junk drawer and extracted a notepad and pen before returning to the table. "I'll start the list with Cheryl at the top."

"But I don't want her to be at the top of the list. She's sweet, and I can't see her killing anyone and then attempting to blow up the clubhouse."

"Who else might have had motivation for killing Eloise?"

"I talked to a woman, Arabelle, or Belle as she likes to be called. She purchased a puppy-mill dog from Shawn and is very unhappy about it." I paused to recall what she'd told me. "Cheryl also said that the condo association's treasurer, Rebecca something or another, bought one and paid big bucks for a purebred poodle, who turned out to be anything but. The dog also has health issues, and Shawn refused to refund her money. If she worked with Eloise, who coerced her into buying the dog, maybe that pushed her over the edge."

"Was this Rebecca person there today?"

"No, but that doesn't mean she didn't meet up with Eloise after everyone left."

"I'm adding Rebecca to the list, and you can talk to her." Tillie wrote on the pad.

I thought for a moment. "Most of today's participants kept to themselves, but from what I gathered, most of them were condo residents. It stands to reason that Eloise could have pressured them all to buy overpriced, unhealthy puppies along with the training sessions. Instead of blaming Shawn, perhaps they took their anger out on her for being Shawn's salesperson."

"Can you get the list and contact information for today's participants?"

"Cheryl has all that info. I'd planned on asking her on Monday."

"Good. You let me know when we'll go visit her. I want to see our number-one suspect in person."

"I'll email her tomorrow and set up an appointment. Would around ten Monday morning work for you?"

"I'll be ready. Should I have Andrew drive us?" Andrew was Tillie's longtime driver. Magazine model worthy, he went to great lengths to keep Tillie safe while keeping her confidences to himself.

"I can drive."

"All right." Tillie stood. "I'll get out of your hair and let you get baking. Do you want me to keep the girls for the night?"

Piper and Missy lifted their heads from where they lay. While, technically, Piper belonged to me and Tillie had adopted Missy after tragedy struck her owner, we shared them. The dogs were BFFs and generally didn't want to be separated even for the night, so we'd purchased an extra crate for both our houses and took turns having them at our homes.

"That's probably for the best. Otherwise, I'll worry about keeping them from scarfing up any little crumb I drop on the floor."

Tillie clicked her tongue, and the dogs climbed to their feet, stretched, and ambled to stand by her side. She clipped on their leashes and blew me a kiss goodbye.

Chapter 8

As soon as I heard the gate close, I turned on my stand mixer and began beating the butter and sugar together for the cupcake batter. Once the mixture was light and fluffy, I added eggs and a generous dose of vanilla then slowed the mixer and added flour, baking powder, and salt, alternating with milk. The birthday girl had requested simple vanilla cupcakes with mermaid-colored sprinkles baked into the little cakes. When the batter was smooth, I removed it from the mixer and stirred in a mixture of teal, purple, pink, and blue jimmies just until combined. After scooping the batter into cupcake tins lined with teal, purple, pink, and blue cupcake papers, I placed them in the oven, set a timer, then repeated the process all over again.

As the cupcakes cooled on wire racks, I started on the buttercream frosting. The birthday girl had decided on a lemon-flavored frosting to go with the vanilla cupcakes. When the butter was light and creamy after being whipped for five minutes, I mixed in confectioners' sugar, a pinch of salt, and freshly squeezed lemon juice until the consistency was suitable for piping. To ramp up the lemon flavor, I added several drops of culinary lemon oil then turned the mixer up to medium high and let it whip for another five minutes. I dipped a clean spoon into the sweet mixture for a taste. Sweet, with a hit of lemony tartness, it was exactly what I'd hoped for.

I'd just finished tinting portions of the buttercream dark lavender, teal, and hot pink when Vannie knocked on the doorframe of the French patio doors.

"Can we do anything to help?" She flashed me a grin as she gazed at the cupcakes and bowls of frosting that cluttered my countertop.

I checked the clock. It was already eleven thirty. No wonder I felt exhausted. "You're just in time to help with the fun part of the cupcakes. Decorating!" I set my mixing spoon in the sink and wiped my hands on a dish towel.

A young woman followed Vannie into my house. She was dressed in a buttercup-yellow sundress that complemented her honeyed skin and amber eyes. Her dark-brown hair fell in gentle waves almost to her waist.

"Em, this is Teresa. Teresa, meet my sister, Emory."

I reached out my hand, which she shook. "Nice to meet you. How was the music and dinner tonight?"

"It was fantastic." Teresa's slow drawl caught me by surprise. I'd expected either a Californian accent, that is, no accent, or a Spanish accent from the years she'd spent in Spain. "You and Brian simply must go one of these days."

"I'd love to, but with Brian's work schedule, it's been hard to make time to do much of anything."

Vannie elbowed me. "Don't let her fool you, Teresa. They just want to hole up and be homebodies when they're not working."

My face heated. "Well… you could be right. But we'll make an effort to get out one of these days."

Vannie walked over to the kitchen sink and washed her hands, and Teresa followed suit. "Show us what you want us to do, and we'll get busy."

I filled pastry bags, fitted with large star tips, with the

tinted buttercream and showed them how to pipe a layer of color to cover the top of the cupcake, dip into the mermaid sprinkles—a mixture of colored jimmies and pearls—then pipe another color of buttercream in a swirling mound over the first layer, and finish by sprinkling with the mermaid sprinkles. To finish off the cupcake, I inserted the mermaid tail, fin pointing upward, into the frosting. I'd attached a short lollipop stick to the colored candy mermaid tail so that inserting it in the cupcake base helped keep the mermaid tail upright.

"These are so cute!" Teresa pulled her cell phone from her pocket. "Do you mind if I snap a pic and send it to my cousin in Dallas? She has a daughter turning six in a couple of months, and this just might be the perfect theme for her upcoming birthday party."

"Sure, go ahead." I filled more disposable pastry bags with frosting so there'd be enough for the three of us to pipe without having to share colors.

Teresa set the mermaid cupcake on the kitchen table and took several photos from different angles. She then spent a couple minutes editing them before texting them to her cousin. Before she'd tucked her phone away, it chimed. She swiped the screen then read the text from her cousin aloud. "You have to teach me how to make those cupcakes! Mia will adore them. Party is set for Nov. 1st. Promise you'll come and bring Vannie."

Teresa and Vannie exchanged a tender look, then Vannie looked down, her cheeks pink.

"Emory, you'll show me how to make them, won't you? My cousin's daughter is going to be beyond excited." Teresa set her phone down and rewashed her hands. "Is the tail hard to make?"

"It's really easy, just time consuming depending on how many you need to make." I went to my pantry and pulled out the silicon molds and handed them to her. "I found these online, but I'll be happy to let you borrow them as long as I get them back."

"Thank you. That'll really help out my cousin." She put the molds by her purse. "How do you use them?"

"Basically, you melt colored candy melts, which you can find at the craft store, fill the tail molds, let them firm up, then pop them out. I brushed them with some edible gold glitter. You probably wouldn't have to, but I attached the lollipop sticks to the backs with some extra melted candy to help stabilize the tails since I'm delivering them to the party."

"We have a large family, so there'll probably be about fifty people there."

Teresa picked up a piping bag, and Vannie showed her how to hold it and squeeze just the right amount of frosting out onto a piece of parchment paper. She practiced a few more times before trying it on a cupcake.

"You can make the tails a couple months in advance as long as they're stored in a cool, dry place." I picked up the teal frosting bag, piped a generous swirl onto the cupcake, then dipped it in the mermaid sprinkles.

"Awesome. I'm visiting my cousin in a couple of weeks, so maybe we can have a mermaid tail–creating party while I'm there." Teresa switched frosting colors and practiced narrow but higher swirls on the parchment before tackling the cupcake.

Teresa chatted about her family, which sounded extensive to me, and I found I really enjoyed her company. Vannie was a bit more quiet than usual, but it could've been because she was allowing me to get to know Teresa.

When the conversation lagged for a moment, Vannie pointed at me with the piping bag she held. "Not to stress you out or anything, but we're dying to know what happened with Eloise this afternoon. We hear you were a hero and kept the clubhouse from blowing to smithereens."

I'd been enjoying the decorating and spending time with

the two women. I'd briefly forgotten about finding Eloise. "It was awful. Whoever did it smeared my buttercream all over her face and crammed a cupcake into her mouth."

"Do you think it was a message?" Teresa asked.

"I really don't know. It was an unfortunate happenstance that I found her." I bit my lower lip. "Besides, if the building had blown up, no one would have known about the butter-cream and cupcake."

"I hope they catch whoever did it. They could have killed you and other innocent bystanders as well." Vannie shuddered. "Give us the deets, and we'll help you investigate as much as we can."

I told them everything that had happened, and they both expressed their horror over Shawn's dogfighting training and the puppy mill.

"Whether or not we find the killer, we've got to close him down and get him convicted." Teresa's eyes had narrowed into slits. "Maybe it's time I adopt a puppy and see if we can gain access to his breeding dogs that way to check out their condition."

"We can't let you go on your own, and he'll recognize us without a doubt." I grimaced. "We're kind of persona non grata at his training program. Missy and Piper had an epic flunk out."

Teresa giggled. "So I've heard. But I think one of my cousins can outfit you with some disguises. He works for a stage production and has access to wigs and is a wizard with makeup. Trust me. You won't even recognize yourself once he's done with you."

"How many cousins do you have?" So far, I'd heard mention of three: the paramedic, the one in Dallas, and now a makeup wizard.

"More than I can count, especially when you take into consideration my second cousins or cousins once removed, whatever that means. Still, we're a very close family and spend holidays and birthdays celebrating together. We all expect to be asked for favors and have favors returned as needed." Teresa held up the cupcake she'd been working on. "I might just have to make these for our annual beach campout next summer. The kids will go crazy over them."

"You're more than welcome to borrow the molds anytime you'd like."

I was thankful when the topic of murder dropped and we moved on to other subjects as we continued to decorate. It was one thirty by the time the cupcakes were done and the kitchen cleaned up.

Vannie stretched and yawned. "We'd better let you get to bed. You have an early delivery tomorrow and a detective to talk to."

"Ugh. Don't remind me." I placed two cupcakes in a to-go box and handed them to Teresa. "Thank you for helping out tonight. I made a few extras, so you're welcome to take these."

"I enjoyed it. Thanks for letting an amateur help out." She took the cupcake box in one hand and gave me a quick hug with her free arm. "Vannie and I are going to plan another outing to the jazz club, and we're going to drag you and Brian there with us. Right, Van?"

"Absolutely." My sister smiled at me with a mischievous grin.

I followed them to the door and watched as they walked, arm in arm, to the gate that led to the alley that ran between my pool house and Tillie's home. They turned, gave me a wave, then disappeared into the night.

After making sure the doors and windows were locked tight and the alarm set, I tumbled into bed and dreamt of smashed cupcakes on faceless heads.

Chapter 9

A loud pounding on the door woke me up from a, finally, deep slumber. I'd tossed and turned for at least two hours after climbing into bed before falling asleep. I blearily looked at the bedside clock. Seven? Who was pounding on my door at seven in the morning, and why hadn't they called first? Tillie and Brian both had keys to my house, so I knew it wouldn't be either of them. I tumbled out of bed and wrapped a fuzzy robe over the ratty T-shirt I'd thrown on just a few hours before and stumbled to the door.

My eyes tried to focus on the large, imposing figure of the man who pounded on the door. It was actually a gentle knock, but with my sleep-deprived headache, it sounded louder than it actually was. I finally noticed the extra-large to-go cup of coffee and a white bakery bag clasped in his other hand. I rushed to the door to bawl out my BFF.

"Brad! What the heck? Do you know what time it is?"

"Hello to you, too, cupcake." He bent over and kissed my cheek. "Eww, did you forget to brush your teeth last night?"

I shoved him away. "Do you have any idea what time I got to sleep last night?"

"Ooohh… did a romantic night keep you too busy to

sleep?" Brad batted his eyes. "Did your dreamy chef come over to console you after finding another murder victim?"

"Argh. You're terrible." I snatched the coffee from his hand and chugged it. "You're almost forgiven since you brought me coffee."

"I know the way to your heart." He dangled the bakery bag. "I've got pain au chocolate and a bear claw."

"Okay. You're forgiven." I snatched the bag and dug out the pain au chocolate and took a bite. "How did you hear about the murder?"

"Did you forget I'm engaged to a detective? And said detective has been thoroughly instructed to notify me any time your name comes up on the police hotline?"

Brad's intended was Detective Gabe O'Neill, who had once been certain I'd been a cold-hearted murderer and arrested me. Since then, I'd forgiven him and accepted his apology, and we'd become close friends. It was a testament to his, uh, tolerance of my meddling in murder scenes that I'd been invited to be Brad's maid of honor in their upcoming nuptials.

Brad snapped his fingers in front of my face. "Wake up, Em. Promise me you're not going to be in the pokey for my wedding."

I swallowed the bite of pastry I'd just bit into. "No! Definitely not. Did Gabe say anything about the detective working the case?"

While Detective Hawkins had seemed grateful to have me snoop around while serving up cupcakes, perhaps he'd been lulling me into a sense of complacency so he could swoop in and pin the murder on me.

"Actually, he had nothing but praise to heap on the detective." He cocked his head and examined my face. "What was your interaction with him like?"

"It was actually quite promising." I took another glug of coffee. "First off, he jumped right in and said he'd read Philip the riot act for spreading gossip and inuendo about me being a murder magnet."

Brad sputtered on the sip of coffee he'd just taken. "Get out! Way to go, Detective Hawkins. Although, Em, there might be some truth to that."

"Oh, shut up." I lightly slapped his arm. Philip was the reason I'd dropped my close friendship with Brad after high school and why none of Brad's correspondence had ever reached me in the years that followed. Needless to say, Brad was not a fan of my ex.

"You said 'first of all.' What happened next?" Brad flicked a crumb of pastry from his shirt where my hand had landed on him. He dug into the bakery bag and helped himself to the bear claw. The bear claw that I'd planned on inhaling next.

"Well…" I let the word hang in the air, drawing out the suspense. I shouldn't have bothered since Brad was busy devouring the bear claw. "Anyway, he said he thought my ability to draw people into sharing gossip and drawing out information with cupcakes was admirable, and I should put my talents to use to help him solve this case."

Brad's jaw dropped open, and a bite of pastry fell to the floor. It was too bad my pups weren't there to clean it up for me. "No way. You're pulling my leg."

"I might be paraphrasing it just a tad, but he definitely implied I should be baking cupcakes and talking to potential suspects."

"Count me in as long as you don't tell Gabe."

I lifted an eyebrow. "Is that wise this close to the wedding? I'd hate for you to get arrested for obstruction of justice, and I'd especially hate it if you were injured or worse. Your groom would kill me then lock me up in jail and throw away the key."

"Whatever." Brad huffed. "I don't want to be left out of whatever you, Tillie, and Vannie are doing. I now know how Carrie must feel when you three turn into the Musketeers."

I laughed. "Carrie has her hands much too full with three

kids and a catering business to worry about what the rest of us are doing."

Brad stuck out his lower lip.

In an attempt to distract him, I tried to change the subject. "Are you and Gabe thinking about kids? We haven't talked much beyond your fabulous honeymoon to Costa Rica."

He wiggled both eyebrows. "Have you and Brian talked about kids yet?"

My face heated, and I wanted to cover it. Brad always read me so well. "We haven't even talked about the 'M' word yet. We're both fine with our status quo of spending a night or two a week together once he gets here after midnight and then Sunday nights together with family dinner."

"Ruh-roh." Brad channeled his Scooby-Doo voice. "What seems to be the problem?"

"I don't know if there even is a problem. We've never discussed future plans." I wiped some chocolate from my face with the napkin Brad handed me. "Brian's always been a free spirit, and I never had expectations when we got together."

Brad circled his hand. "And?"

"We have a great time together, but his heart is in Oceana, and I've got my cupcakes, my family, and you. He's here when he's here, and when he's not, well, I'm just fine."

"That doesn't sound like paradise." Brad finally sat down, and his face took on a serious quality I hadn't seen in quite a while. "You've been together for almost a year now, and you've never talked about your long-term relationship?"

I shook my head. "Tillie also seems to be avoiding the topic, which is so unlike her."

"Whoa. That is troubling." He gave my hand a firm squeeze. "Have you come right out and asked her if there's something going on you should be aware of? If Brian is having second thoughts about being with you, you can be sure he's talked to Tillie about it."

"I doubt it. He knows how much Tillie wants us to be

together. It might be that he's feeling extra pressure from that expectation." I shook my head. "Besides, Brian and I are fine, and from my perspective, neither of us is in any rush to take it to the next level."

"Hmmm." He removed his hand from mine and took another sip of coffee.

"Look at it this way. Brian works late most nights of the week, so I'm not in any hurry to move in with him when I wouldn't see much more of him than I do now." I gestured around my home. "Here, I'm close to Tillie and Vannie, and I'm not so far away from you and Carrie. Moving in with Brian would make me feel isolated."

"You could always ask him to move in with you."

I coughed out a laugh. "I couldn't ask him to give up his four-bedroom home to move into his grandmother's pool house."

"You make a good point," Brad conceded. "Let's change the subject, and you can tell me about the murder and the almost-explosion that you prevented instead."

For the third time, I went over the details of what had happened the previous day. It might have been easier to have had a Zoom chat with everyone and get it over all at once. I knew my mother and Carrie were going to want the details, but I hoped it could wait until our family dinner.

Brad reacted to Shawn's dogfighting training and puppy mill the same way the rest of us had. Disgust and anger clouded his face. He promised to prod Gabe into digging into it. "It sounds like he's covered his tracks, though, by letting his partner take the fall for the dogfighting. Do you have any idea where the puppy mill is located?"

"Not at all. I doubt it would be in a city, because the noise from the dogs and puppies would definitely attract attention. Maybe it's out toward the desert or in some industrial park." I wondered if I should mention that Teresa wanted to get involved. Brad had already seemed sensitive about Vannie helping out in the previous murder investigation I'd had the misfortune of being involved in. I didn't want him to feel like he was being replaced, except I hadn't been kidding when I'd said his groom would kill me if something happened to Brad.

Brad tapped his forefinger on his full lips and raised his gray eyes to the ceiling. "Maybe I should pose as a potential purchaser of a new puppy and see if I can gain access to his breeding site."

Teresa had suggested this, and now Brad had too. Perhaps they were both on the right track. "Funny you should mention that since Teresa, Vannie's new friend, suggested the same thing."

"What? I'm getting shoved out of the sleuthing group already?" His lips turned downward, and he blinked rapidly as if to chase away tears. I knew for certain he was jesting.

"Not at all, you clown."

As I'd suspected, Brad's face immediately brightened, and he laughed.

"Vannie and Teresa went to the jazz supper club up in Seal Beach last night then dropped by to help me finish the mermaid cupcakes. There was no getting around discussing the murder since Teresa's cousin was one of the EMTs who responded to the scene." I picked up Brad's arm and looked at his watch. "I've got to get in the shower within the next fifteen minutes. It won't do to be late delivering the cupcakes to this party, especially since the birthday girl is the investigating detective's goddaughter."

Brad's chuckle filled the room. "I have a feeling you'd better have cupcakes on hand when you meet up with him to give your statement."

I was ready to tell him Detective Hawkins was completely professional when my phone began buzzing with an incoming call. It wasn't a number I recognized, but the call was local, so I answered it in case someone wanted to place a cupcake order.

As soon as I said hello, a gruff male voice responded. "Ms. Martinez, this is Detective Hawkins. As you know, I'm supposed to be attending my goddaughter's birthday party at eleven today, and I'd like to sit down with you and take your statement beforehand. Can we meet at ten?"

"I'm supposed to drop the cupcakes off at their house at ten, so we could meet around ten thirty if that works. Or right now if that's better for you." I wasn't about to offer to meet after the party concluded since I wanted Brian to myself for the afternoon. I pushed Brad's niggly worries about our relationship from my head.

"I'll meet you at the Adkins residence no later than ten thirty. I'm sure they'll let me borrow their library or the study to chat once Leisa and Amanda tell you where to arrange the cupcakes." He sighed. "I'd hoped to avoid the birthday party and keep this professional, but I was told in no uncertain terms that skipping the party wasn't an option. This morning has already turned into a headache, and my afternoon will be even worse by the time I can sneak away from the festivities."

"That will actually work for me. I'll see you then, Detective Hawkins."

He hung up without any further ado.

Brad lifted his eyebrows. "Pray tell, what did the cupcake-loving detective want?"

I lightly punched his shoulder. "Right. As if you weren't listening in. I could smell your coconut shampoo because you were leaning in so close."

Brad didn't bother looking embarrassed. "I only caught every second or third word, so fill me in."

"He's attending the birthday party and will take my statement after I set up the cupcakes." I widened my eyes. "We'll meet in either the library or the study."

"It sounds like one of the larger houses on Lido Isle." Brad swiped his phone open. "What's the address?"

I provided it, and he plugged it into the search engine.

When results popped up, he whistled. "Whoa! Did you know you were delivering to a mansion?"

I took the phone in my hands and practically dropped it once I saw the slideshow of the house. With a modern style, the enormous house had large, open rooms with views over-looking an infinity pool that melted into the bay. "I knew they had serious money based on their willingness to pay a premium for the cupcakes, but I didn't think to actually look at where I'd be delivering."

"I'd better get going. I think you need to do a bit more than a wash-and-dry toilette this morning." He batted his eyes. "You'd better put makeup on and wear a nice dress with heels and pearls."

"I'm only the cupcake delivery person. Besides, I didn't get the uppity-rich-person vibe when I talked to Leisa about what the birthday girl wanted."

Brad narrowed his eyes. "What's their last name?"

"Adkins."

"And what's Mr. Adkins's name?"

"I have no idea. I only dealt with Leisa. And she was quite adamant I call her Leisa and not Missus."

Brad thumbed in information and scrolled on his phone then thrust it into my face. "Is this who you're delivering to?"

A woman with the same caramel-colored skin as the detec-tive smiled with perfectly straight white teeth. She had high cheekbones and emerald eyes that appeared to be amused. She was stunning. Perhaps Brad was right about upping my usual grooming today. Besides, I'd be seeing Brian afterward, and it wouldn't hurt to look my best.

I shrugged. "We talked on the phone and emailed. I never met her in person."

"What does her husband do?"

"What's with the twenty questions?" I might have snapped a bit since I was starting to feel a little insecure about meeting this beauty face-to-face, assuming it was the same Leisa Adkins.

Brad took several deep breaths. "I think you've made cupcakes for the one and only Rod Adkins. Can I help you deliver them?"

I twisted my mouth to the side and looked at my best friend over the bridge of my nose. "Who?"

He slapped his palms over his face. "You've got to be kidding me! Rod is only the greatest first baseman to ever—and I do mean ever—play for the Dodgers."

"Oh."

He peered at me between splayed fingers then dropped his hands into his lap. "That's all you've got to say? 'Oh'?"

"Yeah, well, you know sports isn't my thing."

"I know, but this is Rod Adkins we're talking about." Brad placed his palms together in a prayer position. "Please let me help you deliver the cupcakes. I promise I won't go all fangirl crazy if he's there."

"Yeah… uh, no." I picked up his arm again and checked the time. "And with that, it's time for you to go. So long. Farewell. Thanks for the coffee and pastry."

"I'll remember this, Martinez." Brad stood and pulled me into a warm hug. "Please get me his autograph at least?"

I pushed him away. "You're relentless. I'm sure it's not even the same Adkins you're thinking of."

Brad pretended to pout as he left my house, but the second the door was closed, I sprinted to the bathroom, hoping I'd have enough time to make myself presentable just in case he had been right about the identity of my clients.

Chapter 10

The Adkinses' home was even more striking in person. The online photos hadn't done it justice. I rang the doorbell, and within a moment, Leisa answered the door. And as Brad had predicted, it was the same stunning woman who was married to the best baseball player ever. She wore a dark blue-and-purple ombre sheath dress that hugged her slender figure. Wedge sandals displayed her toes, which had been painted in alternating colors of blue, purple, and teal. I was glad I'd taken time to flatiron my frizzy hair into submission and apply a moderate amount of makeup. My dress was pearl pink and, although casual, didn't look out of place. I'd wisely worn flat sandals that were comfortable enough to wear all day long, in case I never found a chance to sit.

"Emory, it's so nice to finally meet you in person." Leisa held out both hands to grasp mine. It was impossible to not gawk at what must've been a ten-carat emerald-cut diamond ring sitting on her left ring finger. She released one hand and pulled me into the house.

"It's a pleasure meeting you as well. You have a gorgeous home." I stepped into an atrium that soared to the roof, where crystal-clear skylights let in light. Potted palms and ferns dotted the wall spaces, giving it a tropical feel.

"Come. I'll show you where to set up the cupcakes, and then I'll send Rod and Nathan to help you bring in the boxes."

She must've noticed my puzzled look. "Rod's my husband, and Nathan is Detective Hawkins. He mentioned he needed to talk to you about that tragic death yesterday."

"Oh, right. I never caught his first name." I followed Leisa through the wide-open hall that led into a great room. The floor-to-ceiling accordion doors were open, letting in fresh breezes. A sparkling infinity pool took up the far portion of the patio, and the crystalline blue water seemed to spill right into the bay. "Your view is stunning."

"Thank you. We enjoy it."

She led me out onto the patio, where long tables and chairs had been arranged for the guests. Each table had been covered with gossamer fabric in shades of teal, purple, blue, and pink. Two similarly bedecked tables stood next to a glass wall that separated the main patio on which we stood and a smaller grass-covered space, where two small Yorkies romped.

"You can use one of these tables for the cupcakes. I know you said you had platters and serving stands, but Amanda saw these online and just had to have them for the cupcakes."

The serving pieces were works of art, and I couldn't even begin to imagine how expensive they must have been. Iridescent blue, turquoise, and purple glass had been swirled together with threads of gold and then sculpted into patterns reminiscent of the scales on a mermaid's tail. There were oval platters, a large square platter, and two three-tier serving stands with mermaid tails sculpted from glass for the top handles.

"These are exquisite." I brushed a finger against the cool surface of a platter. Instead of finding ridges from the mermaid scales, I encountered a completely smooth surface. "It's like an optical illusion."

Leisa laughed. "I know. My daughter definitely has an eye for art, especially if it reminds her of mermaids."

My cupcakes would seem childish when placed on these serving pieces, but I reminded myself that the birthday girl had chosen the design herself and had approved the photo of my sample cupcake. I'd offered to deliver a few in person before signing the contract, but Leisa had said it wasn't necessary.

"I'll start bringing in the cupcakes and set them up." I looked around, expecting the birthday girl to come bounding in at any moment.

As if she could read my mind, Leisa said, "Amanda is upstairs, getting her hair and makeup done. As soon as you have the cupcakes arranged, I'll have her come down."

This birthday party was turning into the most over-the-top I'd ever catered. Yet Leisa seemed like a kind and thoughtful person and nothing at all like some of the ultrawealthy people I'd worked for before.

"I'm sure she's excited about the party."

"You have no idea." She laughed as she tapped her phone open and thumbed a text. "I told the guys to meet you by your car. They'll carry in whatever you need, and then you and Nathan can use the solarium to talk. No one will disturb you there."

"Thank you." As Leisa led the way to the front door, I followed her back into the house.

"I'll check on Amanda, so if you need anything, let Rod know."

I walked down the steps to the circular driveway and found Detective Hawkins standing with a large man next to my car.

"Emory, let me introduce you to Rod Adkins," the detective said. "Rod, this is one of the best cupcake bakers in Orange County."

Rod, who stood a good foot and a half taller than me, stuck out his large hand. I shook it and felt my hand engulfed by his.

"It's a pleasure meeting you, Mr. Adkins. One of my best friends is a huge fan of yours."

"I'm delighted to meet you as well, but please call me Rod." He flashed a wide grin, white teeth gleaming in his ebony face. His voice held an island cadence that made me think of sand and gentle lapping waves. "And it's always a pleasure to hear I have a fan."

"Show us what needs to be brought in." Detective Hawkins looked at his watch. "I want to have plenty of time to go over your statement."

I piled bakery boxes into their waiting arms, and between the three of us, we managed to bring in all the cupcakes in only two trips. With the mermaid tails needing extra space, I'd had to use taller boxes that didn't hold the usual dozen. Rod led the way back to the patio, and they piled the boxes on the empty table that would, I assumed, hold the catered lunch items.

The two men headed back to the house.

"Excuse me, Detective Hawkins, where should I meet you?"

"Please, call me Nathan. I'm sure we'll hear Amanda's squeals of delight when she sees your cupcakes. I'll come find you then."

I hurriedly began opening the bakery boxes and arranging the cupcakes on the gorgeous platters and tiered trays. A couple mermaid tails needed to be repositioned, but I'd brought a baggie of extra sprinkles to use to cover any frosting imperfections that might have occurred during the transport. Once the cupcakes were in position, I used my phone to take several photos from a variety of angles. And instead of the elegant design of the platters making the cupcakes seem child-ish, they'd ended up enhancing my creations.

Nathan had been right about squeals of delight. I'd had no idea a child could make that piercing a sound. I turned to find a girl my nieces' age rushing onto the patio. Her golden skin sparkled with glitter in the sunlight, and she wore a mermaid costume with a bejeweled bikini top and a long tail that trailed behind her. Her black hair had been piled atop her head with a sparkly tiara nestled amongst the expertly posi-tioned curls. She looked like a fairy tale come to life.

Amanda ran up to me and threw her arms around my torso. "You did it! You made mermaid cupcakes exactly like I wanted."

I hugged her back. "Happy birthday, Amanda. You look beautiful."

"Thank you, and thank you for making this the best birthday party ever." Amanda walked along the length of the table, examining every detail of the cupcakes. "Where did you find the mermaid sprinkles? I looked at the craft store and couldn't find any."

"I bought a bunch of different ones online and then mixed them together." I pointed at the cupcake closest to me. "See how there are three different pearl sizes and one of them is pale pink? They all came separate, same as the different colors of the jimmies."

"What are jimmies?"

"They're the oblong sprinkles. I used teal, blue, purple, and pink."

"Oh, my goodness. I never envisioned it looking this spec-tacular." Leisa slung her arm around her daughter's shoulder. "Honey, let me take some photos of you before everyone arrives."

"But, Mom, I'm going to have to do that when the photographer comes."

"I only want a few of my own. It won't take long."

Nathan stepped out onto the patio. "Emory, are you ready to talk to me now?"

I gathered up the boxes I'd already flattened. "Happy birthday, Amanda. It looks like you're going to have a splendid mermaid party."

"Thank you, Ms. Martinez." Amanda smiled at me from where she stood in front of the cupcake table as her mother took photos.

"Leisa, let me know if there's anything else you'd like me to do before the party starts. You can text or call me." I was supposed to have received the final payment once I delivered the cupcakes but, in the excitement of the moment, had forgotten to ask. With the detective standing there, I didn't feel comfortable bringing it up, so I decided to send her an invoice that evening.

"You did a marvelous job, and I'll be sure to pass along your information to all the other parents attending the party today." She turned toward me and tapped on her phone a few times.

My phone vibrated in my pocket since I'd silenced it when I'd arrived. I didn't pull it out to see who had messaged me. "I appreciate that. If I don't see you before I leave, have a wonderful party."

"I just sent you a Venmo for the final payment. If it doesn't show up, send me a text, and I'll get it straightened out tomorrow."

I pulled my phone out, checked the screen, and tried to keep my face neutral. She had sent me not only the final payment but a very, very generous tip. "It showed up, and thank you so much. I truly enjoyed working with both of you."

Amanda gave me another quick hug, and then I followed the detective into the house.

Chapter 11

He led me past the kitchen and down a hallway that curved along the side of the house. We passed multiple rooms with doors closed, and at the end, a wide entrance opened into a sun-filled sitting area.

While the house's architectural style was modern, the solarium had an old-fashioned gazebo look to it with the octagon shape and the white wood accents that framed the arched windows. The solarium was filled with flowering orchids of every shape, color, and size along with potted palms and ferns. The windows looked out onto a lush garden filled with tropical plants and exotic flowers. A koi pond dominated the center, with lily pads floating in the water. I looked more closely and found colorful orange fish lurking beneath the water plants.

Nathan gestured for me to sit on one of the plush white sofas in the room while he closed the pocket doors to afford us some privacy.

I sat on the sofa that kept me from the garden view. I feared I'd get distracted by the beautiful flowers that made me feel like I was in a tropical paradise.

"Thanks for agreeing to meet with me here, Emory. It's

difficult to be in two places at once." He sat on the sofa opposite me and picked up an iPad that rested on the glass table between us. He swiped it open. "Do you mind if I record our conversation?"

"That's fine." I crossed my ankles and tried to settle my hands in my lap. I resisted the urge to try to pull the hemline of my dress down farther.

"I'm going to have you start with the time you returned to the clubhouse and found Ms. Parker. Tell me not only what you saw but any feelings you had." He sat the iPad back on the table. "Start with the time, or at least the approximate time, you returned to the building."

So I talked. Since I'd told the story three times already, I didn't falter. For the most part, Nathan didn't interrupt me unless he needed clarification, such as how many windows I'd opened, what kind of windows they were, and if any had been unlocked.

My mouth was getting dry, and I cleared my throat a time or two after I'd finished sharing everything I knew.

"My apologies. Leisa left some coffee, tea, and water on the sideboard for us. Help yourself if you'd like something to drink." He closed the iPad.

"Thank you. I think I'll have some coffee. Can I get you anything?"

"Water would be great. Caffeine tends to make my heart rate go wonky." He stood and stretched while I made my way to the sideboard.

In addition to bottles of water, there was a stainless-steel carafe of coffee and a pitcher of iced tea. Cups and saucers had been neatly stacked, and a small crystal bowl held individual packets of just about any type of sweetener under the sun. A small crystal pitcher held cream. Sitting beside the beverage tray, a plate of chocolate chip cookies begged to be sampled. I obliged.

After pouring my cup of coffee—which was surprisingly

hot—I splashed some cream into it and stirred with the silver spoon that sat beside the pitcher. I carried a bottle of water along with the plate of cookies to the coffee table and set them in front of the detective then retrieved my cup of coffee.

After we'd both sipped our chosen beverage and nibbled on a cookie, Detective Hawkins opened the iPad back up. "Are you ready to continue?"

"Yes."

The sounds of children laughing and the murmur of adult voices floated our way. I glanced at my watch. It was after eleven already, and the party had started. I wondered how soon Nathan would need to leave to join the group.

"Don't worry about the time. They know I'm going to be late joining them." He tapped the iPad screen to start the recording. "I'd like for you to talk about your observations of what happened during the potluck lunch that you attended. You don't have to limit it to your interaction or your observation of other people interacting with the victim. I'm just as interested in the overall picture."

By the time we finished, it was almost noon. I'd consumed another cookie and downed two more cups of coffee. A gentle knock sounded on the door.

"Nathan?" The door slid open a foot, and Rod stuck his head into the doorway. "Leisa forced me to interrupt you. Lunch is being served, and she'd like you to join us. Emory, you're invited to stay as well, and afterward, Nathan can continue his interrogation."

"I think we're done with the interrogation." Nathan smiled at me. "You're free to go, Emory, but please stay for lunch if you'd like. I heard we're having an under-the-sea seafood extravaganza."

"Thank you. I appreciate the offer, but I'm supposed to meet my boyfriend for lunch." I was going to be late, but Brian would either make himself comfortable or hang out with Tillie and Vannie until I came home.

"Then let me see you out." Rod slid the pocket doors back into the walls so that the entryway was wide open.

I shook Nathan's hand. "If I think of anything else or overhear any gossip that pertains to the case, I'll give you a call."

"Thanks. I appreciate it."

I followed Rod to the front door. The sounds of laughter, shouting children, and the thump of heavy bass from the speakers playing music filled the air. He opened the door then handed me a large manilla envelope. A sheepish smile crossed his lips. "I hope I'm not overstepping any boundaries here, but you mentioned your friend was a fan. I thought she'd like an autographed picture."

"It's actually a he, and he is going to be freaking out over this! He begged to come with me today so he could fangirl, but I said no." It was my turn to look sheepish. "Honestly, I didn't know you were, well, you. Leisa never said, and I didn't put the names together. Okay, I'm babbling now. Thank you. Brad will treasure this."

"It's the least I could do after you made my little girl's party so special."

I stepped out into the sunshine, waved goodbye, and climbed into my SUV. As I drove down the circular driveway, several young men dressed in uniforms of white button-down shirts and black slacks clustered near the exit. One of them waved at me, so I pulled to a stop and rolled down the window.

"We're here to park your car for you," a blond, surfer-looking kid said. "Valet is complimentary for guests."

"I'm the cupcake caterer, and I'm just leaving."

He looked hopeful. "Do you have any leftover cupcakes you'd like to get rid of?"

"Sorry, guys. I left them all at the house. Maybe there will be some left over after the party."

"Dude, don't be a mooch." A red-haired, freckled kid

punched his arm. "Mrs. A is great about bringing us sand-wiches and stuff, so chill, okay?" They waved at me.

As I headed home, I called Brian on Bluetooth.

"Sorry I'm late," I said when he answered. "The detective wanted to interview me right after I set the cupcakes up. It took a whole lot longer than I anticipated."

"No worries. I'm at your house, taking a little nap with the dogs." Brian yawned. "I hit the waves early this morning and wore myself out."

Despite being an excellent chef and a foodie, Brian worked hard keeping his body trim and in shape. His favorite form of exercise was surfing, but he also hit the gym a few times a week. What he saw in my cupcake-plumped body was anyone's guess, but I was grateful he accepted me just the way I was.

"I'll be there in about fifteen minutes. Do you need me to pick anything up from the market before I get there?"

"Nope. I brought the fixings for chicken fajitas for lunch, and then I'll grill salmon for the family dinner's main course."

Brian always took charge of the main course for our weekly get-togethers and coordinated side dishes with everyone else for a potluck-style dinner. I generally made cupcakes for dessert, especially when I wanted to try out a new recipe. My mother gravitated toward appetizers, and Carrie typically brought a salad or veggie. Brad and Gabe were in charge of the wine, and Vannie baked some type of homemade bread. Sometimes, it was focaccia—once, she had even made focaccia bread art—other times dinner rolls or sourdough baguettes. And Tillie sat back and enjoyed it all while keeping us entertained.

My stomach rumbled. "Yum to both."

The dogs started barking. "I think they say yum to both too or else decided they need to try to scare a cat away. It's been sitting on the wall for the past hour. Piper, Missy, hush."

Brian's stern voice made them both quiet down right away. I wished they'd listen to me that well.

"Really? Does it look scared or lost?" I turned my signal on and merged into the traffic on the Pacific Coast Highway.

"Nope. It's just sitting there, enjoying the sun."

"Maybe you should give it some tuna or water." I slammed on my brakes when a Lamborghini cut right in front of me. I heaved a sigh of relief that it hadn't happened on my way to deliver the cupcakes. I might have had a lot more to repair instead of just the two.

"I think it's okay. If it's still here when you get home, you can decide and see if it has a collar with tags."

We said our goodbyes, and I turned my full attention to the road.

Chapter 12

The rest of the afternoon turned out to be peaceful and relaxing. After I'd taken a look at the adorable cat—it was gray with a white chest and white on each paw that made it appear to be wearing boots—we decided to leave it snoozing in the sun. Perhaps it would get tired of driving the dogs crazy and wander back home. Brian helped me make the apple pie–filled cupcakes for the dinner and decided I should make five dozen for his restaurant for delivery on Wednesday. We batted other cupcake flavors back and forth to go with dishes he planned on creating for the upcoming holiday season. I jotted down notes and entered reminders in my calendar for when I needed to have the experiments finalized. About an hour before dinnertime, Brian left for Tillie's house to start the grill and spend some extra time with his grandmother.

By the time Carrie arrived with her family, the cat was mewling piteously. My six-year-old twin nieces, Kaylee and Sophie, decided the cat needed food and water, so they raided my pantry for a can of tuna to lure it down from the wall. Thomas, Carrie's husband, took their toddler son, Tommy, and the dogs to Tillie's house with the hope the cat might calm down.

"Here, kitty, kitty," my nieces chorused in their quiet little-girl voices. They lifted their towheads and tried kissy noises like they used for my dogs. When the cat didn't respond, they reverted to "Here, kitty, kitty."

Carrie waved a bowl of tuna in the air below the top of the seven-foot wall while I stood on a stepladder to assist the cat down when it appeared ready. Ever so slowly, the cat stood and batted its paw down at the tuna. I took the opportunity to scoop my arm around the cat's middle and brought it back down to the yard.

"Mommy, hurry and give the cat its food before she runs away." Tears shimmered in Kaylee's green eyes. "She's hungry and scared."

Carrie, knowing she'd better act fast before she had two crying girls on her hands, did as she was told. The cat pounced on the bowl and licked it clean once it had eaten every single morsel.

"We can keep her, can't we, Mommy?" Sophie tugged on her mother's sleeve. "She's scared and alone."

Carrie looked over at me with terror in her eyes. I rescued her.

"We have to make sure she doesn't belong to anyone else. Maybe she wandered off and is just lost."

"How can we find her family?" Sophie asked.

"I'll take her to the vet tomorrow and see if she's chipped. If she is, then they'll be able to find her family."

"And if she's not, then we get to keep her!" Kaylee stated it with certainty.

Oh dear. This wasn't going as well as I'd hoped. With Carrie using her home kitchen for catering jobs, she had to pass inspections. With a pet in the house that wasn't blocked access to the kitchen, she'd lose her license. While Carrie might be able to make sure the cat couldn't get into the kitchen, her young children would be likely to undermine all her efforts.

"Let's not plan on adopting it yet. Chances are her family lives close by and is missing her." I stroked the soft gray fur. The cat appeared healthy, well fed, and clean, which led me to believe she had a permanent home.

"What are we going to do with it while we go to Tillie's?" Carrie asked as she looked at her watch. "We need to get going."

"I'll put her in Piper's crate with a clean blanket." I shrugged. "It's the best I can do right now. Tillie can keep the dogs again until I can take the cat to the vet."

Sophie picked the cat up and held it close. Its purrs rumbled in the quiet evening, and it snuggled in to the little girl's chest. Carrie might have a big problem on her hands if I didn't find the cat's owner.

With the cat safely crated but extremely unhappy, we headed to Tillie's house, a mere hop, skip, and a jump across the alleyway. Vannie had included Teresa in our gathering, and I was happy she'd felt comfortable enough to come. Both of the women were in the kitchen, assisting Brian. Brad and Gabe, both looking relaxed and dapper, dispensed drinks. I marched up to Brad and held out the manilla envelope.

He raised his eyebrows. "What's this?"

"Consider it a prewedding gift from your BFF."

Brad carefully broke the seal on the envelope then slowly pulled out the eight-by-ten color photo of Rod Adkins in his Dodgers uniform, complete with his bold signature. "How did you manage to get this? I can't believe it!"

He handed the photo to Gabe, pulled me into a hug, and spun me around. "Thank you, thank you, thank you!"

"You're welcome. Rod is actually a very nice man."

Brad stuck his lower lip out. "You should have taken me with you. I can't believe I missed my one and only chance to meet the legend in person."

"If I ever have the chance to deliver cupcakes there again, I promise I'll take you." Now that I knew that the Adkinses were nice people, I wouldn't feel quite so awkward about taking Brad with me. "But you'll have to promise not to do any crazy fangirl stuff if that happens."

"Fine. I'll try to remain dignified and reserved." Brad took the photo back and stared at it in awe, while Gabe went back to filling wineglasses.

My mother, Addie, greeted me with a kiss on my cheek and hugged her two granddaughters. As usual, she looked immaculate in pressed dark-blue slacks and a sienna angora sweater. My stepdad, Lars, passed a tray of appetizers that included bacon-wrapped scallops, baked brie on toast points, and bites of sashimi impaled on decorative bamboo skewers. I took one of each, and my taste buds hummed with each bite.

Tillie waved at me from the patio, where she'd been lighting citronella candles for the table. I joined her and offered her the glass of wine I hadn't sipped from yet.

"I'm still working on the gimlet Brian made for me." She eyed me speculatively. "Have you made any headway in solving the murder?"

I shook my head then took a sip of the sauvignon blanc. "Detective Hawkins spent an hour and a half interviewing me, but he didn't share any new information with me."

"What's your next step?" Tillie swatted away a moth that had been attracted to the flame.

I ignored her question and changed the subject. "Did Thomas tell you about the cat we rescued?"

"Boy, did he. Brian bet him ten dollars that Thomas would be carting a cat home tonight." Tillie chuckled. "I would've gotten in on the bet if I didn't know your sister so well."

"Brian can kiss his ten dollars goodbye. I'm keeping the cat...."

Before I finished my sentence, Tillie guffawed. "Piper and Missy are going to be two unhappy dogs."

Hearing their names, the two dogs scampered out onto the patio and began sniffing around for any dropped crumbs. My nephew, Tommy, toddled behind them, his sippy cup clutched firmly in one hand and a half-eaten cracker in the other.

I bent over and picked Tommy up, swung him into the air, then covered his chubby cheek with kisses. His giggles filled my heart with happiness. Too soon, though, he struggled to be put back down so he could continue chasing the dogs.

"What I was trying to say is that I'm keeping the cat tonight, and then I'll take it to Missy and Piper's vet tomorrow to see if it's chipped." I waggled my eyebrows. "I'm also going to take the opportunity to find out if she's heard about any puppy mills operating in the area and if any of her clients have had the misfortune of purchasing from one recently."

"That sounds like a good plan. Do you need any help?" Tillie was always the first to volunteer for sleuthing.

"Nothing except that you keep Piper and Missy here until the cat's ownership is resolved." I took a glug of wine. "If it's not chipped, I don't know what I'll do. Carrie, for certain, won't allow the girls to adopt it, and I'm not sure I can turn it over to a shelter even if it's a no-kill shelter."

The sight of cats and dogs in small crates and enclosures, with their piteous mewling and whining, still disturbed me even though it had been several years since my ex and I had visited a shelter to adopt Piper.

"We'll cross that bridge when we get there." Tillie placed her hand over mine. "You have a kind heart, Emory."

Running from the house, around the patio, and back into the house, Kaylee and Sophie jingled their dinner bells, yelling, "Dinner is served."

Tommy toddled behind, trying to imitate them with the plastic bell Tillie kept just for this purpose. We found that in his enthusiastic excitement, he repeatedly hit himself in the head with the bell. When he'd used a metal bell, some bruising and crying had ensued, so the plastic bell, which wasn't nearly as musical as the metal one, had been introduced.

Everyone migrated to the patio—September evenings were still warm enough—with Brian, Vannie, and Teresa carrying in trays filled with food. Soon we were eating the bountiful feast and catching up with each other. I appreciated how everyone avoided the subject of murder until the kids had eaten their cupcakes and had gone upstairs to the playroom Tillie had prepared for them. The adults stayed at the table and lingered over food and wine. Our cupcakes could wait.

My mother, who used to be horrified whenever I was even remotely associated with a murder, was the first to broach the subject. "While I appreciate Vannie letting us know you were safe, a few more details would've been welcomed. We need time to come up with ways to help your investigation. You are investigating, aren't you?"

"It appears that way."

Gabe, who was a Newport Beach detective, choked on the piece of cornbread he'd been eating.

I raised my voice just a bit. "Huntington Beach Detective Hawkins asked me to bake cupcakes and share them with potential witnesses and suspects so that they'd relax and gossip."

Gabe's coughing grew louder. Brad got up and retrieved a glass of water from the kitchen and handed it to his fiancé. "Easy there. It's not your case."

I turned my attention to Gabe. His eyes were red and watering as he gulped down the water.

He finally spoke, but his words wheezed out. "Who put jalapeños in the cornbread? One got stuck at the back of my throat."

"Ooh, ooh, I know how to fix that!" I rushed to the kitchen, filled a glass with milk, then rushed it back to Gabe. "Water doesn't help, but dairy products will soothe the burn."

I winked at Brian. He'd come to my rescue after I'd

inhaled half a hot dog, sprinkled liberally with jalapeños, at the beach. It was before we'd gotten together, and I'd been beyond mortified. But somehow, he'd overlooked my mottled red face and mascara-dripping eyes and decided he liked me. He'd also shared his string cheese with me that day to calm the burning sensation in my throat. Even then, he'd known the way to my heart.

Gabe sucked down the milk then gave a sigh of relief. "I can't believe that helped."

"I can give you the whole scientific explanation, but I'll skip it for now." Brian fist-bumped Brad.

"Thank you. But really, who put the jalapeños in the cornbread?"

Vannie and Teresa raised their hands. Teresa looked mortified, while Vannie looked ready to defend her choice. "Emory told me I needed to conform more to California cuisine, like adding spicy peppers to more dishes."

Oh, great. She was throwing me under the bus, but I had to admire her pluck. Gabe could be, well, Gabe: a detective who had a strong sense of black and white when generally there were gray areas in between. I was happy Vannie was finally feeling like she was a part of the group and didn't feel uncomfortable standing up for herself, even if she was doing so at my expense.

Gabe glared at me then threw back his head and laughed. "Oh, Emory. You do make life exciting in every way possible. Since I'm not even remotely involved in this case, please feel free to not run things by me or ask me any questions that might give me a coronary. We can't have one of the grooms incapacitated before the wedding."

As one, everyone at the table raised their eyebrows then stared at him. Was this really Gabe joking, or had some alien abducted him and replaced him with a clone? He'd always been straitlaced and proper, especially when it came to his job.

He finally noticed our attention and mopped his forehead

with his linen napkin. "Prewedding jitters. The stress must be getting to me."

Brad jabbed his arm but smiled to let Gabe know he was jesting. "Watch what you say. This big wedding was your idea, not mine."

Gabe grabbed Brad's hand and brought it to his lips. "You're right, although it was my family who pushed this big wedding on us, and I just couldn't say no."

"I know, and I'm not blaming you. Just don't take your stress out on me or our friends." He patted Gabe's shoulder.

Tillie piped in. "How many days is it until your nuptials?"

"Only seventy, and there's still so much to do." Brad pointed at me. "I'm making a list and foisting it off on you to complete. Isn't that what maids of honor do?"

I looked at Carrie, who'd been my maid of honor for my first marriage. "Is it?"

She sputtered. "Mother took care of all the details. All I had to do was fit into that hideous dress you chose and march down the aisle, holding onto a bouquet."

I thought she muttered something about drinking copious amounts of champagne, too, but then decided my imagination was getting the best of me.

Now it was my mother's turn to look put out. "There was absolutely nothing wrong with your bridesmaid dress. I thought it was quite elegant."

Too late, Carrie realized it had been our mother's choice of dresses. In fact, the entire wedding had been my mother's doing. Well, it was water under the bridge, as they say. And time to rescue Carrie.

"Sure, Brad, just let me know what needs to be done, and I'll do it." I side-eyed my mother. She still seemed miffed at Carrie's complaint. "Tell us about your honeymoon plans."

The conversation turned to travel after Brad shared that they would be spending ten days in Costa Rica. Beaches, scuba diving, sailing, and hiking were on their agenda for the duration of their stay.

By eight, Carrie and Thomas decided it was time to get their kids home and in bed since the following day was school. As they collected their kids and belongings, Vannie and I cleared the table before meeting them at the door for our goodbyes.

"Auntie Em, call us tomorrow about the kitty. We want to know if we can keep her." Sophie took hold of my hand and pulled me down to her level. "Promise?"

"I promise." I caught Carrie's deer-in-the-headlights look then kissed my niece's cheek. "Don't get your hopes up, kiddo. The kitty looks pretty well taken care of, and I'm sure her family is worried about her."

"Okay. Maybe we can find a kitty from someplace else." Sophie kissed me back, and then Kaylee gave me a quick hug before following her dad out into the evening.

Once the door closed behind my sister and her family, it didn't take long for the rest of us to clean up after dinner. While Vannie and I washed dishes, she hip-bumped me. "Teresa and I have a minimum day on Tuesday. We thought that might be a good time to plan a meeting with Shawn about adopting a puppy. Can you meet us here at one, and her cousin will give us a makeover?"

I tapped on my phone calendar. I had cupcakes to deliver at eleven that morning for a bridge game, and I'd planned on attending to my part-time, work-whenever-I-wanted job for Tillie's son, David. I could go in either before I delivered the cupcakes or after the meeting with Shawn.

"Sure. That'll work." I put the appointment on my calendar. "I'll call Shawn tomorrow morning and pretend to be Teresa and set up our meeting. I think the sooner we can get him to commit to meeting with us the better."

"Good thinking. We thought we'd try to get ahold of him

after we left school, but it wouldn't be until at least four before we could call."

Once the kitchen was sparkling, Brian and I said our goodbyes and headed to the pool house, took care of the cat, and crashed for the night.

Chapter 13

The cat's meows woke me from a sound slumber. I stumbled to the living room and stroked its head, which peeked up from the nest of blankets we'd made in a cardboard box. Brian had cut Piper's old puppy collar down to size and fastened it on the cat. We needed to be able to attach a leash when we took it out for potty breaks so it wouldn't have the chance to run away. The cat didn't seem to mind the collar in the least, which led me to believe it had a family out there.

"Morning." Brian kissed the top of my head then ruffled the cat's fur before stumbling to the kitchen to make coffee. "Would you like for me to go to the vet with you?"

"There's no need. I think I can handle the kitty on my own." I turned and watched Brian putter around my kitchen, enjoying the view of his broad, muscular back. "You probably want to go surfing this morning, right?"

"That had been my plan, but if you want me to help out, I'm yours to command."

I blew him a kiss. "Go surfing. I have a lot of things to keep me busy today."

Brian quickly made avocado toast along with melon and

fresh berries for our breakfast and spooned more tuna into a bowl for the cat. We ate in companionable silence while Brian checked online surf reports and I browsed cupcake ideas on Pinterest.

I used to fix breakfast for Tillie and linger over coffee with her most mornings, but since Vannie had moved in, she'd taken over cooking for the octogenarian. Unless Brian spent the night or I had an early-morning cupcake delivery, I generally joined Tillie for another cup of coffee after Vannie left for work. I wouldn't have time for it this morning, and I missed it.

I cleaned up breakfast dishes, and Brian got ready to leave, dressing in board shorts and a faded white T-shirt. He gave me a lingering kiss that had me wishing we could stay in all morning. He promised he'd be back by six to cook dinner for me. As soon as the pool gate slammed shut, I called the vet and explained the situation. They assured me they'd fit me in if I could be at their clinic within twenty minutes.

I made it to the clinic with seconds to spare. With the cat still nestled in the blanket-lined cardboard box, I carried it inside.

"Oh, good, you made it just in time." The perky young woman had her auburn hair styled in a cute pixie cut. She wore a colorful cat-print medical smock, and her name tag said Sami. She stood and walked to the door that led to the examination rooms. "I'll put you in a room and scan to see if the cat has a chip. If I think it needs medical attention, the vet can see you in about fifteen minutes. Do you have time to wait?"

"Yes. Whatever you need me to do for the cat, I'm fine with."

I followed her back to the exam room. The walls were painted a cheery yellow, and a huge corkboard was covered with photos of pets—dogs, cats, hamsters, rabbits, and even some birds. A plaque situated at the top of the board read

"Our furry and feathered friends." Piper and Missy's photos were on the board as well.

I placed the box on the stainless-steel table, and the vet assistant stroked the cat's gray head while she waved a hand-held scanner over its back. The machine beeped, and a number popped up on the screen.

Sami picked the cat up and cradled it in her arms then placed it on the table. "She's chipped and appears to be in good health. I'll take her temperature and check her ears to be on the safe side."

"I'm so glad. Will you contact the owner?" My sister would be even more relieved.

"I'll give you the website information, but you'll need to issue a 'found pet' alert, which will notify the owners that you have the cat." She shined a light into the cat's ears then prompted her into standing position for a temperature check.

"Oh. I thought I'd leave the cat here, and the owners would come to pick it up from you."

"Unless you'd like to pay boarding fees and hope the owners will reimburse you, we really can't take her in. Besides, she'd be much more comfortable in a home than in a cage here since we're not a boarding facility." Sami placed the cat back in the box and looked at me expectantly.

"All right, I'll take her home and hope the owners pick her up soon. Can you recommend cat food for her? We've been feeding her tuna." I'd have to find out a way to get the dogs acclimated to her in case she stayed with us longer than a day.

"We sell both canned food and dry, depending on your preference." She turned to open the door. "I don't think there's any reason to see the vet. You can pay for the food in the reception area. There's no charge for the scan."

"Thank you. Do you mind if I ask you a question first?" I didn't wait for her response. "Have you seen an increase in puppies with issues due to potentially coming from a puppy mill situation lately?"

She furrowed her overplucked brows. "Why do you ask? Do you think you bought one?"

"Not me, but I met a person over the weekend who is sure their dog is from a puppy mill, and she knew someone else who had the same experience recently."

"I can't give you any details, but yes, there has been an increase in puppies with issues. In all likelihood, it's because of a puppy-mill situation despite it being illegal in California." She studied my face. "Are you asking because you're in the market for a new puppy?"

"No. I'm just concerned because I think I might know who's running the puppy mill in the area. I'd hoped to find out names of who else had puppies with issues to see if I could see a pattern and find proof that this person is behind it then get it closed down."

"Are you law enforcement or something?"

"No. Just a concerned citizen and dog lover."

Sami shook her head. "I'm sorry, but I really can't give out personal information. If you'd like, leave your cell number and email address with me, and I'll pass it on to our clients. I have no idea if they'll want to contact you, but it's the best I can do."

"Thanks. I appreciate whatever you can do."

"I wish I could do more." Her solemn brown eyes flickered with anger. "It's despicable what those puppy mills do to the dogs. If you ever come across anyone looking for a new puppy, tell them to educate themselves on how to avoid lining the pockets of a puppy mill operator, which continues the cycle of abuse on the animals. But the number one thing is never purchase from a pet store even if they say the puppy is a rescue. I'll give you a pamphlet with other tips along with the found-pet-alert information."

I followed Sami to the reception area, where three dogs and their owners sat in orange molded plastic chairs. I indicated I'd take the canned cat food. She bagged it up then handed me a printout with the pet alert website after she'd written down the microchip code. She also handed me a blank piece of paper and indicated I should write down my email address and phone number. After she'd swiped my credit card for the cat food and taken my information, she walked over to a rack by the front door that was loaded with pamphlets. Sami browsed through the brochures then selected one and handed it to me. "Let me know if you need any more. I'm happy to mail them to you if it's inconvenient to drop by."

"Thank you, although at this point, I don't know anyone who's considering getting a pet." I tightened my grip on the cardboard box and fumbled with the sack of cat food and the paper in my other hand.

"Here, let me get the door for you." Sami opened it wide and held it. "Keep me posted about this little one and if her family claims her, and be sure to call us if you have any concerns over her health."

I nodded. After I made my way to the SUV, I made a quick stop at the pet store for a litter box then drove home. As soon as I entered the house and got the cat settled, I pulled up the website for the found pet alert and entered the required information. That done, I sent Tillie a text.

Just returned from vet. Looks like I'll be keeping the cat until owners claim her. R u ok keeping dogs a bit longer?

It took only a moment for the gray dots to appear, indicating she was typing. While I waited for her reply, I picked up the pamphlet on puppy mills and quickly scanned it.

As Sami had indicated, the literature recommended that anyone interested in adopting a dog should first avoid buying from pet stores since most puppies were obtained from puppy mills. If at all possible, the best solution would be to check out dog shelters and adopt a dog that way. But if one really wanted to buy a specific breed, they should try to find someone who allowed their dogs to live in their home as part of the family. Buying local was best, and the pamphlet said that if the breeder didn't allow a buyer into their home to visit the puppies, a puppy mill was probably the reason. Other red flags were if a breeder had a large barn or warehouse on their property and dog noises could be heard coming from the space; chances were it was a puppy mill even if they showed a mother and pups inside their home. Or if a breeder offered to get a buyer any breed of dog they wanted, it was most likely a puppy-mill operation.

The pamphlet included a few heartbreaking photos of overbred mother dogs along with the filthy, crowded conditions the dogs and puppies lived in. It made me sick. If Shawn was involved in something like this, I promised myself that he was going to go to prison for his abuses.

Tillie's text finally came through.

Brian took dogs for run before surfing. They're napping now. I'm fine with them staying here as long as you need.

I smiled at Brian's thoughtfulness. Another text popped up from Tillie.

What did vet say about puppy mills? We're going to put that @#$% away for good!

I wished I could give her more positive news.

I'll call you in about 5 min. I want to schedule appt with that @#$% right away.

She sent back a thumbs-up emoji.

Chapter 14

I scrolled through my phone and selected Shawn's contact info. It dawned on me that I didn't know what breed of dog I should inquire about. Cheryl's dog was a pug, and Belle's dog was a Chihuahua. I decided to see what he had available, and if he wanted me to name a breed, I'd go with a corgi. The Queen of England had made them quite popular.

I punched his number and listened as his phone rang. Expecting to get his voicemail, I jumped when he answered the phone.

"Shawn's Dog Training Solutions." Shawn didn't bother with any social niceties.

"Hi. Is this Shawn? I was given your number since I'm interested in purchasing a puppy."

"Yep. What kinda dog do you want?" His voice was gruff, and he sounded impatient.

"What breed of puppies do you currently have available?" I pulled out a scratch pad and hunted for a pen.

"Who gave you my number?" Shawn's voice was wary.

"I forget her name, but I was talking to a friend in line at Starbucks about buying a new puppy since my dog died. He was twelve years old, so it wasn't unexpected, but, you know, it was still hard to say goodbye." I paused for a breath of air. "And anyway, this lady was standing behind us, eavesdropping. How rude, right? But she gave me your phone number and said you could help."

He sighed, probably thinking I was a ditzy blonde who wanted a pocket-sized puppy to carry around in my purse. "Let me guess. You want something like a Yorkie or Maltipoo."

"Yeah, one of those would work. Or a teacup poodle or Pomeranian. My friend has one of those, and he's just adorbs." I cringed, worried I'd laid it on too thick.

"Okay. I can get you a teacup Pomeranian. It should be available to go home within five days."

"Ooohhh. Thank you," I gushed. "Can I visit the puppy tomorrow? You know, see if it wants to bond with me before I make a decision. Is it a girl or a boy?"

"I have a litter of five puppies, so you can have your choice." Shawn's patience was definitely wearing thin if his brusqueness was any indication.

"Can you text me your address, and I'll drop by after work tomorrow, say around three? I'd like to interact with the entire litter. It's so important to connect with their little personalities, right?" I had a feeling Shawn was wishing he hadn't answered my call.

"Fine. Whatever." He shuffled some papers around. "What's your phone number? I'll send the text."

I rattled off my phone number. Tillie had provided her phone number with my email address when she signed us up for the dog training sessions, and as far as I could remember, I hadn't ever given his company my number. If I had, Shawn just might put two and two together. "We haven't talked about the price yet. What's the puppy going to cost?"

Shawn gave me a quote, and I stifled a gasp. It was at least thirty percent higher than what I thought had already been an extravagant price based on the quick Google search I'd done while we talked. "Sure. Fine. Do you take credit cards, or do I need to bring a check? I don't want someone else to swoop in and buy the puppy I want."

"A credit card is fine, but I'll have to charge you a three percent surcharge. Or you can send me a Venmo or Zelle payment."

"Zelle's fine. Will I be visiting your home or your place of business?" I made a note of the cost on the scratch pad with several exclamation points.

"I'll bring the puppies to my business."

"Hmmm. I'd rather see them in their natural habitat with their mom so they're more relaxed. It's the best way to get an idea of their personalities and if one of them will suit me." I knew I was pushing it, but this was a big sale, at least by my standards, and I hoped Shawn would comply.

"Whatever, as long as you don't mind driving to Norco. But it'll have to be three thirty. I have a training session at one."

"That's right. You train dogs as well. Do you think the teacup Pomeranian will respond well to training? Sometimes the smaller dogs are resistant."

"Lady, I can train anything with four legs." He heaved a heavy breath. "I'll send you the text right now and have you down for three thirty at my home. Is there anything else you need?"

"Nope. And thanks. You've been a big help." The line went dead. It was readily apparent that Shawn really didn't believe in social niceties because he'd never even asked my name.

A few minutes later, my phone chimed with an incoming text. It was from Shawn with his address in Norco. I responded with a "See you soon." Close to forty miles north-east of Newport Beach, Norco had plenty of wide-open land with lots of stables and riding areas. It made sense that if he was running a puppy mill, he'd need to be away from high-density residential areas. I googled his address, and a real estate website popped up with photos of the property. Set against the foothills, the three-bedroom ranch-style house and a warehouse sat on five acres of undeveloped land with some scrub and oak trees. No one else lived close by.

Examining the remote location in which I'd proposed we meet left me feeling more than a little worried. He was one of my suspects for his mother's murder, and if he was the mastermind of the illegal puppy mill, he might turn to violence to protect it. Even with Vannie and Teresa alongside me, we wouldn't be able to protect ourselves should he pull a gun on us. It was time to talk to Tillie in person, and I'd text Vannie afterward. I called Tillie and told her I'd be there within a few minutes, and she promised to have the coffee ready.

Knowing the cat was a loved pet, I wasn't so reluctant to leave her on her own inside my house. But I did make certain she knew where the litter box was and had properly used it before she was left without any supervision. My few minutes turned into ten before I headed across the alleyway which separated Tillie's luxurious bayside mini-mansion and my charming two-bedroom pool house which also belonged to her.

I let myself in through the security gate and then into Tillie's home. The entryway featured a wide, two-storied foyer. On one side, a curved stairway with a wrought-iron railing reminiscent of crashing waves led to the second floor. Straight ahead of the foyer was an equally wide hallway featuring a view of the bay through an entire wall of glass doors. With the generous number of windows and an overhead skylight, the house was bright and airy. Museum-quality works of art lined the hallways, with lighting illuminating each piece. When I'd first begun working for Tillie, I was scared senseless that I'd damage or destroy one of the paintings. I'd relaxed a bit since that first day but still tensed up when the dogs got overly rambunctious.

Piper and Missy heard me enter and came scrabbling down the hallway, their claws trying to find purchase on the travertine floor. After giving them plenty of pets and hugs in response to their yips and nose nudges, I walked to the kitchen, where I found Tillie pouring coffee into the delicate teacups she preferred using. She added a splash of cream to each cup and handed a saucer and teacup to me. "There are some salted-caramel cookies left in the pantry if you'd like to get them out."

I grabbed the cookie tin, brought it to the kitchen table, and offered it to Tillie. She took two cookies, as did I. Vannie had made the cookies the previous Friday, but they were still soft, chewy, and oh so tasty. Perfect with a cup of coffee.

After we'd consumed our cookies and refilled our teacups —one of the many reasons I preferred to drink from a large mug—Tillie tapped the table. "Tell me what you found out about the puppy mill. Are you really going to meet up with Shawn?"

I gave her an overview of what the vet's assistant had told me and then shared my conversation with Shawn in great detail. She almost choked when I told her how much he wanted to charge for the puppy. "After seeing how remote his property is, I don't feel it's safe for us to go out there. I think I need to text him and say something's come up and that I'd like to meet at his office."

"Which is located where?" Tillie plucked another cookie from the tin and nibbled.

"It's in Irvine at an industrial park. There are a lot of businesses there, with people coming and going all the time, even on Saturdays, so I feel it's safe enough." I followed Tillie's lead and helped myself to another cookie as well. "We did half the dog training in the warehouse attached to his front office, while the other half was completed at a couple parks and on a hiking trail."

Tillie chewed her cookie thoughtfully then took a slow sip

of coffee. "This is what I think we need to do. Have Vannie and Teresa meet Shawn in Irvine at three while you and I search his property at the same time. In case there are cameras, we'll wear disguises so he'll never know it's us."

"That might work, although I don't know how much snooping we can do. The warehouse didn't appear to have any windows through which to see what's inside, and I don't want to get arrested for breaking and entering. Your son and grandsons would have some strong words for me getting you in trouble if that happens."

Tillie waved away my concerns. "If we hear dogs barking, we can always claim we thought they'd gotten locked in somehow, and we were trying to rescue them. And it wouldn't even be a lie."

She made a good point. "What if Shawn has people working for him? I doubt they'd be very welcoming, especially if they have an illegal enterprise going on."

"Simple. You show them the text Shawn sent you that proves he invited you there." Tillie lifted her immaculately sculpted eyebrows, which caused nary a single wrinkle in her forehead. She was a firm believer in regular Botox treatments along with having the best cosmetic surgeon in Southern California on speed dial. "That should cover all our bases. If the employee tries calling Shawn to confirm, we'll instruct Vannie and Teresa to keep him from answering any phone calls while they're there, and then we'll get out of Dodge lickety-split."

"You've thought of everything." I bit into the cookie, my mind trying to consider every scenario that might go wrong with the plan.

"Well, not everything. What are we going to do if we do find a puppy mill? Calling 911 seems excessive. Maybe animal control?"

"I think I should start with Detective Hawkins if we find any concrete evidence. The puppy mill might be tied in with Eloise's death. If he thinks otherwise, he'll know who we should notify." I shuddered. I hoped I wouldn't regret letting Tillie talk me into trespassing on a potential criminal's isolated property.

"Don't worry, dear. I'll take my Taser and pepper spray just in case."

"That makes me even more worried." I gave her a stern look. "Why and where did you get a Taser?"

"A gal can't be too careful in this day in age." Tillie shrugged. "It fits perfectly in the Versace handbag David bought for my birthday. I have an extra pepper spray for you too. You should probably carry it with you all the time."

I shook my head. "I'd just lose it or accidentally spray myself."

"Better safe than sorry is my motto." Tillie stood and gathered our teacups and saucers. "I hate to rush our brainstorming session, but I have an appointment in thirty minutes. Andrew should be arriving any moment to pick me up."

I looked Tillie over. She was always stylish, but today, she had dressed up and had applied more than her usual makeup. "Will you be around this afternoon or evening?"

"Don't wait up for me, dear." She winked at me. "I have a committee meeting for the women's shelter silent auction and dinner fundraiser, and then I'm having dinner with Harvey."

"Harvey?" I had a difficult time keeping track of Tillie's male friends.

"He just moved here from New York and joined the country club." Tillie gleefully rubbed her hands together. "I had to snatch him up before Frances Allain got her claws into him."

Frances was Tillie's country club nemesis, although in my opinion, at their advanced age, they should have learned to get along. "You'd better not get too cocky, or Frances might contact your English baron and tell him you're two-timing him. She'll probably hope he'll end up on the rebound with her."

"He wouldn't touch that crow with a ten-foot pole. He's seen what kind of damage she can do to those around her."

I winced at her description of Frances, although Tillie had a point. The woman was birdlike and mean-spirited with a sharp tongue.

"Besides, John and I have an understanding that works well for us." Tillie uncapped a tube of lipstick and dabbed some onto her enhanced plump lips. She must've noticed my wince, because she patted my hand. "You don't need to worry so much. I'm not getting romantically involved with Harvey, and John knows it. But I do want Frances to think the possibility is there."

I couldn't help but shake my head. Perhaps their rivalry kept them on their toes and energized. Who was I to judge? "Go finish getting ready. I'll clean up the dishes and lock up when I'm done."

"Thank you, dear." Tillie stood and air kissed my cheek then smoothed down her black skirt. A designer brand, of course.

I looked down at the two dogs snuffling beneath the table, hunting for crumbs. "I'll take the dogs and see if I can get them and the cat to tolerate each other. I still haven't heard back from her owners."

"Perhaps they're on vacation and aren't checking email often."

"Hopefully that's all it is."

Tillie's phone buzzed, and she checked the screen. "Andrew's here. I'll see you tomorrow at one for our Norco rendezvous disguise makeover. Should we leave here around two so we have some time to do some reconnaissance?"

"Sure. If we find we have too much time on our hands when we get there, we can always find a Starbucks."

"I'll have Andrew drive us." Tillie opened her handbag and checked the contents.

"That's really not necessary. I can drive."

"Andrew will be necessary if we need to make a speedy getaway." She patted her hair. "It doesn't hurt to have a muscular male watching out for us either."

And with that, Tillie swept from the room, spritzing herself with her favorite floral fragrance.

Chapter 15

The dogs and I returned to the pool house, and I left them in the yard to romp around and sun themselves. I wasn't ready to introduce them to our feline guest yet. Once inside, I made sure the cat hadn't gotten into any mischief, and fortunately, she'd done nothing more than jump up on my bed and fall asleep on my pillow. Not wanting to have a curious cat jump into the middle of my cupcakes as I baked, I placed her litter box in my room then shut the door.

Waiting for the butter to come to room temperature, I called Shawn to see if he would meet me at his office instead of home. He was more than amiable and seemed relieved, so we agreed to meet at three. To cover my bases, I asked him for his office address. I didn't need him wondering how I already was in possession of it. Next, I powered up my laptop and sent an email to Cheryl, asking her to call me right away and providing her with my cell number. When her reply didn't immediately appear, I began working on the four dozen apple pie–filled cupcakes that a bridge group had requested.

With the apples chopped into small cubes and simmering on the stove with butter, brown sugar, cinnamon, nutmeg, ginger, and salt, I mixed up simple vanilla cupcake batter using a box mix but added a generous dose of cinnamon and a bit of nutmeg. When the filling and cupcakes were cooled to room temperature, I'd remove a tablespoon worth of cupcake from the center of each one and fill it with the apple pie filling. Swirls of cinnamon-spiced buttercream frosting would top it off. As I worked, my kitchen smelled like autumn, and I had to resist the urge to eat spoonfuls of the pie filling.

I took multiple breaks while working to check on the cat and the dogs. Piper and Missy were content to laze in the shade of the patio cover, and I made sure their water dish remained full. Despite it being autumn, the sun was quite warm. When I peeked in at the cat, she was entertaining herself with a soft ball that one of the dogs had abandoned in my room. She batted it around then pounced on it before repeating the process. I quietly closed the bedroom door and went back to work.

I'd just put in the last batch of cupcakes to bake when my phone rang. I didn't recognize the number but answered anyway.

"Hi, this is Emory." Carrie constantly chided me to throw in "Emory, the cupcake caterer," but I'd resisted. She also thought I should get a separate phone for my business but I had a hard enough time keeping track of one phone.

"Hi, Emory, this is Cheryl. I just saw your email, and I realize I should have contacted everyone after Eloise's horrific death, but as you can imagine, it's been chaotic around here."

"I know, which is why I waited until today to email you. I hoped things might have calmed down after the, uh, incident."

She snorted. "If anything, things are worse today."

"Oh?" I hoped I could nudge her into divulging more information.

"It's nothing I'm at liberty to talk about. Now, what can I do for you?" Cheryl's tone was brisk and businesslike. This was not at all the same chatty person I'd talked to on Saturday.

"I know you're swamped, but I was wondering if I could get the email addresses of all the participants in our dog training group?" I knew I shouldn't share that I was looking into whether anyone else had purchased a puppy from Shawn, so I only told her the partial truth. "Given what you're going through, I thought I could send out a group email, asking everyone to share their recipes from Saturday. I'm sure you don't need any more things added to your responsibilities."

"Really? Do you think it's appropriate to be doing something so trivial when such a horrific death occurred right after we'd been together?"

Well, no, it wasn't appropriate when she put it that way, but I had my ulterior motive, so I pressed on. "I understand what you're saying, but I've found that food often helps me cope with grief. I can collect the recipes and maybe have them printed and bound with a page stating something to the effect that it's in memory of Eloise. I think the majority of the people attending Saturday knew her, right?"

Cheryl's silence began to make me feel uncomfortable. Had my request been in poor taste? My mother would have known, but it was too late to ask her.

"All right. I guess that might be a good idea. We can keep copies of the booklet here in the association's office and pass them out to other residents if they'd like a keepsake."

I blew out a quiet sigh of relief. "Do you have time to send me the email addresses now?"

"I'll get it done after I get back from lunch." Cheryl tapped on her keyboard, the keystrokes clicking in my ear.

"Thanks, Cheryl." I had another few minutes before I needed to rotate the cupcake tins to promote even baking. "Say, where is your office located? Is it in the condo's complex or off-site?"

"It's part of the clubhouse. If you keep walking down the corridor, past the restrooms, you come to the offices. Of course, we keep the doors locked after hours so no one can wander in when the clubhouse is being used for events."

"I guess I didn't really pay attention."

A phone began ringing in the background. Cheryl muttered beneath her breath. "I've got to answer that, but I'll be sure to send you the email list soon."

"Thanks, I appreciate it." Except Cheryl was no longer on the line to hear my thanks.

I continued working on the cupcakes, and as promised, Cheryl's email came in just after one thirty. I opened the email and saved the Word attachment to my download folder. I opened it then scrolled to below the email address and began crafting a message asking for recipes from everyone. I didn't want to make Cheryl suspicious of my motivation just yet. I typed out a rough draft then decided to let it sit for a while as I assembled the cupcakes. Sometimes, words and clarity popped out at me after I gave an email time to rest.

Once the cupcakes were frosted and packaged up, ready to deliver the following day, I sent Vannie a text.

Can you drop by my place when you come home from work? We need to discuss the plan for Shawn.

Almost immediately, the gray dots appeared. She must've had her students doing busywork, so she was free to text.

Do you mind if I invite T? We can pick something up for dinner.

It made sense that Teresa should be involved since we'd planned on using her as the supposed puppy buyer along with her cousin giving us a disguise makeover.

Hope T can join us. Brian is cooking, so I'll let him know to plan for 4.

She sent back a thumbs-up emoji.

I immediately called Brian to let him know Vannie and Teresa would be joining us for dinner, which, being the good sport he was, he didn't mind in the least. He promised to be there by four and planned on serving scallops with fettuccini.

After we disconnected, I stuck two bottles of chardonnay in the refrigerator. Since I'd made a few extra apple pie–filled cupcakes to share, dessert was taken care of.

There was still time left before the gang arrived, so I turned my attention back to the group email. It took a while, but I was finally satisfied with the piece and hoped that Cheryl wouldn't think it was in poor taste.

I'm sure you've heard by now about the loss of Eloise Parker. We're saddened she was taken from us much too soon. As a tribute to her memory and the last day we spent time with her, we thought it might be fitting to compile the recipes from the dishes we shared together. If you're willing, please email your recipe to me along with a photo of your dog and its name, and I will compile and arrange them into a meaningful keepsake. If you'd like to say a kind word or share a memory of Eloise, I'll be happy to include it with your recipe.

If you have any questions or comments, feel free to either email me or call me at 949-555-1234.

Fondly,

Emory Martinez, Piper, and Missy

I wanted to come right out and ask them to include their phone numbers, but I didn't want to raise Cheryl's suspicions. For now, I'd wait until they individually emailed me back, and then I'd ask. Copying and pasting the addresses Cheryl had provided, one by one, I sent off the email personalized to each individual, hoping against hope that one of the people would provide some clues so we could suss out who had killed Eloise.

Chapter 16

By the time the emails were sent, Brian had appeared at my door with Vannie and Teresa behind him. Piper and Missy, not wanting to miss out on any attention, pranced around their legs, whining for attention. Or it could have been that they smelled the scallops and, if I hazarded a guess, bacon that were nestled into the reusable tote bag Brian carried.

I rushed to open the French doors wide. Brian brushed a quick kiss on my lips and hurried to the kitchen, the dogs in his wake. Vannie and Teresa each gave me a hug.

"What have you been baking? It smells amazing." Teresa sniffed the air.

"One of my customers requested apple pie–filled cupcakes." I licked my lips, recalling the way the spiced, tart apple filling complemented the cake while the creamy cinnamon buttercream provided a sweet contrast. Obviously, I'd had to sample one or two to make sure they would meet my customer's expectations. Wink, wink.

"If I know my sister, she made some extras for our dessert." Vannie nudged me. "Right, sis?"

"You know me well." I nudged Vannie back. "If you'd like, you can have one now for a snack and one later for dessert."

"Ooohhh…" Teresa cooed. "Yes. Definitely yes."

"Brian, would you like a cupcake?" I asked. I retrieved two small plates from a cabinet, added a cupcake to each, and handed them over to Vannie and Teresa.

"Thanks, but I'll save mine for after dinner." Brian flashed me a grin then patted his rock-hard abs. "I can't get too crazy with the sweets. Even though you're starting with dessert, would you like me to put together a charcuterie board to go with the wine?"

"I don't think we need a lot of appetizers." Vannie came into the kitchen and grabbed a couple paper napkins. "We can't stay too late or drink much wine. We both gotta find time to grade homework assignments after dinner so we don't end up staying up half the night."

"Oof, I forgot you still had to finish that." Brian pulled a bottle of wine out of the refrigerator along with brown butcher-paper-encased packages. He handed a small package to me along with the wine. "I'll start working on dinner, and Em can slice the smoked Havarti and pour a bit of wine. Just hang out here so I can listen in on your sleuthing planning session."

"We can do that as long as you don't try to talk us out of our plan of action." Vannie licked some frosting from her fingers then washed her hands.

"Moi? Would I ever try and tell you three what you can or can't do?" Brian clutched his T-shirt dramatically.

"You'd never do something like that. You're one of the good guys." Standing on my tiptoes, I kissed his cheek. "Vannie, can you get the wineglasses and more plates while I open the wine?"

"What can I do to help?" Teresa asked.

I handed her a box of crackers and the brown paper package. "You can place the cheese and crackers on a plate. I'll get a cheese knife in a sec."

It wasn't long until the three of us sat down at my kitchen table, sipping wine and nibbling on cheese. Brian stood at the kitchen counter, dicing and chopping veggies for salad. I'd offered to help, but he gently pushed me back to the table.

"I'm on pins and needles." Vannie rubbed her hands together. "Were you able to set up an appointment with Shawn?"

"Yes." The smile I gave Teresa was sheepish. "I pretended to be you, and you're interested in adopting a teacup Pomeranian."

"A teacup what?" Teresa furrowed her brows.

I fished in my pocket for my cell and brought up an image of the adorable dog. "Shawn said he could get just about any puppy you wanted but said a Pomeranian would be available to take home within the next few days."

"That seems so fast." Teresa handed my phone to Vannie.

"It does, but he also charges about a grand more than other breeders, and if you want to use a credit card, he charges an extra three percent."

Vannie whistled. "Maybe it's a good thing he's not the victim, because there's got to be a boatload of people who'd want him dead. That's robbery on top of dealing in puppy-mill dogs."

"Agreed." I took my phone back from Vannie. "Shawn was eager to meet up tomorrow to show us the puppy. He wasn't terribly happy about my request to meet at his home and see the mom and litter together. I claimed it was so I could pick the one with the best personality, and I wouldn't know until I saw the puppy interact in its natural surroundings."

"That makes sense," Brian said as he paused his chopping.

I nodded. "It seemed like the perfect plan until he gave me his address. It's way out in the middle of nowhere in Norco."

Brian gave a sharp inhalation, but to his credit, he didn't try to dissuade me. I jumped in to put his mind at ease, if only momentarily.

"Even with three of us, it doesn't seem prudent to visit him there, especially since we suspect he's running an illegal enterprise on his property." From the corner of my eye, I saw Brian's shoulders relax. "I revised the arrangements for meeting him at his office in Irvine. It's the same building where we did the indoor dog training."

"Did he offer to bring the mother and the entire litter?" Vannie asked.

"I didn't push him on it because…" I gulped, knowing no one would like the next plan. "Because Tillie and I will be going out to the property in Norco and checking it out while you two keep Shawn occupied in Irvine."

I didn't dare glance at Brian. Vannie, however, didn't hold back. "Do you really think that's wise? Maybe you should call the detective and have him send someone out there to check it out."

"I don't think law enforcement can storm someone's private property without probable cause. Us saying we think maybe Shawn's running a puppy mill without knowing it's true isn't going to work." I snuck a peek at Brian. His mouth was a grim line, but he held his tongue.

"It might work," Teresa said. "At least we know Shawn won't be on the property since we'll be keeping him in Irvine. Emory can do some reconnaissance before she and Tillie try to get into the warehouse and see if anyone else is around."

"I'm planning on studying the view from Google Earth to see if there's a way to access the warehouse without driving up the main entrance. I'm thinking we should walk in instead of driving."

"Andrew is going with you, isn't he?" Brian asked. "Not that I don't think you can hold your own, but there's something to be said for safety in numbers."

Did Tillie want to keep her Taser and pepper spray a secret from her grandson? I wasn't sure, so I held my tongue and didn't tell him about her arsenal. At least she wasn't packing a gun... that I knew of. "You're right. Andrew is going with us."

"All right. I think it's probably a good plan then." Brian turned his attention to the stovetop, drizzling oil into a cast iron skillet before he patted the plump scallops dry.

Vannie lowered her voice to barely above a whisper. "Take the extra Taser and pepper spray with you. Just in case."

Tillie must've bought a set for Vannie, knowing I'd decline the gesture. But in this instance, it seemed prudent to have the devices on hand. Flashing her two thumbs up, I chuckled.

"Shall we meet back at Tillie's to compare notes afterward?" Vannie asked. "I'm happy to provide dinner this time since Brian's been doing all the cooking lately. Are you free to join us, bro, or do you have to work?"

"I gotta work. Duty and bills call." Brian kept his eyes on the sizzling scallops. "Em, can you put the salad on the table? I'll take a glass of wine with dinner too."

I hopped up and retrieved the salad. Brian had already dressed it with a citrus vinaigrette, and the multitude of colorful veggies glistened, while dollops of creamy goat cheese dotted the lettuce.

Soon, our conversation ceased as we ate the succulent scallops sitting atop fettuccini that soaked up the flavorful citrus pan sauce Brian had made after plating our food. He was a magician at turning a little wine, juice from whatever citrus he had on hand, garlic, and butter into the most amazing accompaniment to whatever meat he served.

After eating our cupcakes—okay, I'll admit I had another

one—Vannie and Teresa did the dishes then left to finish their schoolwork and lesson plans. Brian and I spent some time working on getting the dogs and the cat to tolerate each other so that, by bedtime, the dogs ignored the cat and the cat— which Brian had nicknamed Boots because of her white paws —ignored the dogs. I considered it a huge success.

Chapter 17

Tuesday morning, Brian and I joined Tillie and Vannie for an early breakfast. Vannie looked sleep deprived, so while Brian fried up a skillet of bacon and scrambled eggs, I poured her a mug of coffee to drink immediately and fixed her a to-go mug to take on her drive to work. The dogs were practically attached to Brian's feet, waiting for a morsel to drop, and their disappointment showed when the food made it to the table with no mishaps.

I stilled Tillie's hand when she broke a piece of bacon in half. "Piper and Missy already ate breakfast at my house. And besides, I don't want them begging at the table."

"Whatever you say, dear." Tillie picked up a napkin with her free hand and tried to surreptitiously drop the bacon on the floor with her other. The chomping noise of the dogs gave away her subterfuge.

Brian thought it was the funniest thing ever, and soon, his belly laughs had us all laughing as the dogs sat up and began begging for more bacon.

"Thanks, I needed that." Vannie swiped at her eyes. She took her plate and put it into the dishwasher. "Sorry to eat and run, but I can't keep those monsters, er, students waiting."

"We'll see you and Teresa back here at one, right?" Tillie asked.

"Yep. That's the plan." She planted a kiss on Tillie's cheek. "Don't ever change, Gram. You're a treasure."

Even though I planned on heading to Tillie's son's home to work that morning, my day was much more flexible than Vannie's. After she'd left, I refilled our coffee cups and snatched another piece of bacon from the platter. The dogs practically drooled as they watched me eat.

Brian checked his watch then looked at the dogs. "Do you want me to take them for a run before I leave?"

"You don't have to. I'm heading over to your dad's this morning, and I'll take them with me and walk there." David Skyler, Tillie's son and Brian's father, lived across the bay from us. Without a bridge to connect the two residential enclaves, either we had to drive ten minutes north then make a hard right and drive ten minutes back south, or we could walk or bike and catch the ferry to take us across the bay, which took about the same amount of time. During the summer when hordes of tourists flooded our area, the ferry was the quickest route, hands down. Besides, the dogs and I got some exercise in, and there were plenty of enticing sights and sounds to keep us entertained, especially around the Balboa Bay Fun Zone.

He stood and kissed the top of my head. "All righty then, I need to get to the farmers' market. I'm meeting up with a couple potential vendors for a supply of local beef."

"But you're a seafood restaurant." Tillie sounded indignant.

"That we are, Gram, but believe it or not, some people aren't fans. I figure if we offer one beef dish, one chicken dish, and one vegetarian dish a night, groups will be happier to book with us if someone doesn't want fish or shellfish."

"I thought you were booking tables out for a month or more," I said. Brian tried hard to not bring work home when he had time off to spend with me. The result was that I wasn't always up to date with the current situation.

"We are, for now. The summer bookings have fortunately trickled over to early October." Brian ran his long fingers through his wavy beach-blond hair, and his green eyes turned dark. "But the lull between mid-October to late November has me concerned that this year will turn out like last fall. It wasn't pretty, and I lost some good employees."

"Have you lined up any marketing plans for that time period?" Tillie asked.

When I'd first started working for Tillie, and way before Brian and I got together, his restaurant had hit a rough patch and had almost gone under. Tillie had swooped in and given Brian the financial support he'd desperately needed. As a result, Tillie considered herself a silent partner, and perhaps she was. Despite my nosy, er, inquisitive nature, I didn't always pry into things that weren't my business.

"I've hired a marketing person, and we'll start some promos within the next couple of weeks." His face flushed pink. "You might not agree with me, but I like giving the underdog, so to speak, a chance. She's young and just starting out, but I like her vision, and her graphic skills are totally rad."

My heart skipped a beat then pounded into a gallop. Was he blushing because he had a crush, or could he be worried Tillie might berate him for not going with a tried-and-true marketing team? I tried to assure myself that Brian was devoted to me.

"Kewl beans, as they say." Tillie fluffed her perfectly coiffed platinum hair.

Brian guffawed. "I think that saying stopped being cool about ten years ago."

Tillie raised her teacup to her perfectly painted lips and took a dainty sip. I often had to wonder if she'd had the color tattooed on, because her lipstick never faded or seem to wipe off. She then lifted her cell phone, scrolled, and tapped a few times. "Let's see… that's chill, that's on fire, that's Gucci. Oohh, I like that one. I'm keeping it. Let's see what Frances Allain has to say when I throw that down."

Tillie's jest seemed to have the desired effect. The tension broke, and I wasn't so worried about the new little miss marketing person.

Brian kissed her cheek. "Ah, Gram, you're one of a kind. But, as the saying goes, G2G2W."

"Whatever, smartie pants." Tillie swatted at him. "But go on. I know you've got to get to work. G2G2W. So there."

"Those *L.A. Times* crossword puzzles come in handy, don't they?" I couldn't help but needle Brian a bit. Tillie could fill out the crosswords in pen, and it kept her mind sharp. Not that I knew whether the *Times* puzzles dealt with acronyms. I could barely fill in the blanks even when someone gave me the answers.

"Wtg." Tillie lifted her palm to me, and I gave her a high five.

"Okay, you two, you can stop ganging up on me." Brian's smile widened as he bent over to whisper in her ear. Although it wasn't much of a whisper because I heard every single word, loud and clear. "Be careful with your Taser and pepper spray. I don't want to see Em injured with a misfire."

Tillie lifted her nose into the air and pursed her lips. "My boy, I have no idea what you're talking about."

With that, Brian laughed, kissed his grandmother on the cheek, gave me a wink, and left. The dogs looked bereft at the loss of their bacon-cooking human.

I stood and began clearing the dishes from the table to load the dishwasher. "How was your date with Harvey?"

"Delightful. Plus, I think I might have convinced him to donate the use of his private jet for one of the silent auction prizes for the fundraiser." Tillie took a sip of coffee. "It'll dovetail nicely with the villa stay on St. Thomas, and it wouldn't surprise me if we raised, at minimum, a hundred grand on those two items alone."

I shook my head. It was still incomprehensible that there were people who wouldn't think twice about dropping that kind of money on a vacation, even if it did benefit a worthy cause. When I'd moved in with Tillie, I'd been flat broke and deeply in debt. But thanks to the generosity of the Skyler family and my cupcake catering business taking off, I'd paid off my debts—well, the debts my ex-husband had stuck me with—and had a teeny bit put into savings.

Tillie's voice pulled me from my thoughts, and her words startled me. I wasn't sure I'd heard correctly. "What did you just say?"

"I said perhaps I should bid on both of the items myself as a wedding gift for you and Brian one of these days." Tillie's blue eyes sparkled.

I almost choked. "Uh, we, uh, haven't even talked about anything that serious."

"I don't know why not." Her gaze drilled into me, and I wanted to look away. "Neither of you are getting any younger, and I've been patient for about as long as I can handle. I'd like to hold a great-grandchild before I pass."

"We really haven't thought that far ahead." My cheeks flamed, and perspiration broke out along my hairline. "Besides, you've got a lot of years left ahead of you, so don't talk like you're on your deathbed."

"Tick-tock, tick-tock." She checked her watch. "You and Brian are my only hope. Theodore's still in prison for another three years, and Vannie has commitment issues. Has she opened up to you about her past?"

Theodore, Brian and Vannie's half brother, had had substance abuse issues and then fled the country after a tragic accident. After finding sobriety, he'd returned home and turned himself in. The judge hadn't been as lenient with his sentencing as the Skylers had hoped given their status within the community. Tillie and her son made biweekly visits to see him, while Brian went once a month. I joined him once in a while, but I still got the feeling Theodore didn't care for me much.

I shook my head. "No. She shuts down whenever she thinks the conversation is even skirting around the topic of her personal life."

"I've suggested counseling, but she says she's fine." Tillie's mouth turned downward. "I just want to see all my grandchildren well-adjusted and happy."

"Perhaps Teresa can get Vannie to open up. They seem to care for each other." I poured more coffee into Tillie's cup then wiped down the counters.

"I hope so."

"I know you want Brian and me to rush toward the altar, but we both have to want that in our own timing." I hated to disappoint this dear, sweet woman who had taken me in and made me a part of her family. "I still have some healing to do after what that snake of an ex put me through, and while I love Brian, I'm just not ready to take that permanent leap. And I don't think he's ready to either."

Tillie sighed. "Brian basically said as much, so I thought I'd try to work on you."

My faced heated, and I felt the urge to stick my head in the freezer.

"Don't look so appalled, dear. You both know what a meddlesome woman I am." She chuckled. "I guess I'll have to be content knowing you both love each other and that all the other stuff will follow when you're both ready."

"I'm sorry we disappointed you, but I'm sure you realize that it has to be the right timing so our relationship lasts."

She snorted. "At least you have Addie and Lars as a shining example of a good marriage. Brian has nothing but his father's ill-advised judgment in picking short-term spouses."

By my count, David had experienced wedded unhappiness four times, with two of his brides meeting tragic ends. The other two spouses, Brian and Theodore's mothers, still received extravagant monthly alimony checks that David constantly grumbled about. He said he'd sworn off marriage, but the rest of the family would never wager on it. David was one of those men who needed to have a pretty wife on his arm without taking the time to find out if the potential bride was a good and decent person.

"Poor Brian. You can't blame him for not wanting to rush into a commitment with me or with anyone else."

"You're right, dear." Tillie stood. "I need to get a few more emails sent to coerce, er, encourage some more high-end donations for the auction, and I know you need to get to work."

I gave Tillie's cheek a kiss then wrapped my arms around her slender shoulders. "You know I love both you and Brian and wouldn't ever do anything to hurt him, right?"

"You're a good influence on this family, and we're all so very lucky to have you." She patted my cheek. "And I love you too. See you at one for our makeover."

As Tillie headed to her office, I couldn't help but have a warm glow fill my heart. It stayed with me until we got to Norco.

Chapter 18

Teresa's cousin, Maurice, was a hoot. My first impression was that he looked familiar, but I couldn't place where I knew him from. Once he broke out singing several refrains of "Back in Time" from one of the *Men in Black* movies, I realized that his appearance and voice resembled the Latin pop artist and rapper Pitbull. He even had Tillie shaking her booty as he segued into some of the artist's other top hits.

Despite his antics, Maurice was a whiz with the wigs, clothing, and makeup, although Tillie wasn't thrilled when he placed a shaggy salt-and-pepper wig on her head and then instructed her to remove all her makeup and false eyelashes. He'd pulled out a beige cardigan with matching corduroy pants for her to try on.

"You're going to make me look old and decrepit," she complained.

"I thought that was the point. Make you look like someone you'll never be." He coaxed her into putting the sweater onto her slender frame. "No one would suspect the too-, too-glamorous Tillie Skyler to be the little old granny helping her granddaughter adopt a puppy."

That answered my question about how much Teresa had shared with her cousin. He knew why we needed good disguises.

"Well, I suppose you have a point," Tillie grumbled.

"Now, darling, just as soon as you have your makeup off, put these on." He handed her a pair of overly large gold wire-rimmed spectacles that could have been popular in the seventies, along with a pair of scuffed brown boots.

"You've got to be kidding me." Tillie wrinkled her nose at the shoes.

"You can't go traipsing around in stilettoes, can you?" Vannie asked. "I'd rather wear your boots than these torture devices."

She stuck her foot up to show the fire-engine-red four-inch stilettoes Maurice had made her wear. She almost toppled over. I grabbed her arm to steady her and heard fabric rip. We both looked down at the thigh-high, skintight black skirt she'd stuffed herself into and saw the ripped seam.

"Oops. Do you have another skirt I can wear that isn't quite so tight? I'm so uncomfortable in this getup." Vannie wrapped her arms, which jingled with oodles of bangles, around the almost-sheer white tank top that clung to her torso. Her wavy platinum wig brushed the tops of her bare shoulders. With the heavily applied makeup, she looked nothing like my sister. "We're adopting a puppy, not clubbing."

"Shush, doll. You look fabulous, and it will only take me a minute to stitch the skirt back up." He jutted his thumb over at his cousin. "I just wish you'd convince her to let me dress her and fix her makeup."

"I'm not wearing makeup, so there's nothing to fix." Teresa stuck her tongue out at her cousin. She wore black skinny jeans with black ballet flats. A cream-colored cashmere tunic sweater completed her ensemble. "We're going with the cover story that I'm the assistant for this pseudo-famous influencer, and the puppy is really for her. No one in their right mind would think I'd want a teacup puppy, no matter how cute they are."

"Yeah, yeah, yeah." Maurice stuck his tongue out at her.

"Now, kids. Behave yourselves and stop your squabbling." Tillie, dressed in the wig, the wire-framed glasses, and cardigan, sans makeup, looked like the proverbial little old granny. She shook her finger at them and made her voice squeaky. "It'll be off to your room with no dinner if you don't stop."

"Darling, you're fabulous." Maurice clapped his hands. "The Playhouse has auditions coming up for a production soon. There's a part in there that would be perfect for you. Shall I text you the deets?"

Tillie looked thoughtful for a moment. "Sure. Why not? YOLO, right?"

Vannie and I gazed at each other with mirrored puzzled expressions. YOLO?

Maurice guffawed. "You only live once. You're so very right."

Tillie patted his forearm, which was heavily tattooed with Māori art. "Let me know when the auditions are and how long the production runs. I'll see if I can fit it into my social calendar."

"You got it." He motioned for me. "Let me finish up your makeup and adjust your wig. I think you mussed it when you kept Vannie from falling."

Maurice had put me in a jet-black, chin-length wig. With sharp angles, the bangs brushed my now jet-black eyebrows, and the bottom wrapped itself around my jawline. I was dressed in black leather pants, a black T-shirt, and a black leather vest. Well, I assumed it was really pleather, because what theater in its right mind would purchase real leather for actresses to wear? Faux black Doc Marten boots and clip-on silver hoop earrings for my ears, nose, and an eyebrow completed the look. Maurice added more dark eyeliner to my eyes then brushed scarlet lipstick across my lips.

He held out a mirror. "There. No one will recognize you, and the boots will make it easier to trek across the terrain."

"Emory, look this way," Tillie called out to me.

I turned, and she began taking photos of my getup. "What's that for?"

"I'm going to text a few to Brian. I'll bet it makes him leave the restaurant at a decent hour once he sees you dressed like this." Tillie winked as I flushed hot. "Vannie and Em, stand together so I can take a few more shots of you together."

Teresa held up her hand in the stop position. "Wait until our mission is over just in case your phone is confiscated. We don't want whoever it is to associate us with you."

"That's a good point." Tillie put her phone back into the brightly colored, crocheted, granny-square-patterned handbag Maurice had given her. The oatmeal-colored yarn trim was frayed in places. It was a far cry from the usual designer purses she favored. "All righty then, let's get the show on the road."

We helped Maurice gather his tools of the trade and carried them to his classic convertible Mustang, which was painted a bright cherry red.

Tillie kissed his cheek then slipped several bills into his hand. I was pretty certain they were all Ben Franklins. "Thanks for doing this for us. We'll have Teresa get the costumes back to you soon."

"My pleasure, ladies." Maurice bent over at the waist and kissed Tillie's hand. "I'll send you the info for the stage production, and in the meantime, call me anytime I can help out."

As he drove past us, he blew kisses. Once he was out of sight, I turned toward Vannie and Teresa. "We'll plan on parking on a frontage road, close to Shawn's property, and start hiking toward the warehouse at two forty-five. Send us a quick text when you're done meeting with him. I'm assuming it shouldn't take longer than a half hour, so we'll plan on not staying much longer than that."

"You'd both better silence your phones and turn on the vibration mode now." Vannie pulled her phone out and, I assumed, did the same. "I'd hate for you to get a spam call and have your cover blown."

I almost giggled. Vannie and Teresa were really getting into the spirit of our investigation with the "mission" and our "cover." But I suppose they were right. Tillie and I both complied with Vannie's suggestion just as Andrew pulled up in the town car. His head jerked as he did a double take at our costumes.

He jumped from the car and opened the rear door. "Mrs. Skyler, I almost didn't recognize you. Are you heading to an early Halloween party?"

Halloween was still seven weeks away, but I supposed some people might be tempted to celebrate this early.

"No, but I'll tell you the plan on our way to our destination."

I hopped into the back seat, buckled in, then gave Andrew the address. Vannie and Teresa waved as we drove away.

PARKED on the frontage road I'd found online, we looked at the steep hillside with consternation. I hadn't noticed the elevation changes on the map I'd viewed. Even with the sensible shoes Tillie wore, she couldn't, or at least shouldn't, attempt to climb the hill. Heck, I wasn't sure I'd be able to easily ascend the rocky hill myself. I pulled the Google Earth map up on my phone and zoomed in.

"Without using the only road to Shawn's residence and warehouse, this is really the only way in." I huffed out a breath. "Tillie, you're going to have to sit this one out with

Andrew. Once I check to make sure no one is around, I'll call, and you can drive up the main road."

Tillie peered out the window and looked up. "Blast my creaky bones and age. But I concede. I can't climb that hill."

I checked my watch. It was already two fifty, five minutes later than I'd planned. Traffic had slowed us down more than I'd allotted for. I took a deep breath in, tried to still my racing heart, and opened the car door. "Okay. I'm going in."

"If we don't hear back from you within twenty minutes, we're coming in, guns blazing." Tillie pulled her Taser from the handbag. "You have your pepper spray, right?"

My heart bolted when, for a brief moment, I thought she'd brought a real gun. "It's in my pocket. I'll call you the second I know it's safe for you to come. If there are employees around, I'll try to sneak around the back of the warehouse to see if I can find any evidence then return here the way I came."

Tillie flashed a thumbs-up before I began the climb.

Chapter 19

Ten minutes later, I arrived at the top of the hill, sweaty and out of breath. A blister had formed on my heel, and I tried not to hobble as I made my way toward the warehouse. It was eerily silent. No birds chirped, squirrels didn't chatter or scamper in the sparse oak trees, and there wasn't even a whimper or a bark anywhere in the vicinity of the warehouse. I felt a huge weight of anxiety lift from my shoulders. We'd gotten Shawn all wrong. He wasn't running a puppy mill, at least not on this property.

With no sight or sounds of other humans in the area, I wasn't so cautious about keeping a low profile as I came closer to the warehouse. The large double doors were mostly closed. A gap of about twelve inches appeared between the doors, which meant the warehouse wasn't locked. I took a good look around, confirmed there wasn't anyone watching me nor were there any other vehicles parked in the gravel parking lot, and strode toward the doors. The closer I came, the stronger the stench became. I used my thumb and forefinger to plug my nose and, with the other hand, gripped the cannister of pepper spray.

I hooked the toe of my boot around one of the metal

doors and pulled it toward me. It easily swung open on well-oiled hinges. The stench almost knocked me over, but not a peep could be heard. I used my T-shirt to cover my mouth and nose and inched into the building as I allowed my eyes to adjust to the dim interior. Two overhead skylights were the only illumination I had, which wasn't much given the cavernous building.

The warehouse was mostly empty aside from several wire crates tipped onto their sides. I assumed they were dog crates given their sizes. The concrete floor was littered with newspapers and piles of, well, animal excrement, which explained the odor.

My phone vibrated with a text. I pulled it from my pocket and peered at the screen. It was from Vannie.

Shawn's a no-show and left no message for us. GET OUT NOW!

Panic seized my stomach, and my heart began to gallop. I started to back out of the warehouse, but as my eyes adjusted to the dim lighting, I noticed a stack of haphazardly piled crates in the left-hand corner nearest to me. I paused as I tried to make sense of the shape among the crates. And that was when it became obvious.

It was the shape of a man. An unmoving man. And there was a huge, dark puddle of something beneath his head that had spread out.

I turned and ran as I stabbed at the numbers on my cell phone. I managed to connect to 911 on the third attempt.

"What's your emergency?"

"I need an ambulance and the police. Someone's been injured, and I'm not sure it was an accident." I could barely catch my breath.

"What's the address?"

I gave it to the dispatcher, having memorized it from all the Google searches I'd done of the property, along with my name and phone number. I'd been through this drill before.

"Is the victim breathing?"

"It was too dark to tell, but I don't know how he could still be alive with all the blood he lost. And I wasn't sure it was safe, so I left the warehouse to call you." I whirled around to make sure no one was following me before I continued loping away from the warehouse. There was no reason to avoid the main road now.

"Do you think there's a perpetrator in the warehouse, or is it environmentally unsafe?"

"Maybe both? It's super dark in there, and I think the warehouse was being used for a puppy mill. The air is practically unbreathable."

"I'll pass the information on to the emergency personnel responding. They should reach you in about five minutes." I listened to her clacking away at the keyboard. "Is there somewhere you can wait that is safe?"

"Yes. I'll wait in the car with my friends." I jumped in before she could ask. "And you don't need to stay on the line with me."

"Call back if you spot any suspicious activity." She disconnected.

I called Tillie, who answered on the first ring. "I just found either a badly injured person or he could even be dead. Have Andrew bring the car up the main road and park near Shawn's house. I'll meet you there. The police and ambulance are on their way."

Much to Tillie's credit, she calmly asked Andrew to drive to the house before starting the interrogation. "What happened? Who is it? Where did you find them?"

"I'll tell you when you get here. Right now, I need to catch my breath." I'd made it to Shawn's rustic porch and bent over at the waist in an attempt to gulp in air. I felt light-headed, so I sank onto the wooden steps, which creaked beneath my weight.

"I hear sirens coming closer. We'll be there in a minute." Tillie disconnected the call.

I called Vannie to let her know I was safe but that there would be a long delay in us coming back home. But instead of letting me get in a single word, Vannie talked right over me.

"Thank God you're safe! We were terrified when Shawn was a no-show." The purr of a car's engine could be heard in the background. "We're almost home. How soon do you think you'll be here?"

"Well, about that. It will be quite a long time, I'm afraid."

"What happened? Are you and Gram safe?"

"We're safe, but I found either a severely injured man or he was already dead. And I couldn't tell if it was Shawn or not."

"OMG! Not again!" Vannie covered the phone with her hand and said something to Teresa, who repeated Vannie's lamenting OMG.

"Look, I have to go. The police just arrived." I disconnected after Vannie made me promise to call her just as soon as we were headed home.

A black-and-white cruiser followed Tillie's town car. Dust billowed behind the vehicles and slowly settled onto the shrubs and scraggly oak trees. No wonder everything seemed colorless; it was caked in gray dust. Once again, I pulled my T-shirt over my mouth and nose as the breeze swept the debris toward me. Fortunately, the billowing dirt didn't last long once the cruiser and the town car pulled onto the gravel parking area.

The officer, who appeared old enough to have retired already, had wispy gray hair that barely clung to his liver-spotted pate and wrinkles on his face deep enough to hide a body. He slowly climbed from his car. I motioned for Tillie to stay put as I stepped forward to meet him.

"Are paramedics and an ambulance on their way?" I didn't think this man would have the strength or the stamina to pull the crates off of the victim, who I strongly suspected just might be Shawn.

"They'll be along in a few minutes." The officer's voice held a slow drawl as his gaze swept over my tight leather pants and upward, stopping at my chest. "Now, what seems to be the trouble, little lady? And why are you out here in these parts?"

I gritted my teeth and reminded myself to stay calm. "There's an injured man in the warehouse. It looks like some crates fell on top of him."

"Well, why didn't you say so in the first place?" He turned to look at the warehouse. "Come on, girl. Show me where the accident happened."

"Just walk through the open door, and you'll find him in the left-hand corner." I truly didn't want to return to the warehouse. "I need to make sure my grandmother is all right."

"I wasn't born yesterday, missy. How do I know you're not going to jump into that fancy car of yours and take off?" He scratched his head with fingers yellowed from nicotine.

Fortunately, the sound of sirens coming down the road saved me from having to answer. It was a relief knowing that responsible humans would be here soon. The officer looked just as relieved as I felt.

I motioned for Tillie to roll down the window as I stepped closer to the car. The officer kept his beady blue eyes on me as I handed her my phone after unlocking the screen. "Send Detective Hawkins a text and let him know about the situation. I have a feeling it's Shawn in there, and there's plenty of evidence that the warehouse, until recently, used to house a gazillion dogs in unsanitary conditions."

"So, in other words, you found the puppy mill?" Tillie's mouth was a tight, grim line.

I almost gagged. I couldn't get the horrific smell out of my nostrils. "It certainly looks that way. At any rate, I think Detective Hawkins needs to get involved."

Chapter 20

The ambulance and a boxy paramedic truck came into view, bringing fresh waves of dust with them. Tillie rolled up the window, and I pulled my T-shirt up over my face once again.

After the vehicles came to a halt, three paramedics hopped from their truck, medical bags in hand, and headed for the officer. I joined them.

"Where is the victim?" the older of the paramedics asked. "A. Brody" was embroidered over his shirt pocket, which I assumed was his name. He might have been in his late thirties and not ancient like the officer, which I was thankful for. It was obvious he was in charge.

"This little lady says he's in the warehouse." The officer jerked his thumb toward me.

"You haven't checked on the victim yet?" The paramedic's face didn't hide his incredulity. "Miss, can you show us where to find him?"

"Do you have face masks or, better yet, gas masks? I think the warehouse was being used as a puppy mill."

"Now look here, gal, you shouldn't be throwing baseless accusations around at law-abiding citizens." The officer hitched his fingers around the belt loops of his trousers and tugged them up his scrawny frame.

"I think time is of the essence here." The paramedics all opened their cases and extracted masks. One handed me an extra, for which I was grateful.

"He's in the warehouse, left-hand corner just as you walk through the door." I reluctantly walked toward the warehouse as I peeled open the plastic wrapper that protected the mask. I slid it onto my face then picked up the pace. "I would have checked on the man's condition myself, but it was too dark to see much. There's also a large puddle of what I think is blood, and it didn't seem possible he could still be alive after losing so much."

Almost as one, they pulled large flashlights from their utility belts. When we reached the entrance, the stench became apparent despite the mask that covered my mouth and nose. I thought I heard one of the men gag.

I stepped inside and pointed to the left. The crates were still in a jumbled heap, and the man hadn't moved since I'd last seen him. Flies darted around our heads the closer we got to the body. The flashlights illuminated the man and the puddle of what was now clearly blood surrounding his head. The light reflected off an aluminum baseball bat, with obvious blood spatters coating it and it had been carelessly tossed next to the feet of the body. The man was definitely Shawn, and it was apparent he'd been murdered.

I felt a hand on my arm, pulling me to a stop. It was the head paramedic, A. Brody.

"There's no need for you to stay in here. Go wait by your car and call 911 and ask them to send out a detective." His voice was muffled by the mask, but I caught every word.

He didn't have to tell me twice to leave, and I practically ran back to Tillie's car. The officer sat in his vehicle, tapping on his cell phone. He never looked up as I approached the town car, and I wondered if he was engrossed in a game, or perhaps a YouTube video held his attention.

Tillie opened the car door, but I motioned for her to remain inside. "The paramedics asked me to call 911 and request a detective. Did you hear back from Detective Hawkins?"

"Yes, and he's en route. Could you tell if it was Shawn?" Tillie handed me back the phone.

"It's him. Let me make that call and get a competent law enforcement person here first, then I'll tell you about it." I made the call, passing along the paramedic's request for a detective to be sent to the scene. The dispatcher promised someone from the county sheriff's department would be sent as quickly as possible.

Next, I sent Detective Hawkins a text. "The victim is Shawn Parker. Riverside County Sheriff's department is sending a detective out as well."

He didn't respond, but then again, if he was speeding to get here, I assumed he wouldn't take the time to text back.

I quickly filled Tillie in on what I'd found in the warehouse. She tsked several times, and when I described the horrid condition that the dogs had been forced to live in, her eyes filled with tears.

"While I'd never wish another human being dead, somehow, I feel like karma caught up with Shawn." Her gaze turned to the warehouse. "What do you suppose happened to all the dogs?"

"I don't know. Hopefully they were rescued and not carted off to some other hellhole."

"I think the detectives should make it a priority to find those poor dears rather than investigate the murder." Tillie pulled her cell phone out. "While you deal with the officials, I'm going to make some calls and see what agency can help us, be it a governmental agency or a nonprofit. Either way, I'm going to make it my mission to make sure every single one of those dogs finds a safe home."

If anyone could get it done, Tillie was that woman.

The paramedics, medical bags clutched close to their bodies, hustled from the warehouse. As soon as they'd gotten several yards from the entrance, they tore off their masks and gulped in clean air. Perhaps I should have told the emergency dispatcher that the detective, along with anyone else who worked the scene, would need a hazmat suit.

The head paramedic walked over to me. Tillie remained in the car, the cell phone clutched to her ear. I'd expected her to jump at the chance to question the handsome paramedics and get the scoop from them. But perhaps she was embarrassed by her hideous costume and didn't want another living soul to see her that way. At least she had her quest to keep her busy until we were released to go home.

"Would you like some?" The paramedic squirted a generous amount of hand sanitizer into his palm then offered the bottle to me. I accepted.

I studied his embroidered name again. What title did you call a paramedic? I was fairly confident it wasn't Officer. "Thanks, Mr., uh, Brody."

"Everyone calls me Brody. You're welcome to do likewise." He inclined his head toward the warehouse. "Is a detective coming?"

"Yes, although I'm not sure how long it will take. He, or I guess it could be a she, will be coming from the Riverside sheriff's office." I rubbed the sanitizer over my hands until it evaporated. "Will you be staying until the detective arrives?"

"I'd better." He squinted at the officer, still sitting in his patrol car with his eyes glued to the screen of his phone, and sighed. "Please forgive the city for sending him. He's the chief's cousin and only serves as a senior volunteer. Thankfully, he doesn't carry a gun. Even though he's supposed to go through training, somehow, the chief lets him skip out."

"It seems odd that he was the one to respond to a potential murder." I felt marginally better knowing that the officer didn't have a firearm on him.

"There was a convenience store robbery a couple hours ago, and most of the on-duty officers are tied up with that." Brody put the hand sanitizer back into his pocket. "Fortunately, there weren't any injuries. Just a few frightened customers and employees."

"I should mention that Detective Hawkins from Huntington Beach will be here in a bit." I bit my lower lip, wondering how much to share. "He's investigating the murder of this victim's mother. We think they might be connected, aside from their relationship."

Brody lifted an eyebrow and swiftly looked me over. It wasn't the sleazy gaze the senior volunteer had given me but more as if he was trying to read what my role in the murders was. Darn Maurice and the black leather he'd forced me to wear. "You undercover? Maybe investigating the puppy mill?"

"Me?" My voice squeaked. "Oh, no. Not at all. I'm a cupcake caterer."

He chortled. "Then how did you get mixed up in all of this?"

The noise of an engine and a cloud of dust announced the arrival of another vehicle, which saved me from having to answer.

Chapter 21

An unmarked, dusty black sedan pulled onto the gravel lot and parked. Once the dust settled, the door opened, and out stepped the skinniest man I'd ever seen. Compared to him, I looked like a balloon.

"That's Detective Lankershim. He's one of the best in the sheriff's department," Brody said. He gave me a nod then strode off to discuss the body with the new arrival.

The detective was short—a good head shorter than Brody. He wore blue jeans with cowboy boots, and a white polo shirt showed off his sinewy arms. It was difficult to guess his age—maybe in his forties—but his dishwater blond hair was still thick and wavy, and he sported a thick handlebar mustache.

The two men disappeared into the cavernous warehouse after each had donned a mask then came out a few minutes later. The detective spoke on his cell phone for a couple of minutes, and then Brody pointed in my direction. The two headed my way.

When they stood in front of me, the detective tucked his mask into his pocket. "I'm Detective Lankershim. You're the one who called in the body, Ms. Martinez?"

"Yes." I tilted my head at the car. "We came out here to

talk to Shawn Parker about purchasing a puppy. He agreed to meet us, and when I couldn't find him, I entered the warehouse."

"What time did you arrive here?" The detective pulled a notebook from his back pocket.

Oh, boy. What if Shawn had security cameras that would show me sneaking up the hillside and onto his property? How would I explain that? "About three? I'm not sure of the exact time since I didn't look at my watch."

He inclined his head at the car. "Would either of them know the exact time?"

This was getting more complicated by the minute, and I felt my cheeks warm. "Well, they didn't exactly drive up to the property until I called them about finding the, uh, body."

Detective Lankershim narrowed his eyes then opened the car door. "I'd like to ask both of you to step out of the vehicle. Now."

"Young man, you don't have to be so snippy. I'm moving as quickly as I can." Tillie reached out her hand as if needing assistance to extricate herself from the car. Surprisingly, the detective took her hand and gingerly helped her to a standing position. Tillie really did belong on a stage, but I wondered if once he found out her true identity, he'd feel less chivalrous.

Tillie stood next to the car, her shoulders stooped forward. Andrew moved to stand next to her, and she threaded her arm into the crook of his elbow and held on tight.

"Your names?" the detective asked as he pointed his pen at each of them.

"I'm Matilda Skyler, and this is my driver, Andrew Miller."

In the couple of years I'd known Andrew, this was the first time I'd ever heard his last name mentioned.

The detective brought his eyebrows together as if puzzling over her name. He looked at her closely then shook his head. "And what brings you here?"

Tillie pointed at me, her hand trembling ever so slightly. "I sent Emory to purchase a teacup Pomeranian for me. I'm a bit of a recluse and didn't want the seller to know it was for me."

"And your relationship with Ms. Martinez is?" The detective continued to study Tillie's features. I wasn't sure her charade was the best plan of action in light of the murder.

"She's my caretaker."

Detective Lankershim took a step back, narrowed his eyes, and tilted his head then turned to do the same to me before returning his attention to Tillie. A smile broke out on his face. "Ah, Mrs. Skyler and Ms. Martinez, you almost fooled me with those disguises. How is it that you're involved in yet another homicide?"

Wait. What? He seemed almost delighted with our subterfuge, but I couldn't figure out how he'd heard about us way out here in Norco.

Before either of us could answer, another cloud of dust announced a new arrival. In the swirling haze, a large, formidable man was visible behind the wheel of the black sedan. Detective Lankershim placed his hands on his narrow hips.

"That's Detective Hawkins from Huntington Beach," I said. "He's investigating the murder of your victim's mother. It happened a couple days ago, which is how we're involved."

"Let me get this straight. You're involved in not one but two homicides? A mother and her son?" Detective Lankershim didn't seem suspicious, as if we'd killed the victims and needed to be interrogated. Instead, he was amused? No, that wasn't quite it. Maybe intrigued at how a senior socialite and a cupcake caterer could keep finding themselves involved in the unsavory business of murder.

Whatever he thought, I was grateful he hadn't handcuffed me and hauled me off for questioning in a dank, windowless concrete room. "That's correct."

Detective Hawkins waited a moment for the dust to settle

then climbed out of the city-owned vehicle. He handed his business card to the Norco detective. "I'm Detective Hawkins, and I hear you have a victim who might be related to a case I'm working on."

"Nice to meet you." Detective Lankershim held out his hand. "I'm Detective Lankershim, but call me Lanky."

His name definitely fit his build, but it wasn't flattering, in my opinion.

"Then call me Nathan, by all means." He turned, frowned at my leather-and-wig getup, then pointed at me. "What kind of trouble has Ms. Martinez found now?"

"It seems like these two had ideas about going undercover." Lanky jerked his thumb toward Tillie.

Nathan must not have noticed the diminutive elderly woman when he'd walked over to us, because he could barely contain his guffaw. "Oh, good Lord. What were you two thinking?"

While Nathan might not have ever met Tillie in person, her photograph was constantly in local newspapers and magazines, touting her attendance at social events and philanthropic endeavors. And it was well known that Tillie and I had solved several murders together in the past in the Newport Beach area. It didn't take a seasoned detective, local to that area, to figure out who the bespectacled old lady was. But that still didn't explain how Detective Lankershim had heard of us.

Tillie huffed. "I shouldn't have paid Maurice so much. My disguise is worthless."

It only made Nathan laugh harder. "All right, you two. I know you have a story to tell, but before we get into it, I'd like to see the crime scene."

"You'd better put on a mask or hazmat suit if you have one." I looked around to see if the paramedics were still around. They weren't, but the ambulance still stood by. "The ambulance crew probably has an extra mask if you need one."

"I've got several in my car." He looked at Lanky. "Can you show me the scene? I take it you haven't begun combing for evidence and bagging."

"Definitely not. This calls for a team of expert crime scene investigators, and Ms. Martinez is correct. They'll need to work in hazmat suits." Lanky visibly shuddered then put his mask back on. "Follow me, Detective."

Once the two men had strode into the warehouse, flashlights in hand, I said, "I'm so sorry to drag you into this, Andrew."

"It's not a problem. We didn't break any laws." He winked at Tillie. "Besides, life is never dull when I'm with you two."

"So true, Andrew my boy, so true." Tillie patted his bulging bicep. "Shall we take a seat in the car while we wait for those two to come back for interrogation?"

"Sounds good to me. That climb up the hill almost did me in." I walked around to the other side of the car and slid in. Tillie, already in her usual spot, handed me a cool bottle of water. I chugged half of it down before remembering there probably wasn't a restroom I could use out here.

My phone vibrated in my pocket. It was a text from Vannie.

When do u expect to b home? Will order in for dinner.

I thumbed a reply, all the while checking for the detectives to return.

Idk. Det. Hawkins just got here. He and other det. have questions for us. I'll text when we're on way.

Vannie sent a kiss emoji.

It reminded me that I hadn't notified Brian about this newest development. I hesitated because I knew he would be super busy prepping for dinner, but on the other hand, if he found out from someone else, he'd be crushed, especially if he worried for my safety. I checked the warehouse, and the detectives still hadn't scurried out. I thumbed as short a message as I could.

Tillie and I safe. Found Shawn murdered and puppy mill abandoned. Talking to 2 detectives. Will head home after done. Come over after work, pls!

I sent two kiss emojis after the first message swooshed into cyberspace. My phone immediately rang.

"Em, are you sure you and Gram are safe?" Brian sounded out of breath.

"We're sitting in the car with Andrew, and there's an ambulance crew thirty feet from us and two armed detectives on the property. We're perfectly safe." It was sweet of Brian to worry, which made me feel bad for having to put that kind of stress on him. But really, it wasn't my fault that I kept finding bodies.

He heaved a sigh of relief. "Okay. I'll have my sous chef close up tonight. I should be over around ten."

"Thanks, Brian. It means a lot to me."

"I would have come over even if you hadn't asked. You know I'm here for you, no matter what, don't you?" There was a catch in his voice. He cleared his throat. "You can tell me all about it when I get there."

"I can't wait to see you."

We said our goodbyes, and Tillie flashed a Cheshire cat grin at me. I ignored her. As I put my phone back into my pocket, the two detectives strode back toward the car.

Chapter 22

Nathan looked a bit green, and he swallowed convulsively, his Adam's apple bobbing up and down each time. I thought his eyes were watering, but he quickly put on mirrored sunglasses so I couldn't be certain that was what I'd seen.

Lanky rested his forearm on the hood of the car and bent over to peer into the back seat. "Ladies, we've decided that due to the condition of the warehouse and the time it's going to take to comb through it for evidence, we'll take a quick statement now. Otherwise, you'd probably be here for hours waiting on us. Since Nathan vouches for you, it's good enough for me. We'll coordinate a time to meet with you tomorrow to go over it in depth if you'll promise to work within our time frame."

Tillie and I both promised, although I hoped the time wouldn't be terribly inconvenient. "Where would you like for us to meet tomorrow?"

"We'll come to your residence if that works for you," Lanky said.

"Perfect. Emory will have cupcakes and coffee ready for

your visit." Tillie practically bounced in her seat. She loved being in the thick of investigations.

"I won't say no to a little hospitality." Lanky licked his lips, but Nathan looked as if he still had trouble with his stomach and didn't say a word.

"All right then, Ms. Martinez, if you'll step onto the porch, we'll ask you a few questions." Lanky opened the car door and ushered me to a cluster of battered plastic chairs. They were caked with dust, so I opted to stand, as did both detectives.

The few questions turned into many, and an hour had flown by before they gave us leave to go. Since Tillie and Andrew hadn't arrived on the scene before I'd discovered Shawn, nor had they entered the warehouse, they were given a pass for immediate questioning. Lanky did note down the time I'd called 911 and called Tillie to tell her I'd found the victim. It had been 3:07, and it was now 5:20. No wonder I felt drained.

After providing our cell phone numbers and addresses, we were finally on our way home... straight into rush hour traffic. I sent a text to Vannie letting her know we'd be home around six thirty or so, depending on the state of the freeways. She said she'd have pizza and salads waiting for us.

"Andrew, would you mind finding a gas station or fast-food place to stop at? I'm in desperate need of restroom facilities." I also wanted to scrub my hands and face in an effort to rid myself of the lingering—most likely imaginary—stench from the warehouse.

"Of course. I should have thought of it before we got onto the freeway. My apologies."

"No worries. I can wait awhile." I held my hand up to Tillie's face. "Do I stink?"

She sniffed. "No, dear. You smell like Christmas tree hand sanitizer."

I leaned back into the buttery-soft leather seat. "Oh, good.

But if I do, you'd better drive with the windows down. I'd hate to ruin your car."

"You're fine. Besides, I'm pretty sure I don't want to breathe in all the exhaust fumes from the traffic around us."

I peered out the window. There were six lanes of bumper-to-bumper vehicles, all going about ten miles an hour... or even less. Several times, we came to a complete halt and just sat there for what seemed like five minutes. Tillie had made a good point about the exhaust fumes. Twenty minutes later, we were parked in front of a fast-food joint sporting golden arches. I left the wig in the car and dashed inside to the restroom. After relieving myself—and struggling for several minutes to get the tight pleather pants back up over my sweaty thighs—I used a generous amount of soap to scrub Maurice's makeup from my face and scour my hands and arms. Dripping wet, I discovered the paper towel dispenser was empty, so I shook myself like a wet dog. It didn't help much.

When I climbed back into the town car, Tillie took one look at me then dug into a white paper sack that released mouthwatering aromas of hot, deep-fried potatoes. She handed me a wad of brown paper napkins. "When your hands are dry, I'll share some French fries with you."

My stomach rumbled while I did what she commanded. Let me tell you, cheap paper napkins don't hold up when sodden. As I rubbed my face in an attempt to dry it, a hundred tiny pieces of disintegrating napkin stuck to my skin. I pulled the back seat mirror down and gazed at myself. I looked like a kindergartener's paper mâché project gone wrong. It gave Tillie the giggles, and soon, I was laughing along as I tried to pick itsy-bitsy pieces of paper from my face and hair. I finally gave up, took the sack Tillie offered me, and shoved a handful of fries into my mouth.

"Thanks," I said once I'd swallowed. "I needed that."

"It was Andrew's suggestion."

"Thank you, Andrew," I said in a slight singsong voice.

Tillie's driver treated her like a queen and, as an extension, me as well. I'd tried baking him goodies—cookies, cupcakes, candy—but he'd always refused, saying he had so many food allergies that he never ate anything he hadn't prepared for himself. I'd quizzed Tillie on other gift items I could bestow upon him and had never come up with anything. He was enigmatic despite my best efforts to get him to talk about himself. Tillie, kind and generous, paid Andrew a princely salary whether he drove for her one hour a week or forty. Her generosity would have to compensate for my guilt over not doing something for him myself.

As Andrew slogged through the unrelenting traffic, I scrolled through my email account. Most of the dog training participants had responded to my request for sharing their recipes. More than half of the individuals had sent their recipe with not a word about Eloise, while the remaining individuals basically said they had nothing nice to say about the woman and there was no need to honor her.

One woman, Karla Rordan, said, and I quote, "If you can't say something nice, don't say anything at all." I seemed to recall a bunny from one of my nieces' movies saying something like that. Apparently, Karla had forgotten her own advice, though, because after she'd typed the recipe into the body of the email, she had gone on a rant about what a tyrant Eloise had been. Luckily for me, she'd included her phone number, and I was determined to talk to her the following day to find out what had made Eloise a tyrant.

With the death of Shawn, though, I felt we had more suspects than we could handle, with many unknown at this point. Anyone who'd purchased an unhealthy puppy would have reasons to kill him, and from the looks of the warehouse, there were multitudes of puppies out there that might have medical issues.

I responded to each email, thanking each person for their recipe. If they hadn't included their phone number, I asked if I might have it just in case I had any last-minute questions about the recipe before I sent the booklet to the printer to be bound. I added the recipe booklet project to my calendar, giving myself ten days to complete it. I should be able to fit it in, right? That was when I remembered I was supposed to provide five dozen cupcakes for Oceana the following day. I groaned.

"What's wrong? Did you eat too many fries?" Tillie asked.

"I just remembered I promised to make cupcakes for Oceana." I scrolled through the joint catering calendar I shared with Carrie. I was a bit surprised she hadn't called or at least texted to remind me. But then again, she had her hands full with three young children on top of running a catering company, and she expected me to be a responsible adult. "And I have another three dozen for a dinner party Carrie's catering tomorrow night. I completely forgot about them both."

"You can bake them at my house while we eat dinner and strategize." Tillie nudged my arm. "You know Vannie isn't going to sit there and let you bake them all on your own. She'll pitch in, and I'll bet Teresa will too."

"I know, but I feel bad that Vannie's always helping me out. The cupcake business is my job, and I'm not paying her." If I could have afforded to pay Vannie an hourly wage, I'd have done it in a heartbeat, but I didn't make enough profit on the cupcakes to do much more than pay for the ingredients and pay myself little more than minimum wage.

It was one of the many, many reasons living rent free in Tillie's pool house was a godsend. David paid me a generous hourly salary plus included me on his company's health insurance plan. But he didn't need my accounting and administrative services much more than a few hours a week, which didn't add up to much. During busy holidays, I frequently worked for my sister's catering company. But as her business expanded, she'd hired help and, lately, hadn't needed me.

"Oh, posh," Tillie said. "I know for a fact Vannie doesn't expect you to pay her. She enjoys spending time with you. You of all people should know that baking together is a wonderful way to get to know each other without the uncomfortable sitting-around-a-table-trying-to-drum-up-conversation problem."

"That's a good point except that while Vannie manages to pry every single secret about my life from me, she never shares anything about herself." I wanted to pout but thought better of it.

"Give her time. I think she's had some dark things happen to her, and it's going to take a while, perhaps even years, for her to learn to trust again." Tillie turned her head away from me. I suspected it was so I wouldn't see gathering tears.

"Has she said anything to you about it?" I placed a hand on Tillie's blemish-free hand.

"Only vaguely hinted. You know what she's like. Clams up or changes the subject if she thinks the conversation is getting too personal about herself."

"All right. I'll try to be more patient, and I'll accept her help in the kitchen whenever she offers." I smiled as Tillie turned my way. "Even though it makes me feel incredibly guilty about taking advantage of her."

Once home, I quickly checked on the cat—she was content—and jumped into the shower to remove the remaining paper napkin shreds from my skin and hair. Dressed in comfy sweats, because I hoped to never wear tight pleather pants again, I headed across the alleyway. As Tillie had predicted, Vannie jumped in, and we got the cupcakes baked and frosted in record time while we ate pizza, drank wine, and talked about the newest murder. Teresa copied down names and phone numbers from the dog training participants' emails, and I made a plan to call both Cheryl and Karla of the Thumper quote. Teresa had come up with the cartoon bunny's name.

Brian showed up at ten, polished off the now-cold pizza, then finished loading the dishwasher for me. With the two dogs in tow, we headed to the pool house, where we snuggled in for the night.

Chapter 23

I woke to the sound of persistent beeping. Thinking it was the alarm clock, I rolled over and punched the snooze button. The beeping continued. Bleary-eyed, I sat up and hunted for my cell phone, which I found stuffed under the covers at the foot of the bed. Somehow, I'd managed to start the timer app, and it had gone off. I tapped the stop button, and the beeping ceased.

Brian and the dogs were nowhere to be seen, nor could I hear them. The cat jumped onto the bed and traipsed across the comforter until she reached Brian's pillow. She hopped into the center, kneaded it a few times, plopped down, and began purring.

I leaned back onto my pillow and scrolled through the notifications. I'd received several new emails and a text from a local number. I opened the message. It was the cat's owners, who were desperate to connect and bring their kitty home. I checked the time. It was seven thirty, and the text had come in at seven. Without wondering if it was too early, I called the owner back.

I identified myself when a woman answered the phone.

"We're so grateful to you for finding our kitty and taking

care of her," she gushed. "We've been worried sick ever since we got back home from vacation last night and didn't find her here."

A child cried in the background, and she shushed it. "I got up at the crack of dawn to hunt for the chip papers to see what I had to do to track Ellie down."

"I wan' kitty. Kittyyyyyy… kittyyy… kittyyy…" the child chanted.

"We're going to get her soon." The woman turned her attention back to me. "Where can we meet? My three-year-old daughter's been asking for her kitty since five this morning."

I well remembered the days when my nieces had been up before the sun at that age. It was exhausting. "Where do you live? I can bring her to you."

I realized that might sound like an invasion of privacy. "Or we can meet at a Starbucks close to your home? I don't mind driving. It sounds like you have your hands full."

"That's so lovely of you to offer after all you've done. But if you truly don't mind, it would be a huge help."

"What's the location of your closest Starbucks?"

"It's on Bison and Macarthur. Is that far from you?" the woman asked just as the child started chanting "kitty" again.

It was quite a bit farther than I'd have liked, but I'd make it work. "It's no trouble. I'll be there in about thirty minutes. How will I recognize you?"

She giggled. "My daughter will be dressed in a gray kittycat Halloween costume. I'm hoping I can get her out of the house without having to draw whiskers on her cheeks."

"She sounds adorable. By the way, my name is Emory, and you'll recognize me by my crazy bed-head red hair and, of course, by your cat."

She thanked me profusely, but I noticed she never offered her name. Oh well. You can't be too careful with personal information these days, and she had no idea what kind of person I might be.

I got dressed in record time then called Brian to see if he was over at Tillie's with the dogs. He wasn't if his labored panting was any indication when he answered.

"It sounds like you're out for a run with the dogs."

"I'm doing sprints with them in the sand and then will hopefully fit in a three-mile run."

No wonder his breathing was labored. I could barely walk in the sand without huffing and puffing. "The cat's owner sent a text. They've been on vacation and just got home last night."

"Oh. That's too bad. I mean, it's good for them, but I was getting used to having Boots around."

"Her name is Ellie, and she belongs to a three-year-old little girl. Apparently, she's been crying and calling for 'kitty' since five this morning."

"Ouch." Brian's breathing quieted, and I assumed he'd slowed to a walk. "Are they coming to pick her up?"

"I offered to meet them at the Starbucks on Bison. I'm leaving now but should be home in about forty-five minutes. Want me to pick something up for breakfast?"

"I'll take an egg-and-bacon sandwich if it's not too crowded."

"Ha! When is Starbucks not crowded?" As I talked, I found the box that still held the towels from when I'd taken the cat to the vet. "Tell you what, I'll make us egg, bacon, and avocado sandwiches when I get home. That way, they'll be fresh and hot instead of us having to reheat something in the microwave."

Brian agreed that was a better choice and that he'd start cooking our breakfast if he beat me home. I suspected he'd cut his run short and have it almost all ready by the time I returned.

. . .

WHEN I PULLED into the Starbucks parking lot, I picked up Ellie and cradled her in my arms. Her purring soothed me, and I couldn't help but think Brian was right. It had been nice having a cat around the house once she and the dogs had learned to tolerate each other. I shook off the thought. We didn't need another pet.

As promised, I spotted a towheaded little girl, her hair pulled up into two high pigtails to resemble ears, standing by the front door. The mom, who was petite and every bit as towheaded as her daughter, hadn't been able to get her out of the house without painting a generous number of cat whiskers on the girl's chubby pink cheeks. She clutched a long, fluffy gray tail in one hand and a glazed donut in the other. Her dark-gray leotard and tights were embellished with white paw prints. It was the perfect costume for a kitty-loving little girl.

The girl screeched, "Kitty!" when she spotted us and dropped her donut and her tail.

I placed the cat in her outstretched arms.

"I can't thank you enough." The young woman raised her hand, which held a fistful of bills, toward mine.

I waved her off. "There's no need for that. It was a pleasure getting to know Ellie. She's a darling kitty."

"It's the least we can do." She tried to place the money into my hand again, but I took a step backward.

"Truly, there's no need. We have pets, and she fit right in." I didn't mention the effort it had taken, but it really didn't matter.

"If you're sure?"

I nodded.

"Thanks. My husband's nephew was house-sitting and keeping an eye on her, but you know young men. He decided to take her to a party close to the beach, and when they lit firecrackers, she ran away. Kids… they can be so irresponsible." She stroked her daughter's hair. "I don't know why he didn't tell us she was missing before we got home. We could've started tracing her then."

That explained how the cat had gotten all the way over to my area, but it didn't explain why her collar was missing. I decided to let it be since all had turned out fine for both the cat and her family. "Maybe he didn't want to ruin your vacation with unnecessary worry? Or perhaps he was trying to find her before you got home. I'm glad she's safe and back with you now."

The mom led her daughter, who was practicing her pretend purring, to their car. A brand-new BMW. The largest size made. I guessed she really could afford the generous reward she'd tried to give me, but I still wouldn't have felt right accepting it.

MY PREDICTION PROVED CORRECT: Brian had breakfast on the table within minutes of me walking in. He'd even taken the time to shower, although his hair, which needed a trim, dripped droplets of water onto his white T-shirt. He was barefoot, and his surfer-style boardshorts were faded and frayed along the hemline. I'd tried to buy more shorts for him, but he insisted the worn look was the style amongst the surfer set.

He kissed me. "Was Boots happy to see her family?"

"She was, and even more importantly, her family was ecstatic to have her back. It was the case of the unreliable house sitter losing her."

I ruffled the ears of both dogs, who'd flopped in the middle of the kitchen floor. They were still damp from the shower Brian had given them to remove the sand from their fur and were tuckered out from the run. But heaven forbid they miss out on the chance that a piece of bacon or egg might find its way to the floor, ready to be gobbled up. I retrieved dog treats from the cookie jar and gave them each a bite.

"Then I'm glad you were able to find her people." He pulled the kitchen table chair out for me and flourished a linen napkin over my lap once I sat. A plate of grilled sandwiches, cut into triangles, sat in the middle of the table along with a bowl of colorful mixed berries. "What's on your agenda today?"

"At some point, the two detectives want to interview me again." I nibbled a sandwich and almost moaned. Brian could make the simplest of foods taste exquisite. "And I have to drop off cupcakes to Carrie's house before three."

"That reminds me, I already put the cupcakes for Oceana into my car. You don't have to worry about delivering them today." Brian took a hearty bite of sandwich and thoughtfully chewed before swallowing. "What kind of investigating do you have planned?"

"You know me so well, don't you?" I lifted my coffee cup in a salute to him. "I'm determined to talk to a couple of the people who participated in the dog training. At least one of them seemed to have issues with both Eloise and Shawn, and the other woman was not a fan of Eloise's in the least."

"You're taking Tillie with you, right?"

"Yep, along with cupcakes to sweeten up the conversations." Vannie had been more than happy to help bake an additional dozen of the apple pie–filled cupcakes. I'd set aside four for the detectives, then I'd take four to Cheryl, and if it worked out, I'd take four to Karla if she'd see us. If she didn't, well, let's just say the cupcakes wouldn't go to waste—rather, they'd go to my waist.

Brian thought our plan was good and was even happier to hear that Andrew would be driving us around again.

Chapter 24

B y the time I'd cleaned up the kitchen and Brian had left for the restaurant, I felt it was late enough to start calling my suspects as soon as I confirmed with Tillie that she'd be available. I called her first.

"I'm assuming you're up for some more investigating today?" I asked while I powered up my laptop.

"Honey, I was born ready. Just tell me what time, and I'll have Andrew here to cart us around." She giggled. "I've already packed my Taser and pepper spray into my Tom Ford hobo bag. It's large enough to fit two Tasers if you want me to bring one for you."

I rolled my eyes. "I seriously doubt we'll have need of either Tasers or pepper spray today."

"It doesn't hurt to be prepared."

"Maybe you have a point. Anyway, I haven't called the two women I'm hoping to question today. As soon as I confirm that they'll talk to me and what time, I'll let you know."

"I'm standing by." Without another word, Tillie hung up on me. Had it been accidental, or was she merely trying to hurry me along?

I called Cheryl first, who wasn't thrilled about my idea of

stopping by to talk about the cookbook and Shawn's death. She claimed she was much too busy but relented when I said I'd bring cupcakes. She finally agreed that she'd carve a few minutes out of her busy schedule if I could be there by eleven thirty.

Karla was a bit more elusive. She first said I shouldn't have read anything into the email she'd sent then said she didn't drink coffee so couldn't meet at Starbucks. When I suggested a tea shop, she said it was too far for her to drive. I could tell the cupcakes were intriguing her, so I pressed harder, and in the end, she agreed to meet me at a park close to her house if I'd bring the cupcakes and an extra-large cup of chai from her favorite tea shop, Teopia. I agreed to meeting her at ten forty-five, although it meant I'd be pushing it to meet Cheryl at the appointed time. I only hoped that the detectives wouldn't pick the same time and undo my careful orchestrations.

I had time for one more phone call before I had to take a shower and get ready for the day. After sending Tillie a text about what time we needed to leave to meet Karla, allowing time to pick up her chai drink, I decided to call Henri. I always thought of him as the man who'd made the bone-shaped dog treats for the potluck. I thought back to which dog belonged to him and couldn't quite remember. A quick look at his email address, henribloomathenribloom.com, reminded me that his dog's name was Blossom, which reminded me that she was a cute schnauzer mix. Although prone to barking more than the rest of the dogs who'd been a part of our group, she hadn't tried Shawn's patience nearly as much as my dogs had.

He answered on the first ring, and I introduced myself. "Hi, Henri, this is Emory. The one putting together the recipe booklet?"

"Oh, yes. I remember you and your two mischievous dogs." He chuckled. "I was actually quite relieved you were part of the group, because it's usually my Blossom and her incessant barking who gets the nasty looks."

I grimaced. "I'm so glad we could help Blossom stay out of that position. I don't know what got into my dogs. They're usually not so naughty."

"Is this the first training session you've done with them?" Blossom's barking filled my ear. "Excuse me a moment. I'm going to let her into the backyard while we talk."

The barking grew distant and then quieted. Henri returned. "There, that's better. You were saying?"

I wasn't, but I picked up where he'd left off in the conversation. "Yes, this is the first time. Missy might have done training before, but not since she moved in with Piper, who has apparently taught her bad manners. But really, the reason I was calling is because I had some questions about Eloise. Did you know her very well?"

"It depends on what you consider well. She's been the president of our condo's association for years and, as such, keeps us residents in line whether we deserve her attention or not." Henri clucked his tongue. "Course, there's been rumors about her, ah, overlooking infractions in exchange for a personal favor or cash, but I don't have any proof that actually occurred."

"I do understand how rumors can take on a life of their own, but sometimes, there's a nugget of truth in there." I hoped that would encourage him to share any more rumors he might have heard about Eloise. I was destined to be disappointed.

"Perhaps, but I don't hold stock in wagging tongues."

It appeared I wouldn't get anything else from him about Eloise, and the little he did share would have to suffice. I changed tactics. "Can I ask you a couple of questions about Blossom?"

"Sure. She's my best buddy." He sounded proud of his dog.

"Did you get her as a puppy?"

"Naw, I found her wandering the beach and took her in. She wasn't chipped and was scrawny as all get-out." Henri chuckled. "She almost ate me out of house and home the first few months, but she settled in, and now it's like her former life never happened."

"She's one fortunate pup." I checked my watch. I had a few more minutes, and then I needed to hit the shower. "How long have you had her?"

"Oh, I guess it's going on three years now."

"Why did you decide to sign up for Shawn's dog training sessions? Was Blossom having some behavior issues?"

"Oh, goodness, no. Blossom is a doll aside from the barking." He huffed. "It was the barking that got Eloise on our case. She claimed our neighbors were complaining, and if I didn't do something about it, I'd be forced to give Blossom up. Quite conveniently, she just so happened to have the application for her son's training program with her and convinced me that if I signed up and paid with a credit card right then and there, she'd smooth things over with my neighbors."

Quite convenient indeed. I had to wonder if the neighbors really had complained or if it was Eloise's excuse for forcing the elderly man to pay an exorbitant amount of money for training that wasn't really necessary.

"Did you and Blossom find the experience beneficial?" I didn't want to come right out and express my own dissatisfaction. I wanted his honest opinion.

"I think Shawn's program is more suited for guard dogs or aggressive dogs who need an extra-firm hand. He didn't do anything to help Blossom's barking aside from telling me to get a bark shock collar or have surgery to remove her voice box."

"That's positively inhumane." I shuddered. "Why did you stick out the entire program?"

He harrumphed. "I paid all that money and thought

maybe we'd get some good information out of the training. And I kind of made friends with Diane Solter, the woman with the boxer, and it was a good opportunity to spend time with her."

I searched my memory and visualized the fifty-something-year-old woman, still trim and with enough energy to match her young boxer. "Does she live at the condos too?"

"No, but her sister does, which is how she came to participate in the training program. Apparently, Eloise caught Diane's dog digging up some of the plants the landscapers had just planted."

I was starting to see a pattern of Eloise coercing people to sign up for her son's program. "How was her experience with Shawn?"

"The same as mine and yours: worthless for the amount of money we paid."

I debated telling him about Shawn then decided the condo rumor mill would be in full force sooner rather than later anyway. "I don't know if you've heard yet, but it appears Shawn was murdered yesterday."

"Is that so?" Henri was quiet for a long minute. "Well, if rumors are to be believed, I suppose karma's caught up with him. Imagine abusing God's creatures the way he's done with no retribution, if what I've heard is true."

I tried to pull more information from the elderly man, but he was done chatting. He claimed he needed to take Blossom for a walk and ended our conversation. I'd really hoped he'd be able to share names of people he knew who might have adopted puppies from Shawn or more names of attendees who had been coerced by Eloise to sign up. Instead, I had to be content with what he'd shared and hope that Karla and Cheryl could shed more light on both the murders.

Chapter 25

"Yoo-hoo," Tillie hollered at my door. "Andrew's here whenever you're ready to go."

I'd just slipped on a pair of comfortable sandals—flats, of course. "Give me a second to fill the dog bowls with some extra kibble and water."

"And I'll give them an extra treat for getting left behind too." Tillie went to the refrigerator and rummaged inside for the bag of homemade treats. The dogs circled around her, tails wagging like mini propellers. She handed them each a piece. "There's my good girls."

When Tillie opened the refrigerator to retrieve another treat, I stopped her. "Save it for later. If they're hungry, they'll eat their kibble."

"You're no fun." But at least Tillie closed the fridge door and ruffled Piper and Missy's ears while I filled their water bowl.

We climbed into the car—Andrew, as always, holding Tillie's door open—and gave him the address, with cross streets, as we drove away. It was rare that Andrew ever had to check a GPS to find out how to get wherever we needed to be. Tillie said he almost seemed to have a Thomas Guide encyclopedic memory. I'd had no idea what she was talking about and had to google it on my phone. I read, with a bit of terror, how people used to have to find routes to a specific place using paper maps that spanned several pages. I'd had some sort of GPS device ever since I'd started driving because Lars had decided it was a way to keep Carrie and me safe.

When Andrew parked in front of Teopia, I jumped out and ran inside. Fortunately, it wasn't terribly busy, so it didn't take long to order and receive three extra-large to-go cups of chai. Once back in the car, headed to the park, I took a sip and immediately wished I'd ordered something else for myself. Overly sweet and flavored with spices that tasted past their prime, the chai was a disappointment. I'd been spoiled by one of David's former housekeepers, who'd frequently made me chai, and I regretted that she'd never shared her recipe with me.

We easily found Karla and her border collie, Joey, standing by a picnic table beneath a trellised canopy. Green, leafy vines grew up and around the posts and had started their progress to cover the top. Ten picnic tables sat beneath the trellis with charcoal grills located on each side of the pavilion. Grass, brown in a multitude of areas, spread out from the pavilion until it reached the sidewalk bordering the parking area. In the opposite direction, a large sandpit covered the ground. Colorful playground equipment and swings waited for children to play. Aside from us, the park was empty.

As we drew near, I finally recognized her. Tall but stocky, Karla was in her forties if I had to guess. Her graying brown hair was chin length and blunt cut. She used cheap plastic barrettes to hold her hair back from her face. She was one of the rare women in our area who never wore a lick of makeup, not even lip gloss.

"Thanks for meeting us, Karla." I set the cup holder containing the three cups of chai on the table. Tillie placed the cupcake box beside it. "I'd like to introduce you to Tillie Skyler. I hope you don't mind her joining us today."

"Nice to meet you, Mrs. Skyler." Karla seemed unbothered with the unexpected guest.

Tillie nodded as she took a seat. "Likewise."

I handed them each a chai then swung my legs over the wooden picnic bench, glad both Tillie and I were wearing slacks. Mine were black, and Tillie had opted for a cream color with tiny embroidered roses along the hemline. Of course, Tillie's were probably from a designer and cost more than I made in a week or even a month, and for her sake, I hoped the bench wouldn't snag her pants or soil them with left-behind dirt or food.

"Did you hear about Shawn's death?" I asked. We didn't have the luxury of small talk because I didn't want to keep Cheryl waiting. Of the two women, I had the feeling she would be the one who had the most information to share.

"No! What happened?" She studied the cup of chai then took a sip.

"The police suspect foul play," Tillie said.

"That doesn't surprise me in the least." Karla set her cup down. "He and his mother both were two peas in a pod."

"Would you mind elaborating on that?" I crossed my fingers beneath the table, hoping she wouldn't clam up since she was the type to quote a bunny.

"What's it to you?" She curled her lip. "You seem awfully nosy for only having taken a few classes with him."

Tillie and I exchanged a glance, and then I turned my attention back to Karla. I let out a slow breath. "I found Shawn, and I feel like I need to know why it happened."

Karla's eyes widened, and she pushed her chai drink away from her. She wiped her mouth with the back of her hand and swallowed noisily. "You found Eloise, too, didn't you?"

"I promise I didn't have anything to do with either of their deaths." I extended my hands, palms up. "Truly. You can call

Detective Hawkins of Huntington Beach, and he'll vouch for me."

Detective Lankershim might have, too, but I wasn't one hundred percent positive. At least not until he took my statement and questioned me. Then I'd know for sure if I was his number-one suspect... or not.

She eyed me warily, then her shoulders relaxed. "Shouldn't it be the police who find the killer?"

"Yes, but..." How to explain that I'd gotten involved in several murder investigations before without sounding whacky?

"Emory has a knack for finding murder victims." Tillie had no such compunctions about blurting out the truth.

Karla's shoulders hunched up again, and she leaned back. "You've been involved in murder before?"

"She has, and she's even been a suspect a few times." Tillie chortled. "Her ex calls her a murder magnet."

Karla clumsily extricated herself from the picnic table bench seat. "I just remembered I have an appointment. Thanks for the chai, but please don't call me again."

Leaving her cup of chai on the table, Karla power walked away, pulling Joey behind her.

I glared at Tillie. "Really? Did you really have to scare her away?"

Tillie lowered her chin and stuck out her lower lip. "I'm sorry. Most people find you intriguing once they hear you've been involved in solving murders before. She sure is a skittish one, isn't she?"

"You didn't tell her I solved murders." I tried to glower, but it was nearly impossible to remain upset with Tillie.

"I didn't?" She tapped her manicured nail against her lip. "I was sure I did."

"No. You. Did. Not." I wondered what kind of bribe I could use to entice Karla to talk with me again. "You confirmed I'd been involved in murders before and said I'd been a suspect a couple times. Then you had to throw in that snake's 'murder magnet' slur on me. It's no wonder she ran for her life."

"Hmmm, when you put it that way, I see why she'd misunderstand." Tillie, unlike myself and Karla, gracefully removed herself from the picnic bench. "Don't worry. We'll catch her another time. Let's go talk to Madam VP at the condos."

I handed her the third cup of chai while I discarded the other two in the trash can.

Tillie took a sip, scrunched her face up, and handed the cup back to me. "Marge spoiled me for anyone else's chai. You didn't happen to get her recipe, did you?"

"No, and it wasn't for lack of trying, but then, you know, it was too late."

"Such a pity." Tillie sighed then took hold of my arm.

Without a doubt, I knew it wasn't the chai recipe Tillie was talking about. I clasped her hand in mine. "Come on, let's go talk to Cheryl. Maybe we'll have better luck if you don't bring up 'murder magnet' again."

Chapter 26

W hen we pulled into the parking lot of the clubhouse, at least a dozen or more cars were already there. Several young men and women, all appearing to be in their early twenties, had gathered in a group. Some were smoking, and a few held soda cans. I wondered if a company had utilized the clubhouse for a meeting. Tillie and I made our way to the entrance and stepped inside. There wasn't a meeting taking place, but long banquet tables had been arranged with chairs lining one side of each table.

I led the way down the corridor to the offices, where we found a beehive of activity. Several young people, similar to those standing in the parking lot, pulled files from filing cabinets and placed them in bankers' boxes before labeling the boxes with a black Sharpie. A staid, older man, his hair completely white, stood to the side and issued orders.

Cheryl came out from one of the back rooms, wringing her hands. A woman close to sixty if her white hair—which contrasted greatly with her overly tanned skin—were any indication, followed right behind her. Cheryl motioned for us to join her, and as we walked back toward the main room, she introduced us.

"This is Rebecca, our treasurer. Rebecca, this is Emory and…" She paused as if searching for a name.

"I'm Tillie Skyler. Nice to meet you."

Rebecca raised her eyebrows as if recognizing Tillie's name, but she didn't say anything.

"You've come at one of the worst possible times, so I'm afraid I can only spare a couple of minutes." Cheryl continued wringing her hands. She led us out onto the pool patio and indicated we should sit at one of the umbrella-shaded tables in the far corner. I handed her the box of cupcakes, which she placed on the tabletop.

I indicated the group of young people still milling around. "What's going on?"

She went back to wringing her hands. "The management company has authorized an unscheduled in-depth audit going back five years. There's strong evidence that Eloise was embezzling money from the association as well as accepting bribes to overlook certain infractions."

Rebecca looked stricken, and her coffee-brown eyes shimmered with moisture. "Since I'm the treasurer, they'll think I was in on it with her, but I swear, I didn't know a thing."

I looked from Rebecca to Cheryl. "Do you think that's why Eloise was killed? Someone found out about the embezzlement and decided to punish her for it?"

Cheryl shook her head. "That doesn't make any sense. With her dead, it'll be harder to trace the money, especially if she hid it in an offshore account or something."

"How much money are you talking about?" I'd thought she'd maybe stolen a few thousand or a bit more, but the effort of setting up an offshore account probably meant the amount was much larger.

Cheryl and Rebecca exchanged a look that I interpreted to mean they weren't sure they should confide in us. Cheryl finally nodded then turned her attention back to me. "There's close to half a million dollars missing."

I tried to keep my shock subdued, but in the end, I couldn't help but squeak out an OMG! "How? I mean, why would the association have that much cash sitting in an account she could access?"

"We were getting ready to break ground on a new fitness facility over by the tennis courts. Plus, there were other improvements needed for our grounds, so between the special assessment of condo owners and the loan the association secured, the money was available." Rebecca covered her face with her palms. "I know the auditors are going back five years, but I'm fairly certain Eloise took the money late Friday afternoon. I want to believe I would've noticed money missing before that when I balanced the accounts each month."

"Are you positive that it was Eloise?" I asked.

Rebecca shrugged. "She's the only one besides me that had access to the account. And on several occasions in the last few weeks, she hinted she was ready for retirement. I even caught her looking at travel websites and cruise packages a couple of times."

"Can the police access the bank's security cameras to verify that she's the one who withdrew the money?"

"No. The money was wired out. The board has a meeting set up with our management company and a financial crimes investigator this afternoon to see what the next steps should be. It's one of the reasons we have the auditors looking over every piece of paper first to make sure nothing else is missing and to give us a clearer picture of what we're facing. The entire thing is way beyond my expertise."

"How did you find out the money was missing?" Tillie asked.

"A vendor called yesterday late afternoon and said our check couldn't be deposited because of insufficient funds." Rebecca massaged her temples. "I logged into the checking account and saw the funds had dipped below five hundred, so I tried to transfer from the reserve account. That's when I noticed the missing money."

All the while Rebecca had been explaining about the embezzlement, a niggling feeling tickled my brain. If Eloise had stolen the money on Friday afternoon, why was she still in town on Saturday? And why had someone killed her and tried to blow up the clubhouse? I recalled the terse argument she'd had with Shawn Saturday afternoon and wondered if it had pertained to her theft.

I relayed my observations of Eloise and Shawn's argument on Saturday. "Did you see them arguing, Cheryl?"

"No. After Eloise's dig about my son, I spent some time in my office. I didn't want to be anywhere around her and risk getting into a public altercation." Cheryl slapped her hand over her mouth, then let her arms drop limply to her sides. "I swear I had nothing to do with her death."

"I can't help but wonder if they were arguing over the money." I gasped as a thought hit me. "What if Shawn killed his mother so he could take the stolen money and then tried to blow up the clubhouse to hide both the murder and the theft?"

"That doesn't make much sense. The digital footprint of the wire transfer would still be there," Rebecca said.

"Yes, but with the explosion and Eloise's death, it would have been quite some time before you noticed the theft, don't you think?" My mind was racing. Shawn had dispensed with his puppy-mill dogs over the past couple of days, given the, er, freshness of the excrement left behind. Why had he done that? As far as I knew, only rumors had floated around that he'd been involved in a puppy mill, and no real investigating had been done yet to spook him.

"You make a good point. Our computers would have been destroyed as well as our emotional well-being. It could've taken weeks if not longer to recreate some kind of semblance of our business." Rebecca bit her lip as tears sprang to her eyes. "And if the explosion had been as gigantic as the fire-fighters said it could have been, there might not have been anything left of Eloise to determine she'd even been there or murdered."

"Which makes me think that whoever killed her stole the money she'd embezzled and set up the explosion to hide their crime. Once the missing money came to light, everyone would naturally assume Eloise had been the culprit and had hidden the money. The killer gets off scot-free with not only the murder but the money as well."

"Dear, there's only one flaw in your hypothesis." Tillie lightly placed her hand on my arm.

I scrunched up my face. "I know, I know... someone killed Shawn, so he probably didn't kill his mother."

"Rebecca and Cheryl, are you free to join us in the conference room now? There are some things we need to go over." The white-haired man who'd been directing the auditors stood about ten feet away. None of us had noticed his approach, and I hoped he hadn't overheard our conversation.

"Yes, we'll be right there," Cheryl said. As soon as the man was out of earshot, she turned her attention back to us. "I think you need to let the police do their jobs. Whoever killed Shawn is still out there, and I'd be devastated to hear that he targeted you because you're asking too many questions."

Chapter 27

Ensconced in the back seat of the town car, Tillie blew out a long breath. "Was Cheryl concerned about you, or was that supposed to be a warning?"

I twisted my lips to the side. "She seems overly stressed by what's going on between the murders and the embezzlement, so I have to assume she's a concerned acquaintance."

"That's a good point." Tillie thought for a moment. "She doesn't seem like a killer. Besides, who in their right mind would blow up their place of business in the middle of their condo residential area? Can you imagine what that would do to property values? I guess you should move her down to the bottom of the suspect list."

"I agree. I never could picture her as a murderer, especially one that strikes twice."

"Back to Shawn. Do you honestly think that there could be two killers if Shawn murdered his mother?" Tillie asked. "It seems more reasonable that only one person did both dastardly deeds."

"I'm just not sure. It's hard to wrap my head around Shawn killing his mother even though they had an intense argument on Saturday. But it doesn't mean that it didn't escalate to violence, given Shawn's penchant for money easily obtained. It's not much of a stretch of the imagination to think he might have wanted to share in Eloise's ill-gotten gains."

Tillie tsked.

"I need to let Detective Hawkins know. I'm surprised he hasn't contacted me about coming to talk to us about finding Shawn yesterday."

"I'm sure he's had plenty to do with two murders now. Maybe the deaths have nothing to do with the puppy mill and the embezzlement. Maybe someone had an old vendetta against their family."

I sniggered. "What Netflix movies have you been watching lately? Something with mob gangsters?"

She ignored my jest. "I might argue with you if we lived on the East Coast, but you're most likely right about the motive for murder, at least with Shawn and the puppy mill."

I nodded. "I'd like to think I'm above homicidal rage, but if Shawn had been alive when I walked into his warehouse, I'm not sure I could have controlled my anger."

"Best keep that to yourself, Emory." Tillie tapped her driver on his shoulder. "Right, Andrew?"

"Consider this a confessional. Nothing you discuss will ever pass my lips unless you instruct me otherwise, Mrs. Skyler."

"You're a good man, and I hope I tell you often enough how much you're appreciated."

"You certainly do, ma'am."

While Tillie and Andrew good-naturedly bantered, I sent Detective Hawkins a text telling him I had some information that might be important. My phone immediately rang.

"Ms. Martinez, you've been at the top of my list to call, but something always comes up before I can connect. Are you going to be home in about an hour? Detective Lankershim and I would like to come talk to you together."

"I'm heading there now and should be home in about twenty minutes. Come to Tillie's house, and you can talk to both of us there, or separately if you want. Do you need her address?"

"I got it from her yesterday before you left." A police radio squawked in the background. "I've got another call coming in, but we'll see you in a bit."

I started to give him a brief overview of what I'd found out then realized he'd already disconnected. I put my phone back into my purse. "Both detectives are going to meet us at your house in about an hour. Will that work for you?"

"I'm assuming they're not giving us much of a choice." Tillie glanced at her watch. "Let's have a quick lunch. I think Vannie left some tuna salad in the refrigerator for us."

"You can have it. I'll put together a green salad with some turkey and cheese slices for myself." I puckered my lips, wrinkled my nose, and shuddered. "She uses Miracle Whip instead of mayonnaise and sweet relish instead of dill... I just can't..."

Andrew visibly shuddered while Tillie poked me in the shoulder. "If you'd try it, the combination might grow on you."

"No, thank you." I swallowed hard. "I'll pass."

"Fine. Just leaves more for me." Tillie crossed her arms. "I don't know why you and Brian both are so finicky about tuna salad."

"And don't forget to add deviled eggs while you're at it. They both deserve real mayonnaise. Not a sweetened wannabe."

"At least Vannie understands and appreciates the nuances of the condiment."

"You both can have it. Just don't expect me to consume it alongside you." I smiled to soften my words.

Once we arrived home, I collected the dogs from the pool house yard and took them to Tillie's home. We quickly made lunch—I avoided adding even a smidgen of the tuna salad to my plate—and ate on the patio overlooking the bay. Now that summer was over, there wasn't the usual steady stream of visitors gliding down the channel in electric Duffy boats. Instead of raucous vacationers, the barks of seals and the cawing of seagulls filled the air.

Once our lunch was over and I'd cleaned up the dishes, I kept an eye on my phone's security app's video feed. The moment the two unmarked sedans pulled up in front of Tillie's security gate, I rushed to the front door to greet the two detectives.

Detective Lankershim reached the gate first. "Thanks for agreeing to see us on such short notice."

"It's not a problem." I held out my hand to shake his. He obliged. "I wasn't sure if you'd recognize me without my costume on."

He flashed me a wry smile. "I did some checking up on you, so I know exactly who you are."

I wasn't sure if that was a good thing or not. I chose to keep my mouth closed and not respond until I figured it out.

Detective Hawkins lingered in his car with his cell phone pressed to his ear as Tillie sidled up to me. Her makeup was impeccable, and she'd fluffed up her hair. From the scent that wafted on the ocean breeze, it seemed she'd also applied perfume with a subtle fragrance of vanilla and nutmeg undertones. It always made me want to bake when I smelled it.

"Detective Lankershim, it's nice to see you again." She bobbed her head at him.

"Ma'am, I appreciate your willingness to speak with us at your home. And please, call me Lanky. There's no need for formalities." He looked over his shoulder as Detective Hawkins strode up. "Nathan. Good to see you again."

"Please come in." I gestured toward the open front door. "Are either of you allergic to dogs?"

They both responded with a no.

"Piper and Missy are friendly."

I led the way up the steps and into the house, expecting the dogs to come barreling toward us. But the hallway remained conspicuously quiet. "When they get excited, they can get a little too friendly, so if they bother you, let me know, and I'll put them in my yard."

"They're on the patio at the moment. We can leave them there for the time being," Tillie said.

But then the dogs caught the scent of new friends and started their excited whining and scratched at the door. "Or not. Emory, please let them in before they do any more damage to the screen door."

I did as she asked, and the dogs scrabbled on the travertine floor to join us. Surprisingly, as soon as they reached the two men, they sat on their haunches and quieted. *Pfff* was all I could think. What was it with my dogs and men?

Nathan, as he'd reminded me to call him when he came into the house, reached down and ruffled both dogs' ears. Lanky was a bit more reserved with them.

"Gentlemen, shall we sit on the patio, and Emory can bring us some coffee and cookies? Or if you'd prefer tea, we have that too." Tillie spun on her heels—yes, she was wearing three-inch heels—and led the way to the deck.

"Coffee would be great," Lanky said.

"Water will be fine for me." Nathan nodded at me as if to remind me of our previous conversation about his issue with caffeine. With everything that had happened, I'd forgotten.

Once the men followed Tillie, I filled three coffee mugs with dark brew and put them on a tray along with sugar, cream, a plate of salted-caramel cookies, four apple pie–filled cupcakes, linen napkins, and a chilled bottle of water. Carefully balancing the tray, I carried it out and placed it on the patio table.

"Thank you, Emory." Lanky grabbed a cookie and bit half of it off. After a few chews, he gulped it down and chugged down the coffee then repeated the process. "That hit the spot."

I set the bottle of water in front of Nathan. "Would you like a glass with ice?"

"No. This is sufficient." Nathan nodded to Tillie. "Mrs. Skyler, if you don't mind, we'd like to chat with Emory first. We can either move to another location or…."

I appreciated that he'd given Tillie the opportunity to sit and wait wherever she was most comfortable instead of playing the bad cop and demanding we do things his way.

"I'll just pop inside and busy myself with committee work. Emory knows where to find me when you're ready to chat with me." Tillie stood, as did the two men, picked up her mug of coffee, and sashayed to the house.

The two dogs watched her go and whined. They knew where the dropped morsels came from, and their source was leaving. I also knew where I'd find her once the detectives wanted to chat with her. She'd be upstairs in her bedroom, the windows opened wide so that she could eavesdrop on our conversation. I resolved to not look up so that the men wouldn't notice the open windows or the platinum-blonde woman pressing her ear to the screen.

Nathan took a sip of water, but so far, he hadn't been tempted by Vannie's cookies or my cupcakes. He tapped on his phone and placed it on the table. "I'll be recording this conversation. Please provide your name, and then let's have you start at the beginning with your arrival at Shawn's Norco property."

"I thought you were here to talk about what I'd found out at the condos this morning."

Nathan took a quick peek at Lanky. "Since Detective Lankershim is here for your statement, let's start with Norco so he can be on his way. You and I can talk about the condo situation afterward."

I should have thought this through and discussed the

various scenarios with Tillie and Vannie. Did we want to admit our subterfuge with Vannie and Teresa meeting Shawn in Irvine so that Tillie and I could sneak onto his property and search for signs of a puppy mill? Or would it be better to come clean and tell the entire truth?

"Ms. Martinez?" Nathan spoke brusquely. "Are you ready to talk, or do you need a moment?"

I took a deep breath. It was better to be completely honest, or else the omissions and white lies might come back to bite us in the derrière. I hoped I wouldn't regret my decision.

Chapter 28

"As you might have surmised from our disguises yesterday, Tillie and I were hoping to find evidence of a puppy mill and then turn that evidence over to you for follow-up." I paused, expecting one of the detectives to lecture me on letting the police do their jobs without me getting involved or putting myself in danger. Instead, they both sat straight in their chairs, their expressions inscrutable, without saying a word.

"It's kind of a convoluted story, so I'll try to make it short." Which I hoped I could do. I blew out a breath, still worried I was doing the wrong thing by confessing Vannie and Teresa's involvement. "I scheduled an appointment for my half-sister and her friend to meet with Shawn at his Irvine office to discuss purchasing a teacup Pomeranian... at the same time I went to the Norco property."

Both detectives raised their eyebrows and leaned forward in their chairs. It appeared I had their attention now.

"Their job was to keep Shawn away while you poked your nose around somewhere you didn't belong?" Lanky appeared displeased.

"I have a text from Shawn indicating he'd meet me at his

Norco property at three yesterday. But once I found out how isolated it was, we decided it would be safest to meet him at his Irvine property." I twisted my hands together and felt my face heat. "The idea to snoop around the property while my sister kept him busy in Irvine just kind of happened."

"Are you telling me that you have a wardrobe of costumes and disguises for spur-of-the-moment snooping?" Lanky shook his head. "I'm not buying it. You need to stop trying to sugar-coat that you trespassed on Mr. Parker's property with the intent of finding evidence of an illegal enterprise."

"Well, when you put it that way, I guess that's what we did." Was he going to arrest me for trespassing, or did he think that I might be a murderer? "But I swear I had nothing to do with Shawn's death."

"We know that." Nathan jumped in. He was apparently playing the good cop to Lanky's bad cop routine. "This morn-ing, Mrs. Skyler's driver provided the toll road account infor-mation and we verified the time you were on the road driving to Norco. The coroner estimates the time of death between ten and noon yesterday. I'm assuming you and your cohorts can verify your whereabouts during those hours?"

"Yes, I can safely say we all have alibis for that time frame."

"We'll get that information from you in a bit, but for now, tell us what you did and what you found once you arrived at Mr. Parker's property." Lanky tapped his fingers on the edge of the table.

I directed my attention to Nathan. Somehow, Shawn's death seemed connected to Eloise's murder, which all came back to the stolen money. It seemed important to go back to where it had all started. "Before we continue, I think it's important to let you know I met with Cheryl, the condo asso-ciation's vice president, this morning. Did anyone tell you about the half million dollars embezzled from the association last Friday afternoon? There's a team of auditors combing through the files, and Cheryl thinks Eloise is the one who stole the money."

Nathan practically jumped up from the chair and grabbed his phone from the table. "No. No one has contacted me. I've got to make a call. If you'll excuse me."

Without waiting for a reply, he entered the house.

"What was that all about?" Lanky took a cupcake this time and sank back into the chair.

I gave him an overview of finding Eloise, the potential explosion, and then finding out she'd probably embezzled the association's money.

"You do get around, don't you." He stated it as a fact, not a question.

"I don't mean too. It just happens." I took a sip of coffee, not that my jittery nerves needed the caffeine. I tried to push Philip calling me a murder magnet out of my mind, but I wasn't very successful. "Do you think it's possible that Shawn killed his mother to get the money she'd embezzled then tried to blow up the clubhouse to cover up both crimes?"

Lanky startled. "Detective Hawkins may be okay with you sticking your nose in where it doesn't belong, but I'm here to get facts from you and not to encourage you to play Nancy Drew."

He'd just confirmed his role as the bad cop to Nathan's good cop. Fortunately, I was saved from having to reply when Nathan returned to the patio, placed his phone on the table, and restarted the recording device. I was dying to know who he'd talked to and what it was about. Maybe Tillie had over-heard the conversation. I'd quiz her later.

"Ms. Martinez, shall we continue with your activities from yesterday, when you arrived at Mr. Parker's property?"

"Can I go back to Eloise's murder? I'm wondering if Shawn could have killed his mother in order to steal the money she embezzled then tried to blow up the clubhouse to hide any evidence." I glared at Lanky. He might not have wanted me to play Nancy Drew, but Nathan had asked for my input and urged me to keep my ears open. "I observed Shawn and Eloise having a pretty intense argument a few hours before I found her dead."

Nathan steepled his fingers and placed them against his pursed lips. He closed his eyes for a brief second, shook his head, and sighed. "I wish you would have told me all of this earlier."

"I texted you as soon as Tillie and I left the condos, and then you said you wanted to focus on Norco first when you got here." I rubbed my cheeks, realizing I'd been clenching my teeth. My jaws ached. "But the more I think about it, both deaths must be linked, and it comes back to the money."

Nathan turned the recording device off. "This goes no further than this table. Agreed?"

Lanky gawped at him, and I nodded.

"I won't give you details, but let's just say that what we found in Mr. Parker's bank account makes much more sense now that I know about the embezzlement, although it's only a fraction of what was stolen." Nathan pointed at me. "Do you have any other insights you'd like to share?"

This time Lanky's mouth gaped open. I ignored him.

"Somehow, the dogs missing from Shawn's warehouse fits in with Eloise's death, especially if Shawn killed her for the money. I'm not an expert"—I glared at Lanky when he snorted—"but it seems like the dogs were only recently removed. With the amount of, uh, excrement left behind, I assume there was a large number of animals. Who took them? Where did they go? Maybe whoever did take them knows something about Shawn's murder."

"We have a team trying to track down the large truck from the tire prints left in front of the warehouse. Do you have anything else?"

I felt horrible bringing up Cheryl's son—I couldn't remember his name—who'd spent time in prison because of

Shawn. But he'd been involved in the puppy mill business before. Perhaps he'd reconnected with Shawn and wanted back in or wanted Shawn to pay for what he'd gone through. I told the detectives everything Cheryl had shared with me.

"Please don't tell her I told you about her son. I know she's had a rough time accepting what her son went through because of Shawn, and she said he refuses to come back to the area. I just thought since he'd been in the puppy mill business before, he might know someone who could have taken the animals off Shawn's hands." I was babbling, and I knew it. Now that I'd mentioned Cheryl's son, I regretted it immensely. He'd paid his debt to society and didn't need law enforcement poking around in his life again.

"We'll do some digging and find out what this person has been up to since being released." Nathan tapped several times on his phone screen then began typing. "I'm going to need to talk to the employees who work for the condo association as well now that the embezzlement has been brought to light. It shouldn't be difficult to manage the conversation with Cheryl and get her to talk about her son."

Lanky tilted his head toward me. "Do you mind if we finish talking about her trip out to Mr. Parker's property? I've got some appointments I need to get to this afternoon."

"Be my guest." Nathan swept his arm my way.

And so I talked for the next thirty minutes, with Lanky asking the same questions in about ten different ways. Once they were satisfied with my answers, they spoke with Tillie for less than five minutes. Before they left, they took down Vannie and Teresa's contact information then told us not to discuss the case with anyone.

Chapter 29

Once I was certain both vehicles had pulled away from the security gate, I sent Vannie a quick text, alerting her that one of the detectives might be contacting her and Teresa. When I didn't get an immediate reply, I hooked my arm around Tillie's elbow. As I led her to the kitchen, I asked, "Did you overhear Nathan's conversation while he was on the phone?"

"I couldn't hear the words, but I could tell he was pretty hot under the collar about something." Tillie starburst her fingers and made an explosion noise.

"Apparently no one thought to notify him about the condo association's embezzlement. He found out from me when I asked if he thought Shawn could've killed his mother in order to take the stolen money for himself and then tried to blow up the building to cover up the two crimes."

"No wonder he was so upset. You'd think someone would have connected the two crimes and called the homicide detective back in to help with the investigation." Tillie put a kettle of water on the stovetop for tea.

"I think, eventually, he would have been notified. Rebecca didn't discover the missing money until late yesterday afternoon and immediately got auditors in there this morning." I pulled a box of decaf Earl Grey teabags down from the cupboard along with two teacups and saucers. "It's hard to imagine someone killing their own mother over money. Wouldn't you think Eloise would have been more than happy to share with her only child?"

"From what you and Vannie have said, it sounded like Shawn created all sorts of trouble over the last several years. Perhaps his mother had had enough and only wanted to run away and forget about him while living comfortably."

"Hmmm, perhaps you're right."

"What's our game plan for tomorrow?" Tillie took the whistling kettle from the stovetop grate and set it on a cast iron trivet to cool to around one hundred and ninety degrees before pouring the water over the bags. She claimed the resulting tea was smoother and more flavorful.

Perhaps she was right, because while I was a coffee fiend, I often found I enjoyed having a cup of tea with Tillie when I felt the need to relax. Or it could have been that Tillie fixed decaf tea in the afternoons and evenings so she'd be able to sleep better, and as a result, I didn't get caffeine jitters like I would if I'd consumed a cup of coffee.

"I still have several dog training participants to call and hopefully visit with in person." I paused as Tillie checked the temperature of the water in the kettle with an instant-read thermometer. "Now that we know Shawn was operating a puppy mill, I don't have to tiptoe around quite so much."

Tillie wiggled her eyebrows. "Yes, you can be just as gossipy as you like. I think the perfect lead-in could be, 'Say, did you hear that Shawn was murdered?' to get the conversation going."

"It might require a little more finesse than that. You'd totally get away with going that route, but I'm not sure I'd get the same results." I went to the pantry and retrieved the last few salted-caramel cookies and put them on a plate while

Tillie filled the teacups with water and began steeping the teabags. It hadn't escaped my notice that Lanky had eaten three cupcakes along with several more cookies while he'd interrogated me. I had no idea how he retained a beanpole figure.

The front door opened, and Vannie called out, "I'm home!"

The dogs rushed from the kitchen and slid around the corner as they yipped to welcome their family member. Tillie retrieved another teacup and saucer, added a teabag, and filled it with water before setting it on the table along with the other two. I added the plate of cookies I'd just filled.

Vannie made her way to the kitchen, with the dogs prancing behind her. "Thanks for the heads-up about the detectives wanting to contact me. I just sent their calls to voicemail. I'll catch up with them later."

She plopped down onto a chair and ran a hand through her red hair. It became wild and frizzy, which was exactly what mine did if I wasn't careful.

"Tough day, sweetheart?" Tillie pushed the teacup closer to her granddaughter while I offered her the plate of cookies.

"Ugh. Why do high schoolers think they know it all?" She chomped down on her cookie as if taking her aggressions out on the treat. "Especially the wealthy, 'I'm so entitled' ones who think just because you don't carry a designer bag or wear five-hundred-dollar shoes or wear a size two you're contemptable."

"Did you find the same kind of attitude when you taught in Spain?" I asked.

She held up her index finger as she finished chewing the piece of cookie she'd just bitten into. "No. Not at all. I was the cool teacher from America, plus most kids there have a different value system than here. I think they're raised to be more family centric and not so catered to so that they become little princesses or princes. I'm not saying all of my students in

Spain were perfect or without problems, but there wasn't such widespread passive-aggressive bullying."

"I'm sorry, dear." Tillie patted Vannie's shoulder.

"It's not your fault." Vannie brushed a crumb off the table and onto her napkin. "Enough about me. Tell me what's new with the investigation and why the detectives need to speak to me."

As I gave her a condensed version of the latest, I took butter out of the refrigerator and pulled ingredients from the pantry to make another batch of salted-caramel cookies. If any of the dog training participants agreed to speak with me in person, I'd have goodies on hand to sweeten them up.

Vannie and Tillie tossed around a few ideas on how to help her students, and then Vannie went to the study to grade homework while Tillie went to her office to make a few calls about some committee meeting or another. Or maybe she was calling Harvey to string him along in an effort to keep him from her nemesis's clutches.

Once the cookies were in the oven baking, which went quickly since Tillie's kitchen contained double ovens with convection, I pulled up the emails from training participants and copied down names with corresponding dog names into a table.

NAME AND DOG **name and breed:**

Emory and Vannie: Piper and Missy / Mix and mini goldendoodle

Cheryl Harris: Precious / Pug purchased from Shawn

Belle (Arabelle) Lawton: Brutus / Chihuahua purchased from Shawn

Henri Bloom: Blossom / schnauzer mix

Simone Peterson (son, Carter): Thor / mini poodle

Rebecca Brighton: Poodle mix purchased from Shawn

Karla Rordan: Joey / Border collie

Diane Solter: Rocky / Boxer
Frank & Nanci Sherman: Ace / Golden retriever
Ralph Morrison: Cooper / Australian shepherd

I PLACED a checkmark next to those I'd spoken with, a star next to those I wanted to speak with a second time, and a square next to those I hadn't connected with.

Karla was at the top of my list, but I needed to think about how to get her to agree to see me again after the fiasco that morning. I also wanted to talk to both Cheryl and Rebecca but not together. I wondered how I could separate the two without raising suspicions. Since I'd talked to Belle at the potluck and knew she had one of Shawn's dogs, I didn't think I needed to talk to her again right away. I'd circle back once I'd made it through the list the first time.

The rest of the dog training participants I still needed to touch base with were Diane, Frank and Nanci, Ralph, and lastly, Simone. I thought I could safely assume Simone had nothing to do with the murders since she had a young son, and their dog, Thor, hadn't been purchased from Shawn.

Once all the cookies were cooling on wire racks, I started calling the people I hadn't connected with. Every single one of the calls got dumped into voicemail. I left a general message for each of them about having questions for the cookbook and hoped they wouldn't blow me off. By the time Tillie, Vannie, and I had eaten dinner and washed the dishes and I trekked back to my pool house with both dogs, I still hadn't heard from anyone. I hoped the following day would prove more fruitful.

Chapter 30

M y twin sister's phone call woke me from a deep sleep at six on Thursday morning. She didn't even give me a chance to say hello. "You've got to help me out this morning, Em."

I sat straight up in bed and clutched the phone tighter. "What's wrong? Are the kids okay?"

"If you call having a stomach bug okay, then they're all just hunky-dory." Carrie sneezed. Twice.

"Are you all right? It sounds like you're catching something too."

My sister groaned. "Thanks to you rescuing that cat, we're now fostering two kittens. Not only am I dealing with my kids picking up the flu that's making the rounds in their schools, but I am apparently allergic to cats." As if to make her point, she sneezed again.

"What do you need me to do?" I asked in between her sneezes.

"Come take the kittens off my hands until the Kittytown Shelter can find another foster home for them. But most importantly, I need you to deliver luncheon at eleven thirty for a bunco group in Dana Point." Carrie blew her nose. "There's sixteen ladies, and it's a buffet of salads and sandwiches. You just have to deliver and set up with no need to stay to serve."

"Do you need me to make the salads and sandwiches?"

"You'd be a lifesaver if you could. I asked Katrina to do it, but she has an important test at school today that she can't miss."

Katrina was Carrie's part-time catering assistant and had worked for my sister for close to a year. She was enrolled in community college culinary classes along with trying to get general education college courses completed with the hopes of going to a four-year university once she saved up enough money. On top of trying to get an education, Katrina was a hard worker and contributed part of her earnings toward paying for her younger brother's medical care.

I guess I didn't answer fast enough, because Carrie broke into my thoughts. "The kids and I are staying upstairs, while Thomas is in the kitchen, as we speak, disinfecting every single surface. You won't catch the bug."

"I wasn't worried about that." Although perhaps I should have been. "I'll be there within an hour. Will that work?"

"Thank you! I was beginning to think I would have to coach Thomas and Mother on how to prep the luncheon and deliver it."

"That's a scary thought." Our mother was not and had never been a good cook. Oh, she could make a mean baked brie for an appetizer and pick out the perfect bottle of wine to accompany it, but even sandwiches were lackluster when she made them. My brother-in-law could grill steak and chicken with the best, but that was about as far as his culinary skills went. His idea of salad was to open a prewashed package of greens and douse it with half a bottle of ranch dressing.

I heard the sound of a crying little boy.

"Tommy just woke up. I need to check on him. Thanks for rescuing me."

"Wait, do I need to make a dessert?"

"No. The hostess has that covered. I gotta go." Carrie disconnected but not before I heard Tommy getting sick.

I shuddered then went to let Piper and Missy out into the yard. While coffee brewed, I took a speedy shower and pulled my hair into a tight bun. I skipped makeup and dressed in black slacks and a white polo shirt with comfy—although quite ugly—shoes. With my largest commuter mug filled to the brim with piping-hot brew, I dropped the dogs off with Vannie, who would alert Tillie that I wasn't around. Even if I'd fed the dogs at home—which I hadn't—Tillie would make sure there was food in their bowls, just in case. It was a good thing the dogs only ate when they were hungry unless a treat or human food was involved. Within thirty minutes of receiving Carrie's call, I was on the road.

Traffic was sparse this early in the morning, and I hit green at almost every traffic light, an almost unheard-of occurrence. Instead of needing the usual twenty to thirty minutes to get to my sister's house, I made it in eighteen. I parked curbside in front of her Craftsman-style home. The house was painted charcoal gray with white trim, and a cheery apple-themed wreath with a large red and white gingham bow decorated the front door. Instead of the usual flowering plants crowding her flower beds, Carrie had taken them out and added lettuce, broccoli, kale, and a variety of herbs. I hoped she'd share her harvest when they were ready to pick.

Thomas waited for me, the front door held wide open. "Thank you for rescuing us."

"I'm happy to help." Mewling kittens could be heard, their plaintive cries coming from the TV room.

He gestured toward the sound. "I'll go feed them and then call the shelter to see if they can find another foster home right away. If not…"

"Carrie already asked, and it's fine. I'll take them home once I finish with the luncheon."

"We'll owe you big time."

"Go take care of the kittens, and I'll get to work." I waved him away. "Let me know if Carrie or the kids need anything to eat, and I can prepare whatever she wants."

"For now, Carrie has everything she needs for the kids upstairs: saltine crackers and pediatric rehydration drinks." He ran fingers through his receding dark-blond hair. "I took some coffee along with a couple muffins to your sister after she called you. I'm kind of her runner whenever she needs anything, but her main concern is making sure you have everything you need, with no interruptions, for the luncheon."

His phone chimed with a text. He swiped the screen then tapped once. "Carrie says you need to leave here by ten thirty-five in case there's traffic getting to Dana Point. I'll get out of your way so you can get to work."

I walked into the pristine kitchen, the smell of bleach hanging in the air. Thomas had taken the responsibility of disinfecting everything to heart. I found a printout of the contract and the list of the salads and sandwiches needed. Carrie had made a couple notations about special requests, such as one sandwich prepared with no mustard and another made without mayonnaise. Other than that, everything was straightforward, and true to Carrie's nature, the ingredients were prepped and organized for assembly already.

Chapter 31

B y the time ten thirty rolled around, I was loaded up and on the road. I'd taken several photos of the ice chests and trays loaded into my SUV and sent them to Carrie in a text. She sent me a kiss emoji back. I got double kiss emojis back when I texted that I'd arrived at the client's house twenty minutes early despite having to wait for the guard at the complex security station to issue me a parking pass.

The 73 toll road had been my friend, and the miles had flown by as I made my way to the southern Orange County seaside town. By the time I'd turned west, toward the coastline, the blue water of the Pacific Ocean glittered in the sunlight in the distance. With its marina, beaches, surf spots, shopping, and restaurants, the town was a popular place for locals and tourists alike.

Carrie hadn't prepared me for the stunning house that sat sand-side. The house was a modern edifice—lots of angled walls and tons of windows—and the view from the front door to the back of the house was wide open. After Mrs. Irye's maid opened the door, I stepped into the foyer, and the white sand and gentle rolling waves beckoned me to continue walking straight through to the open sliding patio doors.

"Emory, it's so delightful to meet you." Mrs. Irye rushed to meet me, her right hand extended. "Your sister called to let me know you'd be delivering our luncheon today, but I have to say, she didn't warn me that you're her twin."

I shook the petite woman's hand. Her short black hair, showing nary a strand of gray despite her age being at least in the early sixties, was held back from her face by an emerald dragonfly barrette. Her cheongsam blouse matched the emerald green of the barrette, and she'd chosen to pair it with white cropped pants and flat, barely-there, nude-colored sandals. "It's nice to meet you, Mrs. Irye. Would you like to show me where you'd like the food set up?"

"Yes, of course." She turned on her heels and glided toward the open sliding doors. "It's such a lovely day I thought we'd eat on the patio before we start our games."

Mrs. Irye, or most likely her maid, had set up a buffet table to the side of the patio. Two additional rectangular tables were arranged with plenty of room between the eight padded folding chairs at each table. All the tables had been covered with emerald-green tablecloths, and flowering orchid arrangements graced each one.

"Thank you. It'll take me a few minutes to set up the food, and then I'll be out of your way." I paused when she lifted her penciled-in eyebrow. "Unless you wanted me to stay and help serve."

"Oh. No. It's not that. I heard the doorbell ring, and I'm expecting the arrival of one of my best friends from college." She gestured toward the maid, who was leading a woman down the open hallway. "We haven't seen each other in a couple decades, and we recently reconnected a few weeks ago after finding each other on Facebook."

As the maid stepped to the side, I saw a woman who

looked quite familiar. It took me a moment before I finally placed her. "Diane?"

The woman pulled away from Mrs. Irye's hug. "Emory? Is that you?"

Mrs. Irye looked from her friend to me and then back at her friend. "How do you two know each other?"

I extended my upward-facing palm toward Diane as if to indicate she should continue. She did.

"We were in a dog training course together recently." She took Mrs. Irye's hand into her own. "It's so good to see you, Laverne, and I can't thank you enough for your invitation to join you today at your lovely home."

I got the distinct impression that I'd just been dismissed. So I hurried back to my SUV and began unloading and carrying the food to the patio. Within twenty minutes, I'd unpacked all the sandwiches and salads and placed them in a tempting arrangement. All the while, Diane didn't pay me any attention but, instead, kept her focus on her hostess.

Finished with the food setup, I waved goodbye to Mrs. Irye, who was now surrounded by several guests, all chattering away. Diane was nowhere to be seen. Mrs. Irye broke away from the group and walked over to me.

"Thank you for such a beautiful setup. I've already sent your sister a Venmo for the final payment." Mrs. Irye shook my hand again. "I can see you out."

One of the guests called out to the hostess.

"There's no need. I can tell you're needed here."

She appeared relieved as additional ladies poured onto the patio. "Thank you, my dear. Now, if you'll excuse me, I must get back to my guests."

I looked around for Diane one last time, and when I didn't see her, I hurried through the house and made my way to the SUV. I'd just opened the door when Diane popped out from behind a parked car. I jumped.

"Sorry, I didn't mean to startle you." She glanced around

then scurried to stand next to me. "I didn't think it was appropriate to bring up the murder in there."

Surprise must've shown on my face.

"Henri said you called him, asking a bunch of questions about Eloise and Shawn. It doesn't take a rocket scientist to figure out your request for recipes was a ruse to nose around." Diane tsked. "As if Henri or I would have anything to do with Eloise's death. That's just preposterous."

Her statement led me to believe that she hadn't heard about Shawn's death yet. I wondered why Henri hadn't told her and I wished I didn't have to be the one to share the news. "I never thought either of you could have had something to do with the deaths, but I hoped you might have observed something that could help out."

"Deaths? Don't you mean Eloise's death?" She pulled her brows together.

Up close, I could tell that Diane was older than I had originally thought. Despite not having a wrinkle or a single sunspot, most likely thanks to a good cosmetic surgeon, I suspected she was still in her early sixties. Her tousled strawberry-blonde hair, paired with a sundress more suited for a thirty-year-old, along with a trim build and an energetic personality, made her seem younger than her age.

"Have you heard that Shawn was killed a couple days ago?"

Diane's hand flew to her throat. "Good heavens! No. I hadn't heard."

"It was murder as well." I studied her face, which had paled. She seemed genuinely distressed, and I felt bad that I'd caused it.

"What is this world coming to?" She wrapped her arms around her torso. "I had nothing to do with either of their deaths."

I peered at the house, but there was no one around to pay

us any attention. "May I ask you a couple questions before you return to the party?"

"Fine. Just be quick about it, please." Diane looked at the sports watch on her wrist.

"Your dog, Rocky, is a boxer, right?" When she nodded, I continued. "Did you purchase him from Shawn?"

"Absolutely not," she sputtered. "I wouldn't have taken those darn training sessions with him had my sister not begged me to. Otherwise she was going to get fined for something my dog did, and it would go on her record. That Eloise is, or was, something else, coercing the condo residents to pay good money to support her son's business. But that doesn't mean I was the one who killed her. Or him. Now, if you'll excuse me, I need to get back to the luncheon."

"Wait. Can I ask one more quick question?"

She huffed. "Fine. Just don't dally."

"Did you happen to hear of any of the other participants in our session having purchased a dog or puppy from Shawn?"

"Why the fixation on Shawn selling dogs? With his business, he probably had a lot of contacts with breeders to facilitate sales."

I shook my head. "He was running a puppy mill, and I found proof of it."

Diane's eyes widened. "Oh no! How horrifying! But I don't recall any of the other attendees saying anything about purchasing their dog from him. Then again, aside from the potluck, there wasn't a chance to socialize at all. I had the distinct impression that Shawn strongly discouraged it, in fact, but that didn't stop Henri from asking me out for drinks."

It was cute the way Diane's cheeks flushed when she said Henri's name.

"I've found three people who'd purchased their dogs from Shawn, and I wanted to make sure no one else had. People need to be aware their dogs may need special attention and medical care, so if you hear of anyone who got their puppy from him, please let me know." I dug into my pocket for a business card.

Diane raised her hand. "I have your phone number from the email and voicemail you left."

"Thanks. I appreciate you taking the time to talk with me."

I had just turned to reopen the SUV's door when Diane stopped me by placing a gentle touch on my arm. I turned back to face her.

"There's one thing you might want to check into." She glanced around as if to make sure no one watched us or could overhear. "I dropped my potluck dish off on Friday afternoon and put it in the clubhouse refrigerator. I had an errand I needed to run after training on Saturday and didn't want my food to arrive late. Henri promised he'd put my Waldorf salad out on the table for me."

"Your salad was quite delicious."

"Thank you, dear." She paused as if to collect her thoughts. "Eloise was in the kitchen, fiddling with the coffeepot. She acted kind of guilty, like I'd caught her doing something she shouldn't. But then she got overly aggressive, asking why I was there, and told me I didn't have permission to use the facilities until the following day."

"That's really odd. What happened next?" Had Eloise planned on blowing up the clubhouse to cover the embezzlement but been caught in the act Saturday afternoon by the killer?

"Nothing, really. She told me to put my salad in the refrigerator and leave. Which I can say I did posthaste."

"I'll let the detective know, and perhaps he can make sense of it."

"Don't be hasty. I'd hate to have the police think I'd misinterpreted her actions. Maybe she was just making coffee, and I read too much into the reaction when I startled her." Diane looked at her watch again. "I really must get back. They're going to think I abandoned them."

"I appreciate all you've shared with me." I lifted my hand to shake, but she'd already scurried toward the house without a backward glance at me.

Chapter 32

Almost as soon as I'd sent Carrie a text letting her know the delivery went well, she sent back a reply.

Don't forget to come pick up the rescue kittens. Pleeaazzzzeeee!!!!!

I smiled at the way she'd spelled please. It was the written version of her daughters' verbal pronunciation when they really wanted something.

On my way now.

Just as I'd put the vehicle into drive, another text came through from a number I didn't recognize. I put the SUV into park and swiped the screen open.

Hi Emory, this is Nanci n Frank. Surfing until 2. Meet at Taco Loco for lunch?

My mouth watered. Taco Loco had the best street tacos around. I quickly thumbed a reply.

See you then.

It was becoming obvious that my voicemail with a generic question about their recipe hadn't fooled any of the attendees. At least the couple had recognized the wisdom of meeting in a public place to set my mind at ease.

The drive back to Carrie's house took longer due to lunch-hour traffic getting from the coastline back to the toll road. As I pulled up in front of the Craftsman house, another text came in from Cheryl.

I found your platters stuck into one of the kitchen cabinets. Can you stop by and pick them up?

Sure. I'll be there in about 20 minutes.

My sister's home wasn't that far from the condo complex. In fact, in some places, it was hard to tell whether you were in Costa Mesa or Huntington Beach. The boundary lines of the two cities seemed to meld together. I jumped from the SUV and found Thomas waiting for me at the door. Again.

"How are the kids?" I asked while I took the tote bag from him.

"Better. All three of them ate some saltines and asked for more food, so I gave them a few slices of banana, which stayed down. They're all sleeping now." Thomas kept his voice to a low whisper. "Let me get the kittens for you, and I'll meet you at your car."

I did as he said, glad my brother-in-law wasn't feeling the need to be chit-chatty. I'd no sooner opened the passenger door when Thomas brought out the cardboard box. Nestled amongst a pink, heart-themed fleece blanket—a product of my nieces' craft efforts, no doubt—two calico kittens snuggled together. He placed the box on the front seat and fastened the seatbelt around the outside of it.

"The girls named them Patches and Tigger."

"I think I can guess which one is which." I laughed as I stroked Patches, with her eye surrounded by a patch of black fur, and then Tigger with her striped fur of black and orange. Both had soft-as-down white chests that extended to their front paws. They both batted my finger. "They're darling."

"Their food is in the tote bag, along with all the feeding and care instructions." Thomas drew his brows together. "The girls are going to be so upset. Maybe you can adopt one of them so they can at least come to visit the kittens?"

"They haven't been told the kittens are leaving your house?"

He snorted. "The kittens came home yesterday afternoon, and by midnight, all three kids were sick. Carrie didn't have the heart to break the news while they were throwing up, and with her allergies getting worse by the minute, she couldn't wait any longer."

My sister had a strange reaction to antihistamines and couldn't take them without her heart racing to dangerous levels for hours. Otherwise, knowing her, she'd have stayed on allergy pills so her daughters could at least keep the kittens until a permanent home could be found.

"Sorry. I didn't think of it that way." I sighed and looked at the kittens. "But the girls understood that, eventually, the kittens would find a permanent home and they'd be leaving them?"

"They understood, but in all honesty, I thought we'd be the ones adopting them, and I suspect the girls were hanging on to hope that would happen too." He sighed. "Carrie had no idea she was that allergic."

"I'll talk to Tillie and Brian and see if it's feasible to keep them, but I'm not going to make any promises just yet." I checked my watch. "I hope Piper and Missy remember that cats can be tolerated."

"Thanks, Em. I'll let you know when the kids feel well enough to visit the kittens. And you, of course." Thomas patted my shoulder. He helped me unload all the catering supply totes and crates then carted them back to the house.

I noticed he never said he'd let me know when the shelter had found a new foster family for the kittens. Well, Brian had mentioned he missed having Boots around. I hoped he meant it.

I made it to the clubhouse in the twenty minutes I'd promised. The parking lot wasn't nearly as busy, and I wondered if the audits had been completed. I called Cheryl and told her I was in the parking lot and explained why I couldn't come in. She said she'd be right out.

Cheryl came through the glass doors, clutching my two platters, with Rebecca right on her heels. Both women were dressed in light-gray slacks. Cheryl wore a cream silk blouse that featured a bow at the neckline, whereas Rebecca wore an oversized zebra-print T-shirt that looked more like lounge wear than office attire.

I opened the vehicle's door and stood to greet them.

Cheryl thrust the platters into my hands. "Where are they? We'd love to see the kittens."

I walked to the passenger side, opened the door, and retrieved the box. The kittens had done remarkedly well on the drive and had remained calm. Sensing there were people around to give them attention, they began mewling. Each woman picked up a kitten and cradled it close, which caused the felines to purr loudly.

"Oh, the sweet dears," Cheryl cooed. "Do you think they're hungry or thirsty? You can bring them inside and let them play for a while after being cooped up in the box."

"Please, won't you come in? I lost my cat a few months ago, and I've really missed having her around." Rebecca kept her gaze glued on Patches. "I still have some cat toys in my desk. You can have them if you'd like."

They were giving me the perfect opportunity to find out more information about Eloise and the embezzlement. "That would be really nice. I'm not terribly organized to care for them yet."

"That's the nice thing about cats. They're very independent, and you don't need much to make them happy," Rebecca said. "Of course, they're not going to complain about getting toys or treats either."

I put the box back into my vehicle, picked up the tote containing the cat food, and followed the women into the clubhouse. It was eerily quiet. "Are the auditors done?"

Cheryl pursed her lips. "Yes, but what a nightmare this has been."

"Were they able to track down the money and return it to the association?" I asked.

Rebecca huffed as she put Patches down. "No. I think the money is long gone. Eloise, or more probably Shawn, most likely transferred it to an offshore account."

"So they were able to determine that Shawn was involved in the theft?"

"They're not saying, but it makes the most sense." Cheryl rolled her eyes. "Eloise wasn't the most computer savvy and was pretty lackadaisical with her passwords. It wasn't uncommon for her to call us in order to dictate an email she wanted us to send from her personal email account. It seems a very reasonable assumption that Shawn would have all her private banking account and password information. He did just about everything for her."

I found it odd that the president of a high-end condo association could be so incompetent, but perhaps she was good at organizing and delegating, which got the necessary work accomplished.

Cheryl placed Tigger on the floor, and Patches immediately pounced on her sister. While the kittens played, I opened the tote and found the kitten food. They came running to me the second the kibble rattled in the bag. I took a small handful out and spread a few pieces on the floor. The kittens daintily nibbled for a bit then went back to playing.

"I'll be right back with a dish of water and the cat toys." Rebecca scurried toward the hallway that led to the offices.

Knowing I had scant minutes to talk to Cheryl alone, I jumped right in. "Do you have any idea who might have hated Shawn enough to kill him?"

She turned toward me, anger blazing across her face. "I know what you're getting at, Emory, and I don't appreciate your insinuation one bit."

Taken aback, I held my hand up, palm facing her. "I didn't mean to offend you. I only wanted to know if you'd heard of anyone abnormally angry after purchasing one of his puppy-mill dogs."

"You mean like me?" Rebecca stood in the hallway, her arms crossed.

I'd really put my foot in my mouth. "No. Of course not. I'm pretty sure no one I've spoken with so far is the killer."

"So you're siccing the police on my son instead." Cheryl's mouth was smashed into a grim line, and if looks could kill, I'd have been dead.

"Your son?" I decided to play innocent. "Why would he have anything to do with it? You told me yourself that he's moved away and isn't in the area."

Rebecca picked up Patches and handed her to me. "I think it's time for you to go. We've got work to do."

Tigger jumped up onto my leg, and I winced at both her sharp claws and my blunder in offending the two women. Even if they had some sort of clue, there was no way I'd get it from them now. I bent down and picked up the second kitten. "I apologize. It wasn't my intention to insinuate anything untoward about either of you or your family."

Neither of them said a word but, instead, continued to glare at me.

"I'll just see myself out. I'm sorry for upsetting you." I stumbled toward the door, wishing I'd brought the box with me as the kittens clawed at my shirt and my hair, which had escaped the scrunchie I'd used to pull it away from my face. I finally made it to the safety of my vehicle and collapsed into my seat after securing the kittens in the passenger seat beside me. An incoming text pinged on my phone.

Ok to meet you at 2:15? We're running a bit late.

With the drama that had played out in the clubhouse, I'd almost forgotten about meeting up with Frank and Nanci. Looking at the clock on the dashboard of my SUV, I realized the later time would work out better. Otherwise, I would have been very late.

See you at Taco Loco. 2:15 is great.

I called Tillie on my hands-free Bluetooth and explained the kittens to her and my need to meet up with Frank and Nanci. She readily agreed I should bring the kittens home, and Piper and Missy could hang out at the pool house until both of us were available to help socialize the animals.

By the time I reached Tillie's house, I knew I'd be lucky to be less than ten minutes late to meet Nanci and Frank. Traffic lights hadn't been kind to me.

The octogenarian met me at the front door—she must've been watching the video feed as I parked—and cooed over the kittens. "I already took Piper and Missy over to the pool house and made sure they had food and water."

One of the very thoughtful things Tillie had done when Piper and I had moved in was to have a doggie door installed so that my dog was free to come and go in the yard as she pleased. And once Missy had joined the household and my nephew started toddling about, she'd had a pool safety fence installed as well. "Thanks. Where would you like me to put the kittens?"

"I thought the kitchen would be best. I brought the litter box from your house for now, and I can keep it in the laundry room." Which just so happened to be situated off of the kitchen.

"Thomas didn't say if they were litter box trained yet." I followed her toward the kitchen. "I have a tote in my vehicle that I'll get as soon as I put the kittens down. He said there was food and instructions. I've been too busy to take a look at the instructions as of yet, but they weren't hungry thirty minutes ago."

Tillie directed me to put the box on the floor in the corner closest to the laundry room. "Maybe we should put the box in the laundry room with the litter box. That way, they'll know where they belong if you want to just shut the door on them to keep them contained."

"I'd never do that to the poor dears."

Lest anyone think that Tillie's laundry room was little more than a closet, it was actually the size of a small bedroom, with lots of built-in cabinets and cupboards, along with a marble-topped island in the center of the room. I also doubted Tillie had ever availed herself of the washer and dryer. She had a housekeeper who'd been a part of the household for at least three decades. Now that Dorie was nearing retirement age, she only came in a couple days a week to clean the house and tend to the laundry instead of working full-time. It worked out well since Vannie lived at the house and took care of anything she thought needed attention. As she'd confided in me, it made her feel less guilty about living rent-free with her grandmother.

I put the box in the laundry room anyway. "As soon as I get the tote with their food, I'm going to have to dash to meet a couple of potential suspects at Taco Loco. Do you mind reading over the instructions? We can talk about where the kittens should sleep when I get home."

"I'm happy to do so." She rubbed her hands together. "And I hope you find out some incriminating evidence for us to work with."

I dashed for the SUV, rushed back into the house, and thrust the tote into her hands. After filling a baggie with some of the cookies I'd baked, I kissed her cheek and ran back out.

Chapter 33

Despite my attempt to avoid traffic by taking surface roads a few blocks from the Pacific Coast Highway, I still ended up being ten minutes late. While stuck at a painfully long traffic light, I sent Nanci a text alerting her to my tardiness. She sent a shrug emoji, which I hoped meant what could I do, it was Newport Beach traffic.

When I finally found parking and located the couple—both dressed in board shorts and T-shirts with sand-crusted legs and bare feet—they had a large plate of loaded nachos on the table along with three plates holding three tacos each. I waved when they noticed me walking down the boardwalk, dodging bikes and pedestrians. Their sun-bleached hair tumbled in damp, curly locks onto their shoulders. During the dog training sessions, they'd both kept their hair pulled up: a man-bun for Frank and a messy bun for Nanci. But now, they'd removed the elastic bands to let their hair air-dry after surfing.

"I'm so sorry I'm late." I placed the bag of cookies in front of them.

"It's cool, and thanks for the cookies." Frank patted the

bench beside him. "We just picked up the food, so it should still be hot. Help yourself."

Neither of them waited for me but instead scooped up thick tortilla chips laden with beans, chicken, cheese, tomatoes, and jalapeños and shoveled them into their mouths. Nanci dolloped some guacamole and sour cream onto the platter to dip her chips into. My stomach rumbled, and I helped myself. My questions could wait. Recalling a jalapeño pepper stuck in the back of my throat some time ago and the coughing fit that had ensued, I cautiously avoided them.

"We weren't sure what you'd like to drink, so we got you an unsweetened iced tea." Frank pointed at his wife, who had just taken a large bite of taco. "Nanci. Pass the tea over, dudette."

Nanci handed the tea to me.

"Thanks. I appreciate it. Let me know how much I owe you for lunch."

She waved away my offer. "It's on us. Besides, you came with cookies. What kind are they?" She put down her taco, picked up the bag, and opened it.

"Salted-caramel. I just baked them last night."

Nanci took one out and handed the bag to Frank before taking a bite. "Mmmm. Can you share the recipe?"

"Sure. It's my sister's recipe, but I'm sure she won't mind me emailing it to you."

Frank took two cookies out and put them on his plate. "I'll finish my tacos first."

Despite Frank being in his forties and appearing to enjoy consuming mass quantities of food—not only did he help polish off the plate of nachos, he ate his three tacos and then took one of mine and one of Nanci's—he was in shape and had well-defined muscles. Nanci's tall, lithe body also reflected her love for the sun and physical exercise, which made it hard for me to guess her age.

Once the meal had been consumed, including the dozen

and a half cookies, I decided it was time to get down to business.

"Do you mind if I ask you a few questions about your dog and your experience with the training sessions?" I stuck a paper napkin, about to blow off the table because of the ocean breeze that had picked up, beneath my cup of iced tea.

"Sure. Diane and Henri both told us you'd be contacting us about the murders," Frank said. He must've interpreted my expression when I wondered why the older pair had been in contact. "After the second training session, we joined them for a glass of wine afterward at Henri's house. Ace hit it off with their dogs, so we've continued the tradition every week, and I expect we'll be setting up weekly playdates now that training is over."

It surprised me that neither Diane or Henri had mentioned their social visits with this couple when I'd chatted with them. Were they trying to hide something, or were they keeping it on the down-low so it wouldn't get back to Shawn? "You've already heard about Shawn's death?"

"Yes." Frank crossed his arms over his chest, which made his biceps bulge. "We had nothing to do with either of the murders."

I held up my palm in a conciliatory gesture. "I never thought you did, but I am trying to piece together what might have led someone else to kill both Eloise and Shawn. Personally, I think it might be because Shawn was running a puppy mill."

The couple exchanged a quick look.

"Did you buy Ace from him?" If I recalled correctly, Ace was a Golden Retriever about eight months old.

They both nodded grimly.

"Has Ace had any medical issues since you brought him home?"

Nanci sighed. "It's nothing worrisome now, but the vet said his joints will have issues as he ages, and he might need some surgeries. And yes, the vet said it was most likely because of how he was bred."

"I'm so sorry to hear that." I flicked a fly away from the remains of the taco on my plate. "How did you come to sign up with Shawn for the training sessions?"

"Shawn charged a premium for his dogs, but he assured us it was because he would work with us to train Ace to our satisfaction, no matter how many sessions it took. This is our second group session," Frank said.

"And you were happy with the training he provided?"

"Not really. Shawn and Spike"—Nanci rolled her eyes —"are a little too intense for our liking, but we know how important it is to keep a puppy socialized. We've met some great people, like Henri and Diane, who are happy to set up playdates for the dogs outside of Shawn's classes."

The couple were so likeable I had a difficult time imagining either of them could be a murderer. "Did you overhear anyone in our class who might have had issues with either Eloise or Shawn?"

They both shook their heads, but Frank answered. "Nothing that would indicate someone hated them enough to kill them."

Nanci pointed her index finger at me. "Why do you care so much? You aren't related to them, are you?"

"I guess you haven't heard. I found both of the victims, and I feel a certain responsibility to find the truth."

"Whoa. That's gnarly," Frank said.

"You really should leave it up to the police to figure it out. It's not like Shawn didn't deserve his fate." Nanci crossed her arms, and her voice hardened. "But in case you take that the wrong way and think we had something to do with either of those deaths, we have an ironclad alibi. After the potluck lunch, we dropped Ace off at my sister's house and boarded a plane for Chicago for a conference. We just returned last night."

"Again, I never thought you'd committed the crime, but I appreciate you sharing your information with me." I had the feeling I'd overstayed my welcome. I disentangled myself from the picnic bench. "Are you sure I can't pay for lunch? It seems the least I can do after intruding into your afternoon."

Frank waved me off. "It's our pleasure. Ignore Ms. Grumpy. She has to go back to work tonight and was already in a bad mood."

"Then I'll get out of your way so you can enjoy the rest of your afternoon." I picked up the plastic bag. "I'll take this so I'll remember to send you the recipe."

The drive back home wasn't nearly as long as getting to the beach had been, and just as I pulled into the garage, Karla called. She wanted to meet up with me immediately at her favorite tea shop, Teopia.

Chapter 34

Karla was nowhere to be seen when I stepped inside the tea shop. Aside from a bored-looking college-aged girl manning the counter, there were only two other people in the shop. The two elderly ladies sat at a four-top with a plate of scones in front of them along with a white teapot and white teacups. I placed an order for Karla's chai and, remembering how awful it had tasted, ordered a bottle of sparkling mineral water for myself.

I'd just placed the drinks on a table, as far from the other customers as I could get, when Karla entered the shop. Her shoulders were hunched, and her eyes flitted around the room. She spotted me and meandered over to the table as if dreading talking to me.

I gestured at the to-go cup sitting atop the table. "I bought you a chai. Would you like to sit here and talk? Or we can go somewhere else if that works better for you."

She plopped down into the chair opposite me, took another look around the room, then picked up the cup. "This'll be fine."

I waited, somewhat impatiently, as she sipped the chai. After all, she'd been the one to ask me to meet. I didn't want to try to pry whatever it was out of her and risk her scurrying out of here.

When she'd drained at least half the drink, she set the cup down and wiped her lips with the back of her hand. "Thanks. I really needed the pick-me-up."

When she didn't continue, I could contain myself no longer. "You had something you wanted to talk to me about?"

Her eyes darted to the door, and I worried she was going to run off again. Instead, she leaned in toward me and lowered her voice to barely above a whisper. I had to strain to hear. "The police questioned me this morning. I'm afraid they're going to arrest me any moment now, and I need your help."

I slumped back in the chair, taken aback. This unassuming woman had never really been a suspect on my list. I had only figured she might have overheard something during the dog training sessions or could corroborate that Shawn had been running a puppy mill, which I already knew to be true. "Perhaps you'd better start at the beginning. How are you connected to Eloise and Shawn aside from the dog training?"

She fidgeted with the cardboard cup in front of her. "I'm —or I guess I used to be—their accountant for both personal affairs and Shawn's business. About a year ago, I found some irregularities in Shawn's accounts." Her eyes darted to the side, and her face flushed red. "Instead of bringing it to the attention of the appropriate authorities once I confirmed he was running an illegal puppy mill, I, ah, um, agreed to an increase in my monthly fees."

I smashed my lips together and dug my nails into the palms of my hands to keep from saying anything condemning her greedy decision instead of rescuing the helpless animals. It wouldn't do to have her run away from me again. When I didn't respond, she continued.

"I saw how much money he was raking in, and a couple months ago, I decided I deserved a nice big raise to keep quiet about his operation." She placed both palms over her face. "That's when both Shawn and Eloise cornered me at my home. Shawn threatened me with bodily harm, and Eloise said she'd created proof that it was me laundering money through Shawn's training business and not the other way around. The police found whatever it was Eloise had put together along with a few emails Shawn had sent reminding me that my life was on the line. They think I killed them both to free myself. But I didn't. I swear it."

I believed her even though I didn't want to. "What do you want me to do?"

"You've solved murders before, and I know you're asking questions about these two. You need to hurry up and clear my name before they arrest me." Karla tried to contain the tears that trickled down her cheeks. "I know it's my fault I'm in this mess, but I don't need a murder conviction on top of being an accomplice to a puppy mill. My life will be ruined enough as it is without spending the rest of it in prison."

It was difficult to feel any sort of sympathy for the woman sitting in front of me, especially when I recalled the state of the warehouse in which I'd found Shawn's body. Still, I argued with myself, she didn't deserve life in prison for two murders she didn't commit. My other self argued back that Karla just might be fooling me, and she really had committed the crimes.

"You're right. I am talking to the people who participated in our training sessions, so I hope you're willing to answer my questions."

"I'll tell you up front, I don't have an alibi for either of the deaths. I live alone and work from my home. I rarely socialize, and my only companion is my dog." She took a long drink from her cup.

"What kind of dog do you have?" I couldn't quite remember, and I hadn't had a chance to review my notes on the owners and their dogs before meeting her.

"Joey's a border collie."

"Oh, that's right. He's the one with a partial white face, chest, and feet while the rest of him is black?"

She nodded.

"I loved how his little ears pointed up every time you pulled out a treat whenever Shawn's back was turned." That was another thing that had disturbed me with Shawn's method of training. He didn't believe in rewarding the dogs' behavior with treats. Barking out orders and issuing minimal praise was his way. Karla and I hadn't been the only ones not to heed the no-treat mandate.

"Joey's purely motivated by food, so I didn't see how we'd survive the class if we didn't cheat just a little bit."

"Did you purchase Joey from Shawn?"

She shuddered. "Not a chance. Do you know what puppy mills are like and how often the puppies sold end up having medical issues?"

I raised my eyebrows, and she must've realized how she sounded. She exhaled a noisy breath and slumped back into her seat. "You must think I'm a horrible, horrible person to let him get away with what he did."

I bit my lip to keep my anger from bubbling over.

"I know how bad it looks, but I didn't do it out of greed." She swiped her hand over her face. "No one but medical professionals know this, and I'd like for you to keep it confidential. Although if people find out I'm an accessory to a puppy mill, perhaps I should be more transparent and explain why I did what I did."

I felt she was stalling with whatever she wanted to confess, so I held back from saying anything.

"I have to have dialysis several times a week and am on a waiting list for a new kidney. Because I'm a self-employed individual, my insurance premiums are sky-high while providing pitiful coverage." She dropped her gaze to the table. "If I don't keep up with dialysis or get a new kidney, I'll die. I had to find a way to get the funds to pay for what the insurance won't cover, and Shawn's business went a long way toward helping."

She was slowly winning over my sympathy, and I could plainly see the desperation in her face. "I'm so sorry you're going through that. Can't your doctor put you in touch with organizations that might help out?"

Karla shook her head. "There's no one to help. Do you know how many underinsured people there are that are in desperate need of insanely expensive medical treatments? Way too many to count."

"Truly, Karla, I'm so sorry." I paused a moment, already knowing her answer. "Have you told the police why you helped cover up the puppy mill?"

"They don't need to know."

"I think they do. If anything, there might be some leniency in charging you, or, if they decide to prosecute and convict, they could opt for probation versus jail time."

"If I'm sent to jail, the taxpayers will have to pay for my treatments." A wry smile flitted across her lips, and then it was gone. "Trust me, I've thought long and hard about it, but I really don't want to go that route. Not unless it's my very last hope for survival."

Chapter 35

K arla's pronouncement lingered with me long after I'd returned home and helped Vannie cook dinner. Tillie and Teresa each cradled a kitten in their arms. Piper and Missy had made peace with having the felines around, and once they'd greeted me, they returned to their positions on the floor beneath the table, waiting for dinner to be served. I longed to share the details of Karla's predicament with my family and friends, but she'd made me promise to keep our conversation confidential. It left me feeling at a loss as to how to help her.

Over our dinner of chicken cutlets served with a lemon-and-caper sauce, parmesan linguine, green salad, and garlic toast, I shared what I'd learned that day. Despite feeling the woman was doing herself a disservice and that people would judge her more harshly, I left out Karla's motivation for turning a blind eye since she'd made me promise to keep it a secret.

Tillie sputtered and pushed away her plate, which still held food. "That kind of greed is hard to stomach. She had to have known the condition those poor creatures were living in. Her not purchasing a dog from Shawn tells you everything you need to know about her. I hope she's ashamed of herself."

"She is very contrite," I said.

"Well, it doesn't make up for the agony those dogs endured." Vannie was just as indignant.

I agreed and was grateful when my phone pinged with a text from Brad.

I'm in alley. R u at Tillie's or home?

At Tillie's. C u in sec.

I stood and slid my phone into the pocket of my stretchy yoga pants. "Brad is out in front. I'll go let him in."

"Oh, good. We need a handsome man at the table." Tillie rubbed her hands together then patted Vannie's arm. "Not that I'm not thrilled to have you beautiful girls with me."

I left the three of them behind as Tillie was telling the story of how she'd met Rock Hudson and shared a martini and cigarette with him in New York. Tillie had a zest for living that I aspired to match.

Brad bounded up the steps as soon as I buzzed open the security gate. He held a white paper sack in one hand and a manilla file folder in the other.

"Whatcha got there?" I pointed at the sack.

"I'll show you once we're in the kitchen." He pulled it out of my reach when I made a grab for the bag. He handed me the folder instead. "Your maid-of-honor duties, milady."

I flipped the file open and gulped. There were three single-spaced pages typed in outline form. "Didn't you guys hire a wedding planner? I thought they were supposed to take care of all the details."

Brad used his free hand to guide me into the house then gave me a gentle shove. "I'll tell you about that fiasco later. For now, I need the kitchen sooner rather than later."

"Okay, okay. You should've just said so." I turned my head so he could see my smirk. "Did you forget to eat dinner, and you're hoping for some leftovers?"

"Now that you've offered, I'd love to join you for dinner. What are you serving?"

I ignored his question as we stepped into the kitchen. Brad sashayed over to Tillie and kissed her cheek, kissed the top of Vannie's head, and extended a fist bump for Teresa. "While Emory is fixing me a plate for dinner, which, BTW, smells fabulous, I'm going to dish up samples of the wedding cake along with three different vegan ice creams to taste. Gabe has a sister and two cousins who are vegans, and we want to accommodate them, and it seems appropriate that my favorite foodies help me decide."

"The cakes aren't going to be vegan, are they?" I recalled going to a party at which a vegan cake had been stacked to create layers, and the weight of the cake had made the entire thing collapse. It hadn't been pretty, but it was still tasty enough, and not much was left by the end of the party.

"The caterer is making vegan cupcakes for them." Brad, having spent many an hour in the kitchen with me, helped himself to five large dinner plates, five salad plates, forks, spoons, and an ice cream scooper. Carefully lifting slices of cake from each container, he arranged six different-flavored pieces of cake on each plate. Next, he scooped vanilla ice cream from three different cartons onto the salad plates. He frowned as one of the ice cream products began to melt and puddle beneath the scoop. He handed the plate to me.

"Unless that melty ice cream is the best in flavor and texture, I think I'd better not consider it since it melts so quickly." He picked up a spoon and dipped it into the scoop in question that sat on my plate. I followed suit.

My eyes widened. "This is vegan? It's fantastic despite it melting."

"What are we, chopped liver?" Tillie waved her arms overhead. "We want a taste too."

Brad quickly placed the plates with the ice cream on the table.

I tasted the other two products and went back to the melty ice cream. "I think this one is the winner, hands down. Maybe there'll be a way to keep it properly chilled before serving at the reception."

Teresa licked her spoon and voiced her agreement. "It definitely is the best. The texture is the closest to real ice cream that I've ever had. What makes it so creamy?"

Tillie remained quiet as she ate all three scoops of ice cream. Her appetite was apparently back.

"The caterer says she whips up a vegan whipping cream first then blends in macadamia nut cream and a bit of coconut cream along with all the other ingredients." Brad took another bite. "I like that the coconut taste is barely there. You wouldn't even notice if you weren't looking for it."

"These are homemade vegan ice creams?" I was amazed. "She should market it. It's better than any other product out there that I've tried."

"She's looking into it, at least to sell locally, but so far, when she tries to produce in mass quantities, the results aren't nearly as good." Brad shoved a plate containing six different flavors of cake my way then placed the remaining plates in front of the other three women. He pointed to each piece as he named them. "We have a vanilla cake with raspberry filling and Swiss meringue vanilla buttercream. Chocolate with chocolate ganache filling and frosting. Carrot cake with cream cheese filling and frosting. White cake with fresh strawberries-and-cream filling and whipped-cream frosting, although the caterer warned us it might be difficult to get good strawberries without paying a king's ransom. Lemon cake with lemon curd filling and vanilla buttercream frosting. And last, a mocha cake layered with a thin layer of mocha ganache and caramel sauce then frosted with whipped mocha ganache."

"Ooohh, I know which one I'll vote for," I said as I forked up a piece of the mocha cake. I almost swooned as the tempting flavors hit my taste buds.

"That's my first choice too." Brad pointed at the remaining five slices. "We've decided to have two cakes, so which flavor should the second cake be?"

Vannie sampled the vanilla cake with raspberry filling first while Tillie tried the lemon cake, and Teresa took a bite of the carrot cake. I took tiny bites of all of them in rapid succession.

Brad looked at us expectantly. "Well?"

Somehow, everyone's focus turned to me. "What? I chose the first cake."

"But cake, or at least cupcakes, is your business. You know what'll work together and what will hold up to the rigors of transporting and weather." Vannie pointed her fork in my direction. "Give us your input, and then we can discuss if we have other opinions."

I supposed if I got to pick my two favorite flavors, it couldn't be all that bad. "I'd skip the strawberries-and-cream cake for sure. Getting tasty strawberries that time of the year is iffy, no matter what premium price you pay, and if the Santa Ana winds decide to blow and the weather heats up to over eighty degrees, the whipped cream won't survive for very long, no matter how much stabilizer the baker adds to it."

"Okay, you make a good point for that one. There's still four to choose from." Brad ate another bite of the mocha cake.

"While I like carrot cake, it seems too rustic for an elegant wedding. And again, if it's a warm day, the cream cheese frosting could have issues sitting out for hours." I sampled a bite of the white cake with raspberry filling then a bite of the lemon cake. "I'm torn. I like them both. Which do you like better?"

"It's exactly why I brought the samples to you. I can't decide between those two flavors." Brad took bites of each piece.

Tillie's eyes sparkled. "You're overlooking the obvious solution. Have one cake be the mocha cake and the second cake can have one lemon tier and the second tier be the white cake. Either flavor of frosting will go well on both tiers."

I sampled a bite of the chocolate cake with chocolate ganache. My eyes widened at the decadent flavor. "I think Tillie's on to something. You've got to add a tier of this chocolate cake to the mocha cake. The combination is heavenly."

"You're a genius, Tillie. Four flavors of wedding cake it will be." Brad swung me around. "Now, can I eat dinner before my sugar high crashes?"

I reheated a plate of chicken with linguine in the microwave and poured him a glass of iced water when he declined my offer of wine. Brad grilled me on everything I'd found out so far about the two murders.

In the back of my mind, Tillie's words kept repeating: "You're overlooking the obvious solution." Somehow, those words applied not only to the wedding cake but to the killer. Something niggled at the back of my brain, and the longer I thought about it, the more convinced I was that there had been only one killer. I hoped I could remember what I'd heard and identify the person who'd murdered both Eloise and Shawn before another tragedy occurred.

Chapter 36

I woke bleary-eyed the next morning, having stayed up half the night baking. After we'd finished dinner, I'd received another text from my twin, begging for help again the following day. She needed five dozen confetti-style cupcakes baked and frosted then delivered to my nieces' elementary school cafeteria by ten for the school's afternoon bake sale. Lucky for me, she'd been able to make enough excuses, so if I stayed for a couple hours to help organize the scrumptious donations, I wouldn't have to return to work the actual bake sale. When I asked how the kids were feeling, all she'd say was they were better, but she was feeling iffy. Considering the sounds I'd heard on the phone the day before, I decided I didn't want to call for any details.

I took a quick hot shower, which I wished could've been thirty minutes instead of five to loosen my tight muscles. But with a years-long drought going on, I opted to conserve water. I popped two ibuprofen tablets with my coffee instead as I pored over the printed wedding-chore pages Brad had given me.

I'd pried the tale of his missing wedding planner from him as he'd walked me home. She'd apparently been swept off her feet by a carnie who'd worked at the Orange County Fair over the summer and had dropped everything to run off with him over the weekend to live life on the road. Well, she hadn't dropped *everything*. All the deposits her high-end clients had given her to plan their lavish weddings had disappeared right along with her. By Wednesday morning, when Brad still hadn't been able to reach her no matter how many bazillion messages he'd left, Gabe had jumped in to investigate. He'd finally pieced together what had happened after talking to her roommates and her mom.

So far, Gabe hadn't made any headway in finding her, but in the meantime, Brad had volunteered to take over the responsibilities of the wedding, which meant me planning it and telling him what he needed to do. Realistically, it would be impossible to find a last-minute wedding planner since they booked their services at least a year or two out.

So there I was, the faithful maid of honor, trying to make sense of everything that still needed to be done. I had to figure out what the wedding planner had actually accomplished or hadn't gotten to yet, but at least Brad had the wedding cake confirmed and the flavors determined. My plan was to create a timeline—I shuddered at the thought, but desperate needs called for desperate measures—then turn a lot of the planning over to my mother. I didn't feel guilty in the least since I knew she'd thrive on the challenge.

At seven thirty, I filled a carafe with coffee made from beans roasted locally in Costa Mesa and headed to Tillie's house. I lugged my laptop with me to do some research on how to go about planning a wedding and what needed to be done and when. Tillie would at least keep me entertained.

The dogs, having spent the night at Tillie's since I'd opted to bake the cupcakes at my pool house, greeted me like a long-lost friend. They scampered around my feet until I got to the kitchen and then went to stand by their food bowls as if starving.

"Don't pay any attention to their begging." Brian took the carafe from me, and once I'd placed the laptop on the counter, he pulled me into a tight hug. "They've been well fed already. Hmmm, I've missed you."

"I've missed you too." I pulled away, expecting to see Tillie grinning from ear to ear. But the room was empty aside from Piper and Missy sitting next to my feet, wagging their tails expectantly. "Where's Tillie and the kittens?"

"Tillie took them with her upstairs when John called." Brian shook his head. "I've got to have the only eighty-some-thing-year-old grandmother who has more men calling for dates than the average thirty-year-old."

"Well, some of us don't want a bunch of men calling us." I kissed him. "One certain guy calling me or showing up to fix me breakfast is all I want."

Brian kissed me back.

"Okay, you lovebirds. Is there more coffee?" Tillie set the kittens on the floor then plopped into the chair. "John's flying in tomorrow, so I'll have a busy day getting ready."

Her grandson lifted his eyebrows. "The house is clean, the refrigerator is stocked, you have three people to cook for you at a moment's notice, and you have a fully stocked wine cellar. What else needs to be prepared?"

"I've got to get to the salon today for a color refresher, and would you look at my nails? I've neglected them for far too long."

Tillie lifted her hand to me, but I could see nary a chip in the polish anywhere. I said as much.

"The pink was fine for summer, but we're in autumn now. The pink just won't do."

"Fine, Gram. Go pamper yourself, and let me know if there's anything you'd like me to do to help get the house ready for John's visit."

Brian set a teacup filled with coffee in front of her.

"You all have everything under control. It's me that needs

the attention." Tillie smoothed down her platinum-blonde hair. She'd grown it a bit longer over the summer, which had brought a slight wave with the just-below-the-chin length. When it was parted on the side, there was a graceful arch to her hair that swooped out from her face and curved into her neckline. I knew she spent a lot more time on her hair than I did. Of course, I never looked half as put together as Tillie either.

"You're beautiful just the way you are." Brian pecked his grandmother on the cheek. "And I think you know it."

"I don't know what you're talking about." Tillie swatted at him before refilling her teacup with coffee. "The bacon smells good. What else is for breakfast, kiddo?"

"How do veggie omelets sound?" He began cracking eggs into a bowl, using only one hand, of course.

"You spoil us." My eyes met his, and I smiled. "And we greatly appreciate it."

By the time breakfast was done and I'd cleaned up the kitchen, Tillie was on her way to her first pampering appointment, and Brian headed to work. I checked the time and decided I'd better start loading the cupcakes for delivery to Sophie and Kaylee's elementary school. Their mother hadn't texted or called me to remind me about my commitment, which worried me. I sent her a text.

Leaving for school with cupcakes in 10 min. How r kids?

I didn't hear back until I'd placed the kittens in the laundry room—with food, water, and litter box available for them—and gotten the dogs settled at my house and the cupcakes secured in the cargo hold of my SUV.

This is Thomas. Carrie has flu, kids r much better.

Ugh. My poor sister. I was grateful Thomas had disinfected the kitchen so thoroughly when I'd cooked at their house the other morning.

Let me know if there's anything I can do to help.

He responded with a thumbs-up emoji.

By the time I arrived at the school, every single parking space for at least a third of a mile in the school's vicinity was taken. I loaded the cupcakes into two totes and made the trek to the assembly room, where I found pure chaos. I left the totes on one of the few empty tables and searched for anyone who looked like they might be in charge. A woman locked gazes with me, and before I knew what had happened, she'd thrust a clipboard into my hand.

"You're late, Carrie. Start checking names off and tell them which table number has been assigned for their baked goods."

"Uh, I'm her sister, Emory. Carrie has the flu, and I'm filling in for her."

"OMG. This can't be happening." The woman, who appeared to be in her early forties, had taken time to apply a liberal amount of makeup that morning. Unfortunately, it wasn't holding up to the stress of the day; her mascara had already smudged beneath her eyes, and her lipstick was half chewed off. Some of her blonde hair had escaped the tight ponytail and now fell limply onto her shoulder. "Well, I guess we'll just have to deal with it. Call out a name from the list and tell them which table number is assigned. And please be sure to make a mark beside everyone you check in."

Before I could acknowledge her instructions, she was off and running to settle a disagreement between two mothers over table placements. I looked at the long list of donors, gulped, and began calling out names.

Three long hours later, I felt and looked just as frazzled as the woman who'd thrust the clipboard into my hands when I'd first arrived. Limping back to my vehicle, I massaged my neck, feeling a stress headache forming. The last few days were catching up with me, and I needed either a long nap or a major dose of caffeine and more ibuprofen. I decided on the latter since I'd planned on working on Gabe and Brad's wedding that afternoon.

By the time I sat slumped in the driver's seat, air conditioning blasting my face, I realized I hadn't checked to see if I had received any messages since I'd stepped foot in the assembly room. I pulled my phone from my purse and saw a string of texts: Brad, Tillie, Brian, Vannie, and Brad again, more from Brad, and finally from a number I didn't recognize. I opened the mystery text first since the first line intrigued me. The text was long, really long, with the spelling complete and punctuation all in place.

We want to apologize for our behavior. Oh, this is Cheryl, in case you didn't know. Sorry for our attitude yesterday. It's been a stressful situation, and I didn't mean to take it out on you. If you're still looking for a home for the kittens, Rebecca and I want to adopt them. I called Kittytown Shelter, and since I know the director, Mitzie Klein, they said we could take the kittens right away, and she'd approve an over-the-phone application for us and waive the adoption fee.

Wow, it paid to know people. But both Cheryl and Rebecca were obviously cat lovers and had already proven their reliability with their two dogs. I felt a twinge of sadness about losing the kittens so quickly but reminded myself they were finding good homes. I continued reading the text.

We close the office at one every Friday. We can either come pick the kittens up from you today or, if you'd rather, you can bring them to Rebecca's house. She lives on 1st Street in Newport. Again, we both apologize for our behavior yesterday, and I hope you won't hold it against us in our desire to adopt the kittens.

I thumbed a quick text, giving her my address and asking that they meet me at two. That would give me about thirty minutes to eat some lunch, make sure the kittens had eaten, and pack up their few belongings. Plus, I was beat and didn't feel like turning around and going back out the second I got home.

Cheryl texted back immediately.

Thank you. We're both so excited. See you at 2.

With time being of the essence, I decided to skip reading the remaining texts for the moment. Brad was probably wondering how the wedding preparations were coming; Tillie probably wanted me to comment on her new nail polish color or hair style; and Vannie and Brian were probably just checking in. They could all wait until I'd placed the kittens in Cheryl and Rebecca's hands.

Chapter 37

O nce home, I settled for shoving some cheese and crackers into my mouth for lunch and guzzled a large glass of water before I went back to Tillie's to retrieve the kittens. Piper and Missy were disappointed I didn't take them with me, but I didn't feel like trying to corral them at the same time I needed to juggle a box of kittens. So I ignored their forlorn puppy-dog eyes and closed the alleyway gate in their faces. I wouldn't be gone long.

The kittens were carousing in Tillie's laundry room when I opened the door. They paused, practically in midair, as they prepared to pounce on a pile of cleaning rags. A drawer gaped open, and more cleaning rags hung over the edges. They'd tipped over the bowl of kibble, and the small nuggets were littered all over the floor.

"All right, you little rascals. Let's get you ready to meet your new families."

I hastily scooped up the cleaning rags and stuffed them back into the drawer. There would be time later to refold the towels and organize everything the way Dorie had left it. I cleaned the litter box then found an empty cardboard box to place it in. Tillie—or perhaps it had been Vannie—had purchased some toys for the kittens. I added them to the box then nestled the kittens back into their fleece blanket.

Except they weren't having it. I'd no sooner detached one from trying to crawl up my arm to get out of the box than the other would spring up and claw its way over the side.

I was on the losing end of the fiasco. Getting flustered and running out of time, I put the kittens back onto the floor then ran the box containing the litter box and toys over to my house after making certain the laundry room door was tightly closed. On the way back to Tillie's, I scanned a couple how-to videos online showing how to corral cats. Still trying to maintain my patience while avoiding their sharp claws, I wrapped each kitten into a towel burrito then laid it in the box. At first, they mewled, and Tigger even hissed, but as I walked them back to my house, they calmed down.

Cheryl and Rebecca were already waiting for me by the gate, and their gazes strayed to the box I carried. "I hope you haven't been waiting long for me. The kittens didn't want to get into the box."

"We just got here." Cheryl reached out and took the box from me and lovingly cradled it close to her chest. Both women peered into the box and cooed.

I unlocked the gate using the keypad code and held it open for them as they stepped onto the patio. Piper and Missy rushed to greet the new guests, and Rebecca bent down to give them both ear rubs.

"I cleaned and boxed up their litter box, and I found some cat toys you're welcome to take." I gestured at the box sitting on the patio table. "Can I offer you something to drink or some salted-caramel cookies?"

"No thanks, I'm fine." Cheryl placed the box holding the kittens on top of the patio table. "But I'd like to use your restroom if you don't mind."

"Let me show you where it is." I turned toward Rebecca, who had a rapt audience in the two dogs. "Feel free to bring the kittens in as well and let them run around a bit before you take them. Piper and Missy can stay out here."

"I appreciate it. It's probably a good idea to tire them out for the drive home." Rebecca picked up the box and followed us in. "What a darling house. Have you lived here long?"

"Thank you. I've really enjoyed living here over the past two years." I couldn't believe how quickly the time had flown by. "Cheryl, the bathroom is down the hall and to your left."

As Cheryl disappeared down the hallway, I put my cell phone on the kitchen counter and retrieved two chew sticks. Throwing the sticks into the grass for Piper and Missy to sniff out, I hoped they'd remain entertained outside for a while instead of demanding to be let in. It was a very rare occurrence that they didn't have access to come and go from the house as they pleased. They'd made their displeasure known by barking, whining, and clawing at the door when I'd blocked their doggie door on previous occasions. Fortunately, the second the sticks were in their mouths, they trotted over to the patio and began chewing away.

By the time I returned to the house, Rebecca had extricated both the kittens from the towels. They climbed over her legs and chased the length of ribbon she held in her hand. She practically giggled at their antics.

"Have you decided which kitten you'll take or which Cheryl will want?"

"I definitely want Tigger. I don't think Cheryl will mind." Rebecca shook the ribbon to get the kittens' attention as they began to wander off to explore.

Cheryl joined us, but instead of picking up one of the kittens, she walked past me and toward the French doors we'd entered through. She gazed out onto the patio without saying a word.

Patches pounced on my foot, so I turned my attention back to the kitten and picked her up. Rebecca stood and wiped her forehead with the back of her hand, the long ribbon trailing from her other hand. Tigger, having lost her playmate, jumped up and tangled her claws in the ribbon. Rebecca extricated the kitten and put her back on the floor.

I was so engrossed keeping Patches's claws from getting entangled in my hair that I didn't notice Cheryl until she was right at my elbow. I held the kitten out to her. "Here's your new mama, Patches. Be good for her."

Instead of taking Patches, Cheryl pointed a gun at me and gripped my arm hard.

"Ow." I tried pulling away, but her grip was too firm.

Rebecca quickly moved to my free side, took the kitten from my hand, and placed her on the floor.

"You should have kept your nose out of our business, Emory. This is all your fault," Cheryl hissed.

I pulled back, horrified that I'd never really considered these two ladies suspects. "What are you talking about? You didn't kill Eloise and Shawn, did you?"

"Did you think we were too old to be vigilantes?" Rebecca sneered. "Those two deserved their fate."

They forced me to sit on the sofa, and while Cheryl stood guard over me with the gun pointing at my head, Rebecca retrieved a roll of duct tape from her purse, which she'd left by the door. I frantically looked around, trying to find something that might defend me or help me escape. Nothing was within my reach aside from a plump cabernet-colored throw pillow. All the while, Cheryl kept her gaze and her gun fixed on me. She even managed to ignore the kittens clambering over her shoes.

I struggled when they began taping my ankles tightly together but gave up when Rebecca slapped me across the face. Once my ankles were immobilized and firmly bound to the leg of the sofa, they bound my wrists. I was grateful they didn't put my arms behind my back first and, instead, allowed my arms and hands to rest somewhat comfortably on my lap.

"What are you going to do with me?"

My dogs hadn't sensed I was in danger yet. I'd given them extra-large chew sticks to keep them busy, so it might be a while before they'd notice and start barking. I could only hope that a neighbor or a passerby would call the police or check on them. Who was I kidding? No one would check on why my dogs were barking, and even if they wanted to, the gate automatically locked whenever it was closed.

"I think the gas stove scenario is worth trying again, but with something a little quicker than an almost-empty coffeepot left on the burner to ignite the explosion." Cheryl almost sounded gleeful. She pulled a device from her purse, which she'd left slung across her body, and waggled it in front of my face. "The internet has so many helpful videos on how to build a timer that will spark an explosion."

"Please, don't kill my dogs." My voice cracked with emotion as I thought about the pain our deaths would cause my family.

Rebecca slapped my face. Again. It wasn't all that hard, but it still brought tears to my eyes. "What do you take us for? We're not monsters. We saved all those poor creatures Shawn kept caged, and we'll make sure the kittens and your dogs are safe as well."

"What are you going to do with Piper and Missy?" Tillie and Vannie would be doubly devastated if they lost both me and the dogs.

"We'll drop them off at the dog park, and eventually someone will figure out they're on their own. You've chipped them, right?"

I nodded.

"Then it'll be fine. Your family will eventually get the dogs back."

"Why are you doing this?"

"I told you. You're a nosy parker. You should have kept on baking cupcakes instead of stirring up trouble," Cheryl said.

Chapter 38

R ebecca began going through my cabinets and drawers in the kitchen, flinging papers to the floor.

"What are you looking for?" I asked.

"We need to make sure you have nothing to incriminate us." Cheryl lowered her voice, apparently trying to mimic the way my voice had cracked. "I want to share all your recipes and honor Eloise."

"That was just a bunch of baloney to cover up you wanting to snoop." Rebecca slammed a drawer shut, and I jumped. "Maybe you handwrote notes, and if not, we'll take your computer just in case."

Had these ladies overlooked the fact that if they blew my house up, any incriminating evidence I might have collected or penned would be destroyed? I wasn't about to share my insight with them, because the longer they hunted for whatever they thought I might have, the longer I had to stay alive.

I decided to see if Cheryl wanted to brag about committing the perfect crime. These two women hadn't been on my radar, and somehow, I doubted Detective Hawkins had considered them serious suspects either.

"Did Eloise really embezzle the condo account, or was that you?"

Cheryl chuckled, not in a friendly manner. "You still haven't figured it out, have you? Is it hard to stomach two old ladies outsmarting you and the police?"

I shrugged. "You obviously meticulously planned this, so it's no surprise that I couldn't figure it out."

Rebecca stomped down the hall that led to the two bedrooms. She didn't pay any attention to me.

"You're right about the planning. I've been looking for a way to get revenge on them both after my son went to prison. I've just been biding my time." Cheryl finally sat down and returned the gun to her purse. "Once I heard about the condo account being set up and funded for the fitness center and upgrades, I knew it would be the perfect opportunity."

"Why did Rebecca get involved?"

"We've been best friends since kindergarten. She's the kind of friend who helps you bury the body, almost literally, as it turns out." She paused when she noticed my raised eyebrows. She lowered her voice. "I look young for my age, and Rebecca has done a little too much sun worshipping her entire life."

"Did Eloise really embezzle the money, or was it you all along?" I asked again.

"You really do have so many questions. It must be maddening to have two old ladies outwit you." Cheryl's smile was gleeful.

This was the third time she'd brought up being old and being smarter. Had she been belittled for her age or her intelligence? Had something happened to push her over the edge?

"Hey, Rebecca," Cheryl hollered, "should I put Emory out of her misery and satisfy her curiosity before she dies or leave her to die wondering what she missed?"

Rebecca poked her head through the hallway entrance. "If you're not going to help me search, I really don't care what you do."

Cheryl waved her away. "Let me have my moment of triumph. I've waited years for this."

Rebecca turned and headed back to the bedrooms. I could hear her muttering to herself, although I couldn't make out the words.

"Now, where were we?" Cheryl rubbed her hands together. "Ah, yes. The embezzlement. That was us. If you'd been sharper, you might have recalled that Eloise was careless with her passwords. I think I specifically mentioned email passwords, but she was the same with not only her bank account passwords but her son's passwords as well. It was a piece of cake accessing the condo account with Eloise's login information and transferring it all to her account. From there, we sent some to Shawn's bank account to make the police think he was involved and the rest to our offshore account that can't be traced. Rebecca was a whiz at setting all that up, and when we get to the Bahamas tomorrow, we'll be living the life."

"And Shawn? Did your son kill him?"

Rage flashed across Cheryl's face, and she leapt to her feet, her hands balled into fists. "Don't you bring my son into this. He knows nothing about Shawn's death."

"Then how did you get the dogs out of Shawn's warehouse? I don't see you or Rebecca being able to secure and drive a large truck to haul them away."

"Shut your mouth. I don't ever want to hear you insinuate Kai had a part in this."

"Give it a rest, Cheryl. She's going to be dead sooner rather than later." Rebecca leaned against the hallway doorframe. "You're the one who felt the need to, what is it, brag? Or is it confess? You might as well tell her the whole story. We need to get out of here as soon as I finish searching the bathroom."

"Fine. Whatever." Cheryl crossed her arms and scowled at Rebecca.

I had the feeling the pair wouldn't be best friends for much longer. "So the truth is Kai played a part in Shawn's murder, didn't he?"

"No! All he did was rescue the dogs." She shook her fist at me. "He had absolutely nothing to do with either death."

"What did he do with the dogs? Sell them to unsuspecting buyers or set up another site to continue the puppy mill?"

"How dare you malign my son! He rescued those dogs and took them to a sanctuary up in Oregon, where he's got a job. He's made amends for his previous life and served his time." Cheryl flew across the room and slapped me across the face. Hard. "I won't stand by while you vilify his name."

Rebecca scurried across the room to her friend's side. She placed a hand on Cheryl's arm when it appeared she was going to strike me again. I was grateful since I already tasted salty, metallic blood on my lips.

"You should apologize, Emory." Rebecca pointed at me and then at Cheryl. "You shouldn't be so quick to jump to conclusions."

"I'm sorry, and I'm relieved to hear that your son has turned over a new leaf."

Cheryl gazed at Rebecca and then at me before returning to the chair. She sat down and continued as if she hadn't just struck me. "After Kai rescued the dogs, Rebecca and I lured Shawn to the warehouse. He was so greedy he fell for us requesting to pick out two puppies to purchase. He couldn't refuse us, either, since we told him we knew about the puppy mill and didn't care. And if he did refuse us, we'd just go to the police with our accusations, so he complied. Just like I knew he would."

I longed to wipe the tears from my cheeks and dab the blood that oozed from my split lip, but I didn't dare move.

Chapter 39

"Cheryl, I didn't find anything. Turn on the gas and set the timer while I load the dogs up." She pulled a package of hot dogs from her purse and held it up. "I think I'll be their new best friend. What do you think?"

Without waiting for an answer, Rebecca plopped the two kittens into their box, picked it up, and made her way to the patio. I heard my dogs yipping in excitement at the prospect of gobbling up hot dogs, and then there was silence.

"But why? Why would you do all of this?" I wanted to gesture with my hands, but their being bound together made it cumbersome.

"I've told you. You're a nosy parker, and you should've stuck to baking." Cheryl began to walk to the kitchen.

"That's not what I meant. Why did you kill Eloise and Shawn? Was it for the money?"

"Revenge is a dish best served cold, and the money is the cherry on top." Cheryl flipped on the kitchen lights and picked up the timer device.

"What did Eloise do to Rebecca? I see how you might want revenge because of what Shawn did to your son, but why pull Rebecca into it?"

"You really shouldn't be so judgmental, Emory, especially about circumstances you know nothing about." Cheryl cackled. "Eloise had an affair with Rebecca's husband and broke the marriage up. Rebecca needs her job and can't afford to quit, especially when she got swindled out of a decent alimony settlement. All this time, Eloise has been poking at Rebecca, belittling her, and essentially setting herself up to be murdered."

"Was it Rebecca who smeared Eloise's face with my buttercream?"

"You bet it was. It seemed a fitting little insult, messing up Eloise's perfect makeup and hair with something gooey and sticky sweet right before I bashed her head." Cheryl's face contorted into a sneer. "Eloise was always going on about how bad sugar was for you and that's why Rebecca and I were chubby. The witch even told Rebecca, too many times to count, that her weight was why she couldn't hang on to her husband and that's why he betrayed her. Trust me. She deserved what she got."

I didn't agree but held back my retort. It wouldn't pay to anger Cheryl and have her conk me over the head and incapacitate me. I wanted to remain fully aware and try to find a way out before the house blew up. A cold chill slithered up my spine when the tick-tick-tick started sounding from the device in Cheryl's hand.

"I think ten minutes should be long enough for Rebecca and me to be far enough away when the blast happens. Don't you think?" Cheryl cackled again. "I have the exact same stovetop at home, so it'll only take me a few seconds to get the gas going, then night-night, Emory. You should be unconscious, if not already dead, before the big boom."

I heard clicking as she turned all four knobs on. I had no idea how she bypassed the starter that would ignite the burner flame, but it was obvious she'd done her research and knew exactly what to do. And then, without another word, Cheryl scooped up my laptop and cell phone and ran from my house without a backward glance at me.

Unsure how long it would take for the gas to knock me out, I struggled against my bonds. I tried ripping the duct tape from my ankles, but with my hands bound, I couldn't make any headway. I stood and tried to drag the sofa with me, but that too was impossible because of the weight. Collapsing onto the sofa, I bent over and rested my head on my bound hands, which rested on my knees.

And then I suddenly remembered a video Brad had shown me when I first had an encounter with a murderer. It had made the rounds on YouTube several years before. The video claimed that if you raised your arms over your head, pulled your hands outward—even if they didn't move—then, as hard as possible, swung your arms down, catching the duct tape on your leg, just above the knee, the duct tape would tear.

The sulfur smell of gas hit my nostrils, and a trickle of sweat ran down my back. Time was running out. How many precious minutes had I already wasted? Did I have five minutes left? Or was it even less? With nothing to lose, I lifted my arms and forced them down over my knee. Pain jolted through my wrists. While the duct tape hadn't ripped clean off, there was progress. Sitting on the soft sofa and not being able to move my legs into a more advantageous position probably contributed to it not working the first time around. I scooted forward so my behind barely sat on the couch and tried again.

That time, it worked. I felt dizzy with relief—or was I dizzy because of the gas? My free hands fumbled with the duct tape that bound my feet. Using my fingernails, I clawed at the tape and finally tore a strip, which allowed me to begin unwinding the tape from my ankles. I couldn't ignore the dizziness that made my head swim and my vision blur. I scrambled for the French doors and, very carefully, opened them wide and rushed out into the fresh air.

Knowing that the timer was clicking down to detonate my house, I gulped in a lungful of air then rushed back in. With trembling hands, I turned all the burners' knobs to off, grabbed up the timer device, and ran as if my life depended on it. I'd barely made it out the gate and stepped into the alleyway when the timer dinged and a spark zinged my hand. Tears coursed down my cheeks as the realization hit that less than ten seconds had stood between me and death.

Chapter 40

U nsure if Tillie was home, I keyed the code into her security gate then rang her doorbell. I didn't have it in me to return to the pool house for my phone or my keys unless there wasn't an alternative.

A minute later, Tillie opened the door.

"What happened to you?" She eyed me up and down, concern flooding her face.

I looked down and found duct tape still trailing from my ankles and wrists. Red welts had appeared on my wrists, and I clung tightly to the timer device. "Can you call 911 for me? We need Detective Hawkins, the police, and the fire department. Cheryl and Rebecca tried to blow me up, and they dognapped Piper and Missy."

I wasn't sure about the fire department, but I wanted to make sure no lingering gas issues remained before I stepped foot back into my house. I sank down onto the steps and cradled my head in my hands. A headache was beginning to build, and all I wanted to do was hug my dogs.

Tillie pursed her lips, pulled her cell from her pocket, and made the call.

True to form, when a Skyler called for help, every agency

showed up in record time, including an ambulance I didn't think I needed.

When the first police officer arrived, I told him to get someone over to the dog park to rescue Piper and Missy and gave him their descriptions. I reached for my phone in my back pocket to send him a photo then remembered Cheryl had taken it along with my laptop. He immediately got on the radio. Another officer approached me, and I rattled off Cheryl and Rebecca's descriptions, although I had no idea what vehicle they'd been driving. They must've parked around the corner, because I hadn't noticed their car when I'd returned to my house from Tillie's.

The firetrucks appeared with sirens blaring and lights flashing—there were three of them along with the paramedic truck—and blocked the entire alleyway. Our neighbors were just going to love us... not. Several firemen approached me, and I explained the attempt at blowing up my house with the gas burners and the timer device. I handed it to one of them.

They trailed off to inspect my house, and a paramedic took their place to examine me. Since the dizziness had subsided and my headache hadn't gotten any worse, he advised me to seek medical treatment if the symptoms worsened. After taking photos in case the detective needed them for evidence, he gently removed the remaining duct tape from my wrists and ankles. He then rubbed an ointment into the abrasions left behind when I'd yanked the tape away in my haste to escape.

Tillie handed me a glass of water and two ibuprofen, which I gulped down just as Detective Hawkins hustled down the alleyway.

Before he reached me, I tugged on Tillie's slacks. "Can you let Brian know what's happened but make sure he knows I'm okay first before you go into any details?"

"You should call him." Tillie extended her cell toward me.

I jutted my chin at the detective making his way toward

me. "I don't think he's going to be happy if I get on the phone now, and I don't want Brian to hear about this from anyone but you."

"You're right. I'll leave you to the detective and make the call." Tillie disappeared into the cool interior of the house.

The detective climbed the steps and sat down beside me. "Ms. Martinez."

"Detective Hawkins." The situation seemed too grave to call him by his first name.

He rubbed his jaw. "When I suggested you bake cupcakes and chat with people, I didn't mean for you to go and get yourself almost blown up."

"It wasn't my intention." I tilted my head to get a better look at his face. "Did you suspect Cheryl and Rebecca?"

"They were suspects, of course, but they weren't at the top of my list." Detective Hawkins opened his iPad. "The money transferred into Shawn's account made me more inclined to follow your theory that Shawn killed his mother and that an unknown rival had killed Shawn and confiscated his animals for their own gain."

"Are puppy mills that big a problem?"

"There seems to be a surge right now. The perpetrators have learned to team up with unscrupulous pet stores—where it's illegal to sell puppy-mill animals—by claiming their puppies are rescue dogs. Granted, it's not as lucrative as selling them as purebred, but there's still a big enough market for both the pet store and the breeders to make a profit."

"That's just despicable." I hoped Cheryl hadn't been lying when she'd said her son had taken Shawn's animals to a sanctuary. I told Detective Hawkins what she'd said, and he promised to try to track them down.

"Are you sure you don't need medical attention?" he asked when he caught me massaging my temples.

"I'll be okay. I think it's just stress and maybe the lingering effects of the gas. I really wasn't exposed to it that long."

"Do you feel up to telling me how this"—he swung his arm around to encompass the clusters of emergency vehicles —"came to be?"

"Believe it or not, it started with two little kittens named Patches and Tigger." I tried to smile, but my lips wouldn't comply. Not yet, at least.

"You're kidding me, right?"

I shook my head. "Long story short, I wound up with two foster kittens. Cheryl and Rebecca said they were interested in adopting them and came by to pick them up."

"They sure fooled you." Detective Hawkins tapped something into his iPad.

"Actually, I'm pretty sure they intend on keeping the kittens." I shivered. "But because they appealed to my heart-strings, I never saw their bad intentions toward me. While I was distracted with getting the kittens ready to go home with them, Cheryl pulled a gun on me, and then they tied me up with duct tape."

He looked down at my red, rashy wrists. "How'd you get away?"

"Do you remember those videos going around YouTube a few years ago about breaking duct tape binding your wrists?"

Detective Hawkins's mouth formed an O. "That really works? I assumed they were pranking, and I never thought to try it."

"It works, although it took me two tries." I rubbed my right wrist, which throbbed. "Cheryl also said she watched some videos on how to make the timer to spark the gas after the coffeepot didn't do the job at the clubhouse."

"Do you know if both the women were responsible for Eloise and Shawn Parker's murders?"

"Cheryl definitely confessed to it while Rebecca tore my house apart, looking for any evidence I might have against them."

His eyebrows rose to alarming heights. "Like blowing up your house wouldn't destroy anything you might have had?"

"That's exactly what I thought. Maybe they didn't know how big the explosion would be and didn't want to worry about any paperwork left behind." I blew out a breath. "It was all on my laptop, which they took."

"That's a shame. It would have been helpful to have any notes you might have had."

"Oh, I still have access to them. I have my files automatically backed up to cloud storage several times a day."

He chuckled. "Of course you do."

I rubbed the back of my neck, the tension making my headache worse.

"Perhaps you should rest up. We've got an APB out for the women, and I have a team going through traffic cams to find out the make, model, and license plate number of their vehicle. Don't worry, we'll find them."

"How did you manage that? You haven't spoken to anyone but me since you got here."

"I was kept apprised on my way here and started people searching while I drove."

"That's very efficient."

"I like to think that's my middle name." His smile was bashful, as if he wasn't certain he should be making a joke just yet.

I gave him a half smile in return. "What about my dogs? Have you heard if they've been found yet?"

"The officers dispatched to the dog park have instructions to personally text me the second they find them." Detective Hawkins looked at his phone. "How are your dogs with men in uniform?"

"Piper was around my ex quite a bit and had no issues, but it's been a couple years. I have no idea about Missy." I thought a moment. "Do the officers have treats or hot dogs with them? Piper and Missy have never met a stranger they haven't befriended when treats are involved. It's how Rebecca got them to go with her."

"I'll let them know. They can probably beg some treats from other people at the park if needed." He swiped his phone on and tapped out a text. "I promise I'll call you the second I hear that they're safe."

It dawned on me that there were a few dog parks in the area, including the dog beach in Huntington Beach. Surely Cheryl wouldn't be so cruel as to dump my dogs there? "Detective Hawkins, do you know what dog park the officers are checking?"

"Let me ask." He tapped out another text, and within a moment, his phone vibrated. "They said they're at the Newport Beach one on Avocado but see no signs of your dogs."

"There's a dog park off the 55 over by the fairgrounds. If Cheryl and Rebecca were driving to the airport to catch a flight or heading out of state, they'd pass right by that one." I nervously rubbed my hands together, worried that my dogs would never be found.

Detective Hawkins tapped in a phone number and made a call instead of texting. While he gave the officer directions to the dog park, I watched the firefighters leave my patio and head toward their firetrucks. The fireman who'd first talked to me headed my way. Brian and Vannie trailed him, weaving their way around the clusters of emergency personnel still hanging about.

"Ms. Martinez, we've finished inspecting your house, and it's safe to enter." He looked at the detective, who still had his cell phone to his ear. "Although you'd better wait until he gives the all clear. They're probably going to want to collect forensic evidence on top of the report I'll have for him."

"Thank you."

He dipped his head then left to join his crew.

I hurried down the steps to meet Brian and Vannie. They gave me a sandwich hug.

"I'm so relieved you're safe. I got here just as soon as I could." Brian's lips grazed my hair.

"Tillie sounded frantic when she called me." Vannie took a step back then smoothed my frazzled hair from my face. "Are you really okay?"

"I promise, I'm fine aside from a little headache."

Brian released me when Detective Hawkins joined us.

"Emory, the two officers are heading to the second dog park. I'll call you the second I hear anything." He looked at his watch. "Can I schedule you for a formal statement tomorrow afternoon, say about one? I can meet you at your house."

I reached for my back pocket, where I generally kept my phone, to add the appointment to my calendar. It wasn't there. I blamed my exposure to the gas for my forgetfulness. "Ugh. I keep forgetting they took my phone, so you can't even call me when our dogs are found. Vannie, let me have your phone."

She unlocked the screen and offered it to me. I opened Messenger and found my name then clicked on the cupcake I'd set as my profile photo. It took a moment, but then my phone's location showed up on the 91 Freeway. Could they be heading to Shawn's property in Norco? I showed the screen to Detective Hawkins, who called it in.

"We'll have someone waiting at the Norco property in case they stop there. The CHP have been notified to be on the lookout for the two women, but unfortunately, I haven't heard back about the make and model of the car."

"I'll bet they dropped the dogs off at the dog park next to the fairgrounds. Let me give you Vannie's number, and you can call her when our dogs are located." I rattled off the number, and Detective Hawkins entered it into his contacts.

"Now, about getting a statement from you tomorrow. Will one o'clock work?"

"That'll be fine. Do you know if I can go back to my house today?"

"They should finish processing it within the next couple of hours. I'll have an officer let Vannie know via text." He shook my hand then nodded at Brian and Vannie. "I promise, I'll call the second your dogs are found."

Chapter 41

The second the detective was out of earshot, Vannie whirled around to face me. Her face was pale, which made her freckles seem all the more vivid. "What happened to Piper and Missy? Why are they missing? They're not hurt, are they?"

"They were dognapped, but Rebecca promised they'd drop them off at the dog park and that you'd be able to easily find them." I didn't mention that the two women had had no intention of me being able to find the dogs.

My choice of words wasn't lost on Brian, and he pulled me into another tight hug. "Come inside. We need to check on Gram. Vannie was right, she did sound frantic."

Looking around, I spotted Detective Hawkins already speaking with a group of officers. He didn't need me any longer, so I followed Brian into the house. We found Tillie sitting at the kitchen table, her hands toying with an empty teacup. She'd never looked so fragile or vulnerable in all the time I'd known her. I knelt in front of her.

"I'm fine, Tillie, and we're going to get Piper and Missy back, safe and sound." I grasped her cold hands and gently rubbed them to warm them.

Vannie started a kettle of water for tea, and Brian retrieved the brandy from the cupboard. He poured a generous amount into the teacup and placed it in front of Tillie. I released her hands so she could take a sip, which she did. Her hands shook as she tried to set the teacup down, so I took it from her and placed it on the saucer.

"I feel like this is all my fault." Tillie's voice was tremulous. "I get caught up in the thrill of trying to help you find out whodunit, but you're the one who always ends up paying the price. And now our dear, sweet dogs are out there, lost, because of me. I might have lost all of you."

"Tillie, please listen to me. You didn't do this. This entire tragedy rests solely on Cheryl and Rebecca's shoulders. If they hadn't wanted revenge or allowed greed to color their judgment, none of this would ever have happened." I took her hands back into mine. "I survived, and the dogs will too. Justice will be served instead of those two women living their lives out on a beach in the Caribbean. And do you know why?"

Tillie's lips quirked at the sides. "I'm sure you're going to tell me even if I want to continue to wallow in guilt and self-pity."

"You're darn right I'm going to tell you." I kissed her cheek then rose to sit in the kitchen chair beside her. My head still felt a little wobbly. "It's because we cared enough to find justice for two unlovable people. No matter that they were terrible people, especially Shawn, they still deserved to have their killers caught and prosecuted."

"You sound like a superhero, my dear." Tillie picked up the hot cup of tea Vannie had prepared for her. She took a sip, and I was grateful her hands no longer shook as she set it back down.

Vannie set a mug of tea in front of me along with a plateful of cookies. "I think some sugar and caffeine will help you too."

"Thanks. I really didn't eat lunch today, and I'm feeling kind of shaky." I nibbled on a cookie.

Brian moved to stand behind my chair and kneaded my shoulders with his strong fingers. I sank back into the seat and concentrated on allowing my tension to ease.

"You practically have rocks in your shoulders. Van, pour some brandy in Em's mug. I think she needs it more than Gram."

I covered the tea mug with my hand. "I'll pass. My head still feels a bit woozy from the gas exposure or maybe from the adrenaline. I'm not sure that alcohol is the best thing for me right now."

Vannie came to the table and sat on the other side of me. "Do you feel up to telling us what happened? If not, I understand."

The brandy must've perked Tillie up, because her eyes brightened, and her shoulders weren't slumped any more. She reminded me of a wilted plant that had just received a good watering. "You'll feel much better if you share all the details with us. Plus, it'll be good practice for when you have to talk to the detective again."

"Gram…" Brian almost growled. "She doesn't have to talk about it if she doesn't want to."

I covered his hand with mine and gave it a squeeze. "It's all right. I think I do need to talk about it and dissect what happened."

I gave them as many details as I could, and just as Tillie began asking questions, Vannie's phone rang. We froze in place. I willed it to be Detective Hawkins bearing good news about Piper and Missy.

The phone rang again, and Tillie hissed, "Answer it."

Vannie grabbed the cell, tapped the screen, and raised it to her ear. "Hello?"

I could hear a male voice speaking but couldn't determine

who it was or what he was saying. Vannie's face was tight with worry, and then she relaxed. Relief flooded my body when she smiled broadly.

"Thank you, Detective. You have no idea how happy your news makes us." She disconnected and gripped Tillie's hand. "Piper and Missy are on their way here. The officers found them cavorting with other dogs at the park, having a blast. They said both dogs look unharmed and were happy to gobble up some of the treats the officers had before jumping in the back seat of the car. Oh, he did say they were both pretty muddy, so we might want to be prepared with a garden hose and towels to clean them off when they get here."

Brian jumped up from the table. "I'll get their leashes and get the hose ready."

I started to stand, but Vannie gently pushed me back down. "You sit and relax with Tillie. You've both had a trying day."

"But I want to see the girls when they get here." I sounded like a disappointed child, but I also felt like I'd been responsible for the dogs and had endangered them by allowing them to be dognapped, no matter the outcome.

"Why don't you sit out on the patio, and we'll wash the dogs out there." Brian chortled. "You and Gram can tell us how we're doing it wrong and then get sprayed with doggie water when they shake to dry off."

"It sounds like a plan to me." Tillie stood, and we walked together to the patio, arm in arm.

Within fifteen minutes, a very muddy pair of pups had jumped onto my lap and covered my face with doggie kisses despite Brian's very best efforts at containing them. I believed they somehow knew I had been in danger and wanted to reassure themselves that I was safe. Already muddy and wet, I jumped into the fray of shampooing and bathing the dogs. It didn't take long before all of us—except Tillie, who remained looking chic—were soaking wet, and it turned into a water fight. Giggling like schoolkids, we splashed and played with the dogs, which turned into the best way to begin healing my heavy heart.

Chapter 42

Two days later

Once again, our family gathered for our Sunday dinner. Carrie and her family had completely recovered from their bout of flu, and Piper and Missy showed no lingering effects from the dognapping. It probably didn't hurt that while they'd been spoiled before, they were now over-the-top spoiled by everyone in the family.

For the first thirty minutes after they arrived, my nieces and nephew chased Piper and Missy around. When the kids finally settled into the playroom to play with the kittens—which we'd adopted once Cheryl and Rebecca had been taken into custody—we caught everyone up on the arrest of the murderers.

"It's what we suspected. Once Cheryl and Rebecca left my house, they headed to Shawn's property." I handed my mother a glass of chardonnay and poured another for Vannie. "Detective Lankershim was there waiting for them thanks to Vannie and me sharing our iPhone locations with each other."

"Good heavens," my mother exclaimed. "Why would they go back to the scene of the crime?"

"They were greedy. Apparently, at some point, Eloise had

bragged about the amount of cash her son kept in a safe at his house. They thought they'd be able to figure out a way to open it and take it with them." I handed Brian a glass of wine when he came up behind me. "They were thwarted from searching right after killing him when a UPS truck made a delivery, and they worried they might be placed at the scene of the murder if they hung around."

"How much cash are you talking about? A few thousand doesn't seem worth the risk, especially with the amount they'd already embezzled," Thomas said.

"According to what Cheryl told Detective Lankershim, who shared the information with Detective Hawkins, who finally told me..." I drew in a breath to extend the suspense. "It was over two hundred grand."

Thomas whistled. "Who keeps that kind of cash on hand?"

"Someone who's running an illegal enterprise," Tillie said as she took the glass of wine I'd just poured.

"Detective Hawkins also told me they arrested Karla for her part in laundering the proceeds from the puppy mill. She downplayed her part in the enterprise when she talked to me about it, but the detectives found out the truth." I still hadn't shared her health issues with anyone, and as far as I was concerned, she was the state's problem now. She'd turned a blind eye to the plight of the animals, and she deserved whatever prison sentence was handed down.

"Did you hear if they found the dogs taken from Shawn's property?" Brad asked.

"They're all safe and sound at a dog rehabilitation center in Oregon." I'd almost cried when Detective Hawkins had shared the details. "The center is on a twenty-acre farm, and there are professionals who work with the abused mother dogs to help them overcome their trauma. The staff also works hard to find appropriate homes for the puppies, with the adoptee families knowing that potential health issues may be in the dogs' future."

"So Cheryl did tell the truth about her son?" Vannie asked.

"Yes, and he has a solid alibi for the time of the murder. From what I gather, Kai took the opportunity while in prison to gain an education and has dedicated his life to helping rescued puppy-mill dogs." I grimaced. "He was devastated when he found out about his mother and Rebecca."

"I hope those two women are put away for life after trying to kill you and then dognapping my granddogs." Mother, who'd never been overly fond of my dogs, or of any dogs for that matter, had actually ruffled their ears and slipped them each a treat when she'd arrived. Then she'd wrapped me in a tight hug and held me close for several minutes.

"Between the two murders, the attempted murder, the dognapping, the catnapping, and the embezzlement, I think it's safe to say they won't be getting out until they're very, very old women," I assured her.

"Speaking of catnapping, are you sure you're up for keeping both the kittens?" Carrie asked. "I feel bad dumping them on you, but I was desperate. Between the allergies, the kids having the flu, and then me coming down with the crud, I was at my wits' end."

"It's fine. The dogs seem to have accepted Patches and Tigger into the household, and there are three of us to share cat duties," I answered.

"And we want to help take care of them, too, Auntie Em," Kaylee said as she entered the room. She cradled Tigger in her arms as she walked, moving very calmly compared to her usual rambunctious frenzy.

"Me too, me too," Tommy babbled as he trailed his sister.

Sophie brought up the rear, holding Patches as if the kitten was a fragile piece of glass. "Do they need to eat? Can we feed them?"

"They don't need dinner, but you can give each of them a treat while we put dinner on the table. And then it'll be time for you to eat." I went to the treat cupboard, which held more treats than any pet should ever need, selected a foil bag, and pulled three treats out. I broke the treats in half and handed two pieces to each of the kids. "You can take turns feeding these to the kittens."

Piper and Missy, not wanting to miss out on their own treats, went through their short repertoire of tricks unbidden—sit, high-ten, and lie down—before pawing at my leg. I took another foil bag down and went through the same process I'd done for the kittens. Once the kids had fed the kittens, I gave them the dog treats to dole out then left them to entertain themselves while I helped bring the food to the table.

It didn't take long for all of us to settle in and pile our plates high with the delicious meal Brian had prepared. He'd gone the comfort route of creamy, cheesy pasta and garlic bread.

"Brad, dear," my mother said when there was a lull in the conversation, "Emory has given me a copy of everything that needs to be done for your wedding. Can we sit down and go over the entire list on Tuesday?"

"Uh, sure, Addie." Brad gave me the side-eye, which I took to mean he wasn't terribly happy that I'd tossed his wedding planning to my mother. "What time shall I come to your house?"

"Ten is probably best since it'll take a good part of the day to go over all the details. And let's meet at Emory's house. She needs to be in on the planning." Mother gazed at me with a smirk on her face. "It'll be good experience for when she plans her next wedding."

Brian, who'd just taken a sip of wine, choked and coughed. Tillie pounded on his back while my nieces clamored to be my bridesmaids. My face blazed hot, and I felt like crawling beneath the table to join Piper and Missy.

Carrie, who, forgivably, was still feeling a bit weak and clearly wasn't thinking straight, piped up, "Oh! Did you get engaged this week, Em and Brian? I can't believe you didn't tell me when it happened. Have you set a date yet?"

Tillie chortled so hard she almost couldn't catch her breath. "Priceless. This is just priceless."

Brian's face turned cherry red, which probably matched mine if the heat infusing my body was any indication.

I held my hands up in a T shape. "Time out, people. We're not engaged, and this is Brad and Gabe's big day, not Dump on Em and Brian Day."

Mother raised her wineglass to me and winked as Brian took my hand in his.

"Sorry to disappoint everyone, but we've decided to take it slow for now." Brian looked to me as if for confirmation, and I nodded.

Sophie and Kaylee were disappointed, but they quickly got over it when Brad and Gabe asked them to help pass out small mason jars containing votive candles during their reception before the dancing began. My sister looked more than a little worried, but Gabe reassured her that the mason jars were actually plastic, not glass, and the candles were battery operated and did not burn with real flames. She relaxed after that and enjoyed the chatter between her daughters and Brad on what colors the wedding would be and what kind of dress they should wear. Brad, bless his heart, offered to have the florist make flower crowns for the girls to wear.

Once my nieces turned their attention elsewhere, he pointed at me and mouthed, "Make a note." Apparently, I wasn't getting out of the wedding-planning duties quite as easily as I'd imagined.

The evening was a balm to my soul, and I was grateful to Vannie for instigating the weekly get-togethers. I told her so while we washed dishes after dinner. "Next time, you should invite Teresa back if that's something you both would enjoy."

She smiled coyly. "Maybe, but we're taking a page from your book and taking things slow for now."

I hugged her. "I want you to be happy and not feel like you can't invite anyone to our dinners, whether they're just friends or otherwise."

She hugged me back. "Thanks. I appreciate it, and so does Teresa."

By the time the family left, it was nearly nine. Brian grabbed the leashes for Piper and Missy then whispered the magic word, "walk." Both dogs sprang to their feet and scrabbled for the front door. Brian held out his hand to me. "Care to join me for a walk?"

"I wouldn't dream of missing it." I joined my hand with his, then we broke apart to say good night to Tillie and Vannie.

"Be good, you two." Tillie chortled again.

It made me happy to see her in such high spirits after the close call I'd had on Friday.

"On second thought, forget being good. Just have some fun."

"We'll do both, Gram." Brian kissed her cheek, and I followed suit before blowing Vannie a kiss.

With the dogs whining at the front door, we half jogged to reach them. Leashes clipped on, the dogs pulled us out the gate and down the street for half a block before stopping to sniff every single weed or solitary tree. Brian picked up the pace and led us through several streets, where I'd never ventured before. He finally stopped in front of a house that hosted a For Sale sign on the meager lawn.

"Emory, I know we agreed to take it slow, and I'm in no way trying to rush you." He paused for a breath and gazed into my eyes.

My heart skipped a beat and then began pounding. It sounded louder than a booming bass drum. I tried to swallow, but my mouth was suddenly dry.

"I'd like to be with you more than a couple nights a week, and I desperately want to see your beautiful face every morning when I wake up." He swung his arm out to gesture at the house. "I know you want to remain close to Tillie, and this house is only a five-minute walk from hers. Okay, maybe more if you let the dogs sniff their way to her house. What would you think about moving in with me?"

"Oh, Brian, you don't know how happy that makes me!" I flung my arms around his neck, kissed him, then took a step back. "But what about your house? I know you've put a lot of effort into making it your home, and I don't want to be the reason you regret giving it up."

He brushed his fingers along my cheek. "It's not a home if you're not there. And if you don't like this house, we can look for something different."

I was all too aware of home prices on Balboa Island, and I also knew Brian's restaurant had experienced some financial difficulties in the past. I certainly wouldn't be able to contribute toward the purchase price or the mortgage, which worried me. "But how can we afford something here?"

Brian dropped his hand. "Are you looking for excuses for not moving in together? If you're not ready, please just say so."

I took his hand back into mine and kissed his cheek. "Yes, Brian, I do want to move in with you. I'm just hung up on the logistics. But I'm very grateful for your thoughtfulness in taking my relationship with Tillie into consideration. And Vannie too."

"Actually, Vannie and Tillie both are the ones who helped me see how it could be done." He grinned. "I think Vannie has her sights set on moving into the pool house if you decide to move in with me."

"I don't want you to think you have to buy another house to move into with me just because they want us to." I was slightly horrified at the thought. What if it didn't work out with Brian? I'd be homeless all over again.

"Emory, I've wanted this for a long time but wasn't sure how to make it work. They helped me with details and have been keeping their ears and eyes open for houses that come on the market that are close enough for you to walk to Gram's." He gestured back at the house. "This just came on the market today. Would you like for me to set up an appointment to see it soon?"

I lowered my head and hoped Brian wouldn't see the heat rushing to my face. "I'd love to, but, ah, you do realize I'm almost broke? I really can't help much with the mortgage."

He lifted my chin with his finger. "It doesn't matter. One of the reasons I've put this decision off until now was because I've been waiting for my thirtieth birthday."

I raised an eyebrow. "Which happened three weeks ago."

"Exactly. My maternal grandparents set up a trust for me, and I couldn't access it, except for educational purposes, until I turned thirty. And here we are."

"Your trust is large enough to purchase a house on Balboa Island?" My jaw must've dropped, because Brian laughed and kissed me.

"Yes, but definitely not large enough to purchase a water-front house the size of Tillie's."

"I… I don't know what to say." Naturally, I was happy, but part of me was frightened. "I don't want you to think I'm taking advantage of you by not being able to contribute much to the mortgage."

Brian shook his head. "Gram warned me you'd be worried about it. She and her attorney have come up with a solution to put your mind at ease. Hopefully."

"She really is determined to make this work for us, isn't she?" I couldn't help but grin at Tillie's meddling ways.

"You have no idea."

The dogs tugged at their leashes, ready to return home, so we obliged and began walking.

"They suggested that my trust purchase the house and the title remain in the trust's name. That way, you and I get to live rent free. Historically, property is a great investment, because if you hang on to the property long enough, the value always increases."

"What about your house in Laguna? Aren't you going to miss it?"

"If I'm with you, it means nothing to me."

He pulled the dogs to a stop and told them to sit. Remarkably, they listened to him.

Brian brushed hair from my face. "What do you say, Emory? Will you help me find a house where we can make a home together?"

I gazed into his dark-green eyes, the same eyes that had captured my attention from the first time I'd met him and made me think of calm pools of water deep in the forest. "Yes, Brian. I'd love to live with you, and I can't think of anything that I've ever wanted more."

Recipes

Golden Apple Cocktail Cupcakes

MAKES 12 CUPCAKES

Ingredients

Cupcakes:

1 1/4 cups all-purpose flour

1 teaspoon baking powder

1/2 teaspoon baking soda

1/2 teaspoon salt

1 teaspoon cinnamon

1/4 cup plus 1 tablespoon Sour Apple Pucker schnapps

2 tablespoons Goldschläger liqueur

1/2 cup unsalted butter, melted

1/2 cup granulated sugar

1/2 cup brown sugar

2 eggs

1/2 cup (3 ounces) peeled and grated apple

Buttercream Frosting:

3/4 cup unsalted butter, room temperature

5 cups confectioners' sugar

1/2 teaspoon cinnamon

1/2 teaspoon salt

1 1/2 tablespoons Sour Apple Pucker schnapps

1 1/2 tablespoons Goldschläger

Optional Garnish:

Cinnamon sticks

Instructions

Cupcakes:

Preheat the oven to 350 degrees F. Line a 12-cup muffin tin with paper liners.

In a medium mixing bowl, whisk together flour, baking powder, baking soda, salt, and cinnamon. Set aside.

In a liquid measuring cup, mix together the Sour Apple Pucker and Goldschläger.

Using an electric mixer, whip together the butter and sugars on medium speed for 2 minutes. Beat in eggs, one at a time, until well blended. Alternating in three additions, add the flour and the liqueur mixture. Mix until combined, but don't overbeat. Stir in the grated apples.

Divide batter between the prepared muffin cups. Bake 18 to 20 minutes or until a skewer inserted into the center comes out mostly clean. A few moist crumbs clinging to the skewer is fine.

Allow to cool in the muffin tin for 5 minutes then remove to a wire rack and cool completely before frosting.

Buttercream Frosting:

Using an electric mixer, cream the butter until light and fluffy, about 3 minutes. Beat in the confectioners' sugar, cinnamon, and salt until combined.

Add 1 tablespoon Sour Apple Pucker and 1 tablespoon Goldschläger. Add additional Sour Apple Pucker, 1 teaspoon at a time, if buttercream is too stiff, until desired consistency is reached. Beat the buttercream on medium-high speed for 5 minutes until light and fluffy.

Transfer the buttercream to a piping bag fitted with a large star tip.

Pipe swirls of buttercream onto the cupcakes when they are completely cooled. If desired, garnish with cinnamon sticks.

Golden Apple Cocktails
MAKES 1 COCKTAIL

Ingredients
1/2 ounce Goldschläger
1 ounce Sour Apple Pucker schnapps
Optional Garnish:
A small apple cut into thinly sliced rounds

Instructions
Fill a cocktail shaker with ice and add the Goldschläger and Sour Apple Pucker schnapps.

Vigorously shake until thoroughly chilled then strain into a prepared martini glass.

Garnish with apple slices if desired.

Apple Pie-Filled Cupcakes
MAKES 16 TO 18 CUPCAKES

Ingredients
Cupcakes:
1 box vanilla cake mix

Ingredients called for on box: eggs, water, and oil

1 teaspoon cinnamon

1/4 teaspoon nutmeg

Apple Pie Filling:
1 pound tart apples, peeled, cored, and chopped into 1/2-inch cubes

2 tablespoons unsalted butter

1/4 cup brown sugar

1 teaspoons cinnamon

1/4 teaspoon nutmeg

1/4 teaspoon ground ginger

1/2 teaspoon salt

Buttercream Frosting:
3/4 cup unsalted butter, room temperature

1/2 teaspoon cinnamon

1/2 teaspoon salt

5 cups confectioners' sugar

3 to 4 tablespoons frozen apple juice concentrate, defrosted

Optional Garnish:

Cinnamon sticks

Coarse demerara sugar

Instructions

Cupcakes:

Preheat the oven to 350 degrees F. Line two 12-cup muffin tins with paper liners.

Prepare the cupcakes according to the cake-mix package directions, adding the cinnamon and nutmeg to the bowl with the dry mix.

Fill the muffin cups 3/4 full with the prepared batter and bake for 17 to 20 minutes, until a wooden skewer inserted into the center comes out mostly clean. A few moist crumbs are fine.

Remove the cupcakes from the tins and allow to cool completely on a wire rack.

Apple Pie Filling:

In a medium-sized saucepan, melt the butter. Add the remaining ingredients, stirring until combined and the apples are coated with the mixture.

Cook over medium heat until the apples soften, about 12 to 15 minutes. Stir frequently and lower heat when the filling begins to bubble. Cook until the sauce thickens and begins to evaporate.

Remove from heat and cool completely.

Buttercream Frosting:

Using a stand mixer, beat the butter until creamy, about 3 minutes on medium-high speed. Reduce the speed to low and add the cinnamon and salt. Once combined, slowly add the confectioners' sugar.

Once the sugar has been incorporated, add 3 tablespoons of the defrosted apple juice concentrate. Increase the speed to medium high and beat until light and fluffy. If needed, add additional apple juice, 1 teaspoon at a time, until the desired consistency is reached.

Transfer the buttercream to a piping bag fitted with a large star tip.

Putting it together:

Using a rounded teaspoon measuring spoon, scoop out the centers of the cupcakes.

Spoon the cooled filling into the centers, packing it in.

Using a large star tip, pipe swirls of the buttercream over the tops of the cupcakes. Sprinkle with demerara sugar and garnish with cinnamon sticks if desired.

Apple Oatmeal Cookies

Ingredients

1 cup old-fashioned rolled oats (not instant)
2 ounces apple crisps (I used Tree Top brand)
1/4 cup frozen apple juice concentrate, defrosted
3/4 cup unsalted butter, room temperature
1/2 cup granulated sugar
1/2 cup brown sugar
1 egg
1 teaspoon vanilla
1 1/2 cups all-purpose flour
1/2 teaspoon baking soda
1/2 teaspoon salt
1 1/2 teaspoons cinnamon
1 cup white chocolate chips

Instructions

Add the oats and apple crisps in a small bowl and sprinkle the apple concentrate over the mixture. Stir together until combined. Allow to rest for at least 20 minutes so the oats absorb the juice.

Cream the butter and sugars together for about 2 minutes. Add the egg and vanilla and beat until combined.

Whisk together the flour, baking soda, salt, and cinnamon. Slowly add to the butter mixture and mix until fully incorporated.

Beat in the oat-and-apple crisp mixture then mix in the white chocolate chips.

Cover the mixing bowl with plastic wrap and refrigerate for 1 hour. Remove from refrigerator and allow to sit at room temperature while the oven preheats.

Preheat oven to 350 degrees F and line baking sheets with parchment paper.

Form the cookie dough into walnut-sized balls and place on the prepared baking sheets.

Bake one sheet at a time for 9 to 11 minutes, rotating the sheet halfway through the baking time. Edges should appear golden brown.

Remove from oven and allow the cookies to rest on the baking sheet for 5 minutes then place them on a wire rack to cool completely.

Store in an airtight container in the refrigerator for up to 5 days.

Caramel Apple Pie Bars

Ingredients

Crust:
1/2 cup unsalted butter, melted
1/4 cup granulated sugar
1 teaspoon vanilla
1/4 teaspoon salt
1 cup all-purpose flour

Apple Pie Filling:
2 large apples, peeled, cored, and thinly sliced
2 tablespoons all-purpose flour
3 tablespoons brown sugar
1/8 teaspoon salt
1 teaspoon cinnamon
Pinch of cloves

Topping:
1/2 cup old-fashioned oats
1/3 cup packed brown sugar
1/2 teaspoon cinnamon
1/4 cup all-purpose flour
1/4 teaspoon salt
1/4 cup unsalted butter, cold and cubed

Your favorite caramel sauce

Instructions
Crust:
Preheat the oven to 300 degrees F. Line an 8-inch square baking dish with foil or parchment paper, leaving enough to hang over the edges. Spritz with nonstick baking spray and set aside.

Mix the melted butter, sugar, vanilla, and salt together in a medium bowl then stir in the flour until well combined. Firmly pat the mixture into the prepared baking dish.

Bake for 15 minutes then remove from the oven and set aside while you prepare the rest of the dish.

Increase the oven heat to 350 degrees F.

Apple Pie Filling:
Toss the sliced apples with flour, sugar, salt, cinnamon, and cloves until apples are evenly coated. Set aside.

Topping:
Combine the oats, brown sugar, cinnamon, flour, and salt in a medium-sized bowl. Cut the chilled butter in with a pastry blender or fork until the mixture forms small crumbs.

Assembly:
Layer the apples tightly on top of the crust. Press down to pack them in.

Sprinkle the topping evenly over the apple layer, pressing gently.

Bake for 30 to 35 minutes, until the topping is golden brown.

Remove from the oven and allow to cool for at least 30 minutes then place in the refrigerator until thoroughly chilled, at least 2 hours.

Using the foil or parchment overhang, lift the bars out and cut into 16 squares.

Drizzle with your favorite caramel sauce right before serving.

Store in an airtight container in the refrigerator for up to 3 days.

Tip:

Recipe can be doubled and baked in a 9 x 13-inch baking dish. Bake the crust 18 minutes, and extend the assembled baking-dish baking time to a total of 45 to 50 minutes.

Maple-Glazed Apple Blondies

Ingredients

Apple Filling:

2 large apples, peeled, cored, and finely chopped

2 tablespoons brown sugar

1 tablespoon unsalted butter

1/2 teaspoon vanilla extract

1 teaspoon cinnamon

1/4 teaspoon salt

Blondies:

1 cup unsalted butter, room temperature

1/4 cup granulated sugar

1 cup brown sugar

2 eggs

1 1/2 teaspoons maple extract (or substitute vanilla extract)

2 cups all-purpose flour

1 teaspoon baking powder

1/2 teaspoon salt

Maple Glaze:

2 tablespoons unsalted butter

1/4 cup pure maple syrup

1/4 teaspoon maple extract (or substitute vanilla extract)
1/2 cup confectioners' sugar

Instructions

Preheat the oven to 350 degrees F. Line a 9-inch square baking dish with foil or parchment paper, leaving enough to hang over the edges. Spritz with nonstick baking spray and set aside.

Apple Filling:

Combine the apples, sugar, butter, vanilla, cinnamon, and salt in a medium-sized saucepan. Cook over medium heat for 5 minutes, until the sugar dissolves and the mixture is hot. Remove from heat and allow to cool while you prepare the blondies.

Blondies:

Using an electric mixer, cream the butter and sugars until light and fluffy, about 3 minutes.

Beat in the eggs, one at a time, until thoroughly incorporated. Add the maple extract.

In a separate bowl, whisk together the flour, baking powder, and salt. Slowly add to the butter and sugar mixture and stir until combined.

Spread half the batter evenly over the bottom of the prepared pan. Spread the apple mixture over the batter layer then top with the remaining blondie batter, spreading evenly.

Bake for 28 to 33 minutes, until the edges and top are golden brown.

Remove from the oven and allow to cool on a wire rack for 20 minutes then spread the glaze over the top. Cool the bars completely before cutting into squares.

Maple Glaze:

Place the butter, maple syrup, and maple extract in a medium-sized microwave-safe glass bowl. Heat for 60 seconds in the microwave then stir until the butter is melted. If needed, heat in additional 15-second intervals, stirring well each time.

Stir in the confectioners' sugar until the glaze is smooth. Cool for 5 minutes then pour over the warm bars.

Allow the bars to cool completely before cutting into squares.

Store in an airtight container for up to 2 days at room temperature or in the refrigerator for up to 4 days.

Cinnamon-Apple Fritter Bread

Ingredients

Apple Filling:
2 apples, peeled, cored, and chopped into small cubes

2 tablespoons granulated sugar

1 teaspoon ground cinnamon

Brown Sugar Mixture:
1/3 cup brown sugar

1 teaspoon ground cinnamon

1/4 teaspoon nutmeg

Bread Batter:
1 1/2 cups all-purpose flour

1 1/2 teaspoons baking powder

1/2 teaspoon salt

1/2 teaspoon cinnamon

1/2 cup unsalted butter

2/3 cup granulated sugar

2 eggs, room temperature

2 teaspoons vanilla extract

1/2 cup whole milk

Glaze:
3/4 cup confectioners' sugar

1/2 teaspoon vanilla extract

1 tablespoon whole milk

Instructions

Preheat the oven to 350 degrees F. Grease and flour a 9" x 5" loaf pan or spritz with non-stick cooking spray that contains flour.

Apple Filling:

Sprinkle the chopped apples with 2 tablespoons granulated sugar and 1 teaspoon ground cinnamon. Toss to coat the apples then set aside.

Brown Sugar Mixture:

In a small bowl, combine the brown sugar, 1 teaspoon ground cinnamon, and nutmeg together. Set aside.

Bread Batter:

In a medium-sized bowl, whisk flour, baking powder, salt, and 1/2 teaspoon ground cinnamon together. Set aside.

In the bowl of a standing mixer beat the butter with 2/3 cup granulated sugar on medium speed until light and fluffy, about 2 to 3 minutes.

Add eggs, one at a time, and beat until incorporated. Mix in vanilla extract.

Add the flour mixture to the mixing bowl and stir until blended on low speed.

Add the milk to the batter and stir just until it is completely incorporated.

Putting it together:

Drain any liquid from the apple mixture and discard liquid.

Spread half the batter into the bread pan and top with half the apple mixture. Sprinkle half the brown sugar mixture on top of the apples.

Layer the remaining batter into the loaf pan, then repeat adding the remaining apples and brown sugar mixture.

Pat the brown sugar mixture down on top of the batter

then, using a butter knife, swirl the brown sugar and apple mixture through the batter.

Bake for 50 to 60 minutes. Bread should be golden brown and feel fairly firm to the touch. A wooden skewer inserted into the center should come out without any doughy batter clinging to it. Apples may cling to the skewer making it appear that the bread might not be done, so use the touch test as well.

Allow the bread to cool in the pan for 15 minutes. Invert bread onto a plate and then transfer to a serving platter, right side up.

Whisk the confectioners' sugar, vanilla, and milk together until the glaze is smooth. Drizzle over the warm bread.

Let the bread cool before slicing.

Apple Bundt Cake

Ingredients

Cake:
1 1/4 cup vegetable oil
2 cups granulated sugar
2 eggs
2 teaspoons vanilla
3 cups all-purpose flour
1 1/2 teaspoons baking soda
1 teaspoon salt
1 1/2 teaspoons cinnamon
1/2 teaspoon nutmeg
Pinch of cloves
1 cup chopped pecans
1 cup shredded sweetened coconut
3 cups apples, peeled, cored, and finely chopped

Optional Drizzle:
3/4 cup confectioners' sugar
1/4 teaspoon cinnamon
2 tablespoons apple juice

Instructions

Preheat the oven to 325 degrees F. Heavily grease then sprinkle with granulated sugar to cover the surface of a 10-inch (12-cup) Bundt pan. Set aside.

Using a stand mixer, beat together the vegetable oil and sugar. Add the eggs, one at a time, and beat well after each addition. Mix in the vanilla.

In a medium-sized bowl, whisk together the flour, baking soda, salt, cinnamon, nutmeg, and cloves. Slowly add to the sugar mixture and mix until well combined.

Stir in the pecans, coconut, and apples, then spread batter into the prepared Bundt pan.

Bake for 60 to 65 minutes, or until a long skewer inserted into the center comes out clean.

Let cake cool in the pan on a wire rack for 10 minutes. Invert the cake onto a serving platter and remove the Bundt pan. Allow cake to completely cool.

Drizzle:

Mix the confectioners' sugar, cinnamon, and 1 tablespoon plus 1 teaspoon apple juice together, stirring until completely smooth. Add additional apple juice to the mixture if a thinner consistency is desired. Drizzle over the cooled cake and allow to set for 30 minutes before serving.

Cinnamon Apple Coffee Cake
with Streusel

Ingredients

Cinnamon Streusel:

1 1/2 cups all-purpose flour
1/2 cup brown sugar
1/4 cup granulated sugar
3/4 teaspoon salt
1 teaspoon cinnamon
1/2 cup unsalted butter, melted
1 teaspoon vanilla

Cake:

1/4 cup unsalted butter, room temperature
1/2 cup granulated sugar
1 egg
1 teaspoon vanilla
1/2 cup sour cream
1 cup all-purpose flour
1/2 teaspoon salt
1/2 teaspoon baking powder
1/4 teaspoon baking soda
1 large tart apple, peeled, cored and chopped

Instructions

Preheat the oven to 350 degrees F. Grease an 8-inch round cake tin and line with parchment paper. Set aside.

Cinnamon Streusel:

Stir together the flour, sugars, salt, and cinnamon, then slowly pour in the melted butter and vanilla. Stir until the butter is fully incorporated. Set aside.

Cake:

In the bowl of a standing mixer, cream together the butter and granulated sugar. Mix for 3 minutes on medium speed then beat in the egg. Add the vanilla and sour cream and mix until thoroughly incorporated.

In a separate bowl, whisk together the flour, salt, baking powder, and baking soda. Slowly mix into the butter-and-sugar mixture and stir just until combined.

Spread half of the batter on the bottom of the prepared cake tin. (It will be a thin layer.) Spread the apple chunks over the batter then sprinkle 1 cup of the cinnamon streusel over the apples. Spread the remaining batter into the cake tin and top with the remaining streusel.

Bake 35 to 40 minutes or until a skewer inserted into the center of the cake comes out mostly clean.

Cool in the cake tin for 15 minutes, then place the surface of a plate on top of the cake. Invert the cake onto the plate and remove the cake tin. Place a serving platter onto the bottom of the cake and invert so that the streusel is on the top. Allow to cool completely before serving with a dollop of whipped cream or a scoop of vanilla ice cream.

Salted-Caramel Cookies

Ingredients
 1 cup unsalted butter, room temperature
 1 cup brown sugar, packed
 1/2 cup granulated sugar
 1 egg + 1 egg yolk
 1 teaspoon vanilla
 1/4 cup caramel sauce
 2 1/2 cups all-purpose flour
 1/2 teaspoon baking powder
 3/4 teaspoon baking soda
 1 teaspoon salt
 1 11-ounce package Kraft Caramel Bits
 Good-quality flaky sea salt

Instructions
 In the bowl of a stand mixer, beat the butter until creamy, about 2 minutes. Add the brown sugar and granulated sugar to the butter and beat on medium-high speed for about 3 minutes.

 Add the egg and egg yolk and beat until thoroughly incorporated. Mix in the vanilla and caramel sauce.

In a medium-sized bowl, whisk together the flour, baking powder, baking soda, and 1 teaspoon salt. Slowly mix into the butter and sugar mixture.

Stir in the caramel bits by hand, then cover the dough and refrigerate for 1 hour.

Preheat oven to 350 degrees F and line a baking sheet with parchment paper.

Roll the dough into walnut-sized balls and place on the prepared sheet. Bake for 9 to 11 minutes, or until golden brown on the edges.

Remove from the oven and sprinkle a few flakes of sea salt onto each cookie. Allow the cookies to cool on the baking sheet for 5 minutes then remove to a wire rack and cool completely.

Slow-Cooker Apple Cider Meatballs

Ingredients

30 to 40 frozen, premade meatballs (or your favorite recipe, par cooked)

2 cups apple cider

1/2 cup maple syrup

2 tablespoons apple cider vinegar

3 tablespoons soy sauce

1 teaspoon fresh grated ginger

1 clove garlic, minced

2 teaspoons cornstarch mixed with 1 tablespoon cold water

Instructions

Spray the slow cooker with cooking spray, or use a liner if your slow cooker isn't nonstick.

Add the apple cider, maple syrup, apple cider vinegar, soy sauce, ginger, and garlic to the slow cooker and stir.

Add the meatballs to the sauce and stir to coat the meatballs. Place the lid on the slow cooker.

Cook on high heat for 3 hours or on low heat for 6 to 8 hours. Stir once or twice during the cooking time.

Remove the meatballs from the slow cooker. Return the slow cooker to high heat and cover. Bring the sauce to a simmer then stir the cornstarch mixture in. Stirring often, cook an additional 3 to 4 minutes, until the sauce thickens.

Return the meatballs, stirring to coat with sauce. Turn the slow cooker to warm heat.

For a main course, serve over egg noodles and garnish with green onions. For an appetizer, skewer meatballs and garnish with a slice of apple.

Apple Sausage Tortellini

Ingredients

12 ounces chicken apple sausage, sliced into thin rounds
3 garlic cloves, minced
2 tablespoons all-purpose flour
1 14.5 ounce can lower sodium chicken broth
3/4 cup heavy cream
1/4 cup apple juice
1 package (8 to 10 ounces) refrigerated cheese tortellini
1 medium apple, peeled, cored, and chopped into small cubes
2 large handfuls baby spinach, roughly chopped
1/4 cup grated Parmesan cheese plus more to serve at table
Salt to taste

Instructions

Heat a large skillet over medium-high heat and add the sausage. Cook until it begins to sizzle and the slices begins to brown. Reduce the heat and add the garlic, stirring to combine. Cook until the garlic softens, but do not brown.

Sprinkle the flour over the sausage and cook 1 minute, stirring constantly. Slowly, and stirring constantly, add the chicken broth. Scrape up any brown bits sticking to the bottom of the skillet. Once incorporated, add the cream and apple juice. Cook until mixture comes to a boil, stirring constantly.

Reduce heat to medium and add the tortellini and chopped apples. Bring to a simmer and cook 7 to 8 minutes, stirring occasionally, until the tortellini is tender.

Remove from heat and add the fresh baby spinach, stirring until wilted.

Stir 1/4 cup Parmesan cheese into the dish. Season with salt to taste.

Pass additional Parmesan cheese when serving if desired.

Apple-Pumpkin Dog Treats

Ingredients

3 tablespoons natural, unsalted peanut butter
1 medium-sized apple, cored and grated to equal approx. 1 cup
1/2 cup pure pumpkin puree
1/4 cup water
1/2 cup old-fashioned oats
2 cups whole-wheat flour

Instructions

Preheat the oven to 350 degrees F. Line a baking sheet with parchment paper and set aside.

Place the peanut butter in a large bowl and heat in the microwave for 30 seconds. Add the grated apple, pumpkin puree, and water and stir until well combined.

Stir in the oats then gradually add the whole-wheat flour until a thick dough forms. Turn out onto a lightly floured surface and knead a few times to bring the dough together and form a ball.

Roll out dough to 1/8 to 1/4 inch thick and cut out shapes

using your favorite cookie cutter. Reroll scraps as necessary and cut into shapes.

Place the cutout shapes on the prepared baking sheet.

Bake 20 minutes for thinner treats and up to 30 minutes for thicker treats. The treats should be lightly browned on the bottoms and dry to the touch.

Remove treats to a wire rack and cool completely.

Refrigerate in an airtight container for up to 5 days or freeze for up to 3 months. Defrost at room temperature before allowing pet to consume.

Dedication

For those who believe
Love is love

Acknowledgments

It's true that it takes a village to create a book. I'd like to thank my husband, Dan, for reading and editing my manuscript several times. Not only that, he also toted my pink cupcake carrier to his golf group on numerous occasions to collect a wide variety of comments and critiques on my cupcake recipes from his peers. And to all my taste testers, thank you for your suggestions and encouragement with each tweak I did on the recipes.

Thank you to Janet Clause and Kathleen Costa for beta reading. Your comments and suggestions were invaluable in making this book so much better. And to Dan for having an engineering mind to make suggestions to keep my books (mostly) logical.

I greatly appreciate the talents of cover designer Karen Phillips. She captured the vision of my book and made it all the more special by managing to fit in the two special doggies in my life. And to the incomparable Lisa Kelley for the title she created for me. It helped inspire the plot!

To all the bloggers who help me spread the word about my new releases and put up with my last-minute requests to review, I owe you a debt of gratitude! Readers and authors alike are fortunate to have you in our community. A special thanks to all the lovely people who follow my blog, Cinnamon, Sugar, and a Little Bit of Murder, and share in my love for delicious food and mysteries! You inspire me to create stories and recipes to share with family and friends.

About the Author

Kim Davis lives in Southern California with her husband and puppy, Missy. When she's not spending time with her grand-daughters or chasing her energetic pup, she can be found either writing stories or working on her blog, Cinnamon, Sugar, and a Little Bit of Murder or in the kitchen baking up yummy treats. She has published the suspense novel, A GAME OF DECEIT, the Cupcake Catering cozy mystery series, and the Aromatherapy Apothecary Mystery series. She also has had several children's articles published in several magazines. Kim Davis is a member of Mystery Writers of America and Sisters in Crime.

BUTTERCREAM BETRAYAL

Cupcake Catering Mystery Series Book 5

Cinnamon & Sugar Press

ISBN 979-8-9853601-0-3

ISBN 979-8-9853601-1-0

ISBN 979-8-9853601-6-5

Cover Design by Karen Phillips

Edited by Red Adept Editing

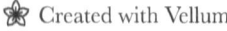 Created with Vellum

Also by Kim Davis

The Cupcake Catering Mystery Series

SPRINKLES OF SUSPICION

One glass of cheap California chardonnay cost Emory Gosser Martinez her husband, her job, and her best friend. Unfortunately, that was only the beginning of her troubles.

Distraught after discovering the betrayal by her husband and best friend, Tori, cupcake caterer Emory Martinez allows her temper to flare. Several people witness her very public altercation with her ex-friend. To make matters worse, Tori exacts her revenge by posting a fake photo of Emory in a compromising situation, which goes viral on social media. When Tori is found murdered, all signs point to Emory being the prime suspect.

With the police investigation focused on gathering evidence to convict her, Emory must prove her innocence while whipping up batches of cupcakes and buttercream. Delving into the past of her murdered ex-friend, she finds other people had reasons to want Tori dead, including Emory's own husband. Can she find the killer, or will the clues sprinkled around the investigation point the police back to her?

Praise for Sprinkles of Suspicion

"…there is enough action, including a few surprises—plus baking—to maintain a steady momentum. The breezy book concludes with a collection of unique recipes. An engaging cozy best enjoyed with a plate of cookies." – *Kirkus Reviews*

"The mystery, characters, and mouth-watering recipes will charm readers until the very end." – *InD'tale Magazine, Crowned Heart Review*

"You are going to love this delicious new cozy mystery! Kim Davis pens characters who come to life and a story you won't want to put down, not to mention recipes that will make your mouth water. Don't miss this scrumptious treat! – *Paige Shelton*, New York Times Bestselling author of the Farmers' Market, Country Cooking School, Dangerous Type, Scottish Bookshop mysteries, and Alaska Wild suspense series

"Sparkling prose, a deliciously twisty plot, and a colorful cast of characters make this debut cozy a surefire winner!" – *Linda Reilly*, author of the Cat Lady Mysteries, Deep Fried Mysteries, and the Grilled Cheese Mystery series.

"A delightful new cozy with a cool California setting and an imminently likable heroine." *Ellen Byron*, Best Humorous Lefty Awards winner and author of the Agatha Award winning and USA Today Bestselling Cajun Country Mysteries, The Catering Hall Mysteries, and the Vintage Cookbook Mystery series.

"This story moves along at a great pace and doesn't lag anywhere. There is always something happening, drama, twists, and yes, cupcakes. So well-plotted, I was totally taken in by the entire story and flabbergasted when the real killer was revealed." *Escape With Dollycas Into A Good Book*

CAKE POPPED OFF

Cupcake caterer Emory Martinez is hosting a Halloween bash alongside her octogenarian employer, Tillie. With guests dressed in elaborate costumes, the band is rocking, the cocktails are flowing, and tempers are flaring when the hired Bavarian Barmaid tries to hook a rich, hapless husband. Except one of her targets happens to be Emory's brother-in-law, which bodes ill for his pregnant wife. When Emory tracks down the distraught barmaid, instead of finding the young woman in tears, she finds her dead. Can she explain to the new detective on the scene why the Bavarian Barmaid was murdered in Emory's bathtub with Emory's Poison Apple Cake Pops stuffed into her mouth?

With an angry pregnant sister to contend with, she promises to clear her brother-in-law's name. As Emory starts asking questions and tracking down the identity of the costumed guests, she finds reasons to suspect her brother-in-law has been hiding a guilty secret. Her search leads her to a web of blackmail and betrayal amongst the posh setting of the local country club crowd. Can Emory sift through the lies she's being told and find the killer? She'll need to step up her investigation before another victim is sent to the great pumpkin patch in the sky.

FRAMED AND FROSTED

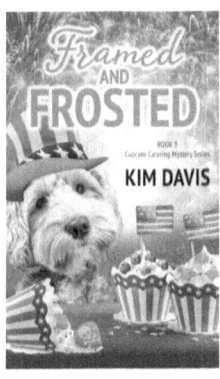

Framed and Frosted, the third book in the Cupcake Catering Mystery series, finds cupcake caterer, Emory Martinez, working at a Laguna Beach society Fourth of July soiree, with her sister and their new employee, Sal. With a host who seems intent on accosting both catering employees and guests alike, things go from bad to worse when he accuses Sal of murdering his long-dead son.

As the crescendo of exploding fireworks overhead becomes the backdrop for cupcakes and champagne, a deadly murder occurs. Can Sal and Emory explain why the cupcake the host ate, after shoving a trayful of buttercream-frosted cupcakes onto Sal, resulted in his death? Or will the detective and guests alike believe that Sal is a murderer? Emory and her octogenarian employer, Tillie, whip into action to find out who framed Sal after he was frosted by the victim.

FROSTED YULETIDE MURDER

Set against the holiday cheer of twinkling lights, costumed carolers, and a festive line of extravagantly decorated boats participating in the annual Christmas boat parade in Newport Beach, California, cupcake caterer Emory Martinez finds that the Grinch has crashed

the party. Together with her sister Carrie, Emory is catering a delectable feast of holiday cupcakes and cookies aboard a luxury yacht for the new Mrs. Blair Villman and her guests.

Sparks fly when Carrie comes face-to-face with the hostess, who just happens to be Carrie's high school frenemy, and old grievances are dredged up. Adding fuel to the fire, Blair's stepson brings his mother, the former Mrs. Villman, to the party. Instead of celebrating holiday cheer, someone seems intent on channeling the Burgermeister Meisterburger and shutting down Blair's party permanently. When Emory finds a body aboard the yacht, she needs to discover who iced the victim before the Scrooge ruins not only her livelihood but her freedom as well.

MUDDLED MATRIMONIAL MURDER

With only two weeks left to finalize the arrangements for the nuptial ceremony and reception for Emory Martinez's best friend, Brad, and a Thanksgiving feast to plan, she has enough to keep her busy. But when Emory and Brad stumble across the body of his former stalker, with a wedding gift marble muddler lying next to the body, it soon becomes apparent someone is intent on framing the groom before vows can be exchanged.

How did the victim locate Brad, and how did she end up being murdered at the scene of the impending nuptials? Was someone so desperate to stop the wedding that they'd resort to murder? Or was she killed for revenge? As the countdown to the wedding speeds by, it'll take Emory and her family and friends pulling together to pick through the muddled clues to clear the groom's name.